THE
COUNTERFEIT
CANDIDATE

BRIAN KLEIN

THE COUNTERFEIT CANDIDATE

LEVEL
BEST BOOKS

For Charmaine and Jessica.
My first readers, greatest supporters
and loves of my life.

Prologue

According to accepted twentieth century history, on 30 April 1945, Adolf Hitler and Eva Braun said their final goodbyes to a small group of close friends and colleagues who'd gathered in a sitting room, deep inside the underground bunker in Berlin. The pair retired to the Führer's personal study where, a few hours later, they took their own lives. Braun bit down on a wafer-thin glass cyanide ampoule and Hitler shot himself in the right temple, using his own Walther PPK pistol. The bodies were then carried above ground, via the bunker's emergency exit, and buried in the Reich Chancellery Garden, after being doused in petrol and set alight.

Thirty-six hours earlier, the couple had married in a simple ceremony, where they declared they were of pure Aryan descent and free of hereditary disease. The only witnesses were the Minister of Propaganda Joseph Goebbels, Hitler's private secretary Martin Bormann and his personal valet, Heinz Linge. The service was followed by a modest lunch of spaghetti in tomato sauce, one of the Führer's favourite meals, prepared by his personal chef, Constanze Manziarly.

Hitler was dressed in full Nazi uniform and Braun wore a calf-length black dress, broken up by a print of small white roses around the neckline. The Führer then dictated his last will and testament in which he declared he chose "death over capitulation" and left his vast personal fortune to the Nazi

i

Party.

Three months after the Nazi regime declared unconditional surrender, the victorious political leaders met in the German city of Potsdam, just outside Berlin, for a post-war conference to discuss the new order in Europe. On 17 July 1945, Stalin and Truman sat down for an intimate lunch in one of the small banqueting suites inside the spectacular Cecilienhof Palace. The only people present were their respective foreign secretaries, Molotov and Byrnes, who acted as translators. Truman was astonished when Stalin disclosed that rumours of the discovery of Hitler and Braun's bodies were fabricated and that a painstaking search by his Red Army soldiers of the Reich Chancellery grounds had failed to discover any sign of the Führer's remains. Stalin was convinced Hitler had escaped his clutches.

Chapter One

6 January 2012

Buenos Aires

The tunnel was almost finished. It had taken three hugely determined men eight months to construct and ran straight from the basement of the Café Torino directly underneath the safe depository of the Banco Estero. The eminent bank was one of the oldest in Argentina and stood, imperiously, on Avenida Cabildo, deep in the heart of the fashionable Belgrano district of Buenos Aires in the north-east of the city. The hundred-foot tunnel had state-of-the-art ventilation, sensor-activated lighting and pure wool carpet flooring. The enormous underground structure was a magnificent feat of engineering. The small gang had worked every night and weekend for eight months and between them had moved over four thousand five hundred cubic feet of dirt, making nearly three thousand wheelbarrow trips.

Pedro García rested the drill by the side of the newly formed earth wall. He stopped chewing, carefully removed the gum from his mouth and stared up at the twelve-inch-

1

thick concrete ceiling, appreciating they had finally reached the floor of the depository. Pedro allowed himself a rare smile as he stroked his straggly salt-and-pepper beard. He hadn't shaved since the very first day the drilling had begun.

"Guys, this is it. We are standing directly underneath twelve hundred beautiful boxes and only God knows what's inside them."

One of his two comrades leapt across the shagpile carpet and bear-hugged his leader. "I'll tell you what's in them – new lives for all of us." Ricardo Gonzales was the youngest of the three robbers and by far the most impetuous. "Pedro, you said we would do it and we have. I love you, old man."

Ricardo was a stunning hulk of a man. He stood six foot six in his bare feet and his body was honed to within an inch of its life. When he wasn't digging tunnels, he was working out seven days a week in his local gym and had done far more than his fair share when it came to heaving wheelbarrows full of dry earth.

The third man shook his head slowly. "Ricky, it's not done yet. Nothing is done until we are lying on a beach somewhere faraway, with more money than we know what to do with."

At sixty-three, Sebastian Ramos was the oldest of the three and by far the most cautious. He'd spent two long spells inside the notorious Caseros Prison, in the south district of the city, for robbery and firearms offences and that meant this job was his last roll of the dice.

Pedro picked up the power drill and started to walk back down the tunnel. "It's 6 a.m. The world above us is waking up. Right now, we rest and at midnight we start the final drilling and then we have the whole weekend to enjoy those boxes."

Pedro was a patient man. He'd been planning the job for

over ten years. The financial crisis that hit Argentina in 2001 had been brutal. It had wiped out his meagre life savings, just as it had for millions of his fellow countrymen. The trigger for the economic meltdown had been a catastrophic run on the banks as people perceived they weren't holding enough cash to cover their deposits. The public lost confidence in the banking system and chose to keep their cash and valuables at home or open safe-deposit boxes. Ten years after the crash, there were over five hundred thousand boxes being rented from banks. One for every eighty residents: a staggering ratio.

Pedro was one of them, but his box, located in the vault of the Banco Estero, was different from the rest. It was permanently empty.

He'd opened it in January 2009 and had made regular visits to the bank on the first Monday of every month. Over time, he'd memorised the internal layout of the vault and had mapped the exact positions of the twelve hundred boxes. The living room walls inside his tiny one-bed flat were covered with large hand-drawn designs. They displayed the layout of the boxes inside the vault and were colour-coded, depending on their size. Pedro knew that, even with a clear run of forty-eight hours over a quiet weekend, there wouldn't be enough time to drill open all the boxes. He calculated that three men, working as a team, could manage roughly ten per cent, so that meant targeting the biggest ones, of which there were one hundred and twenty.

Pedro was a former soldier who'd left school at eighteen and served for seven years in the First Tank Calvary Regiment as a mechanic. Once he left the army, he'd landed a job as a heating and air-conditioning engineer and those skills proved to be invaluable when it came to constructing the ventilation system required for a hundred-foot tunnel.

In March 2011, the lease for a rundown café came up for sale in the Belgrano District and Pedro was the only person who showed any interest in acquiring it. Café Torino had first opened its doors in the mid-eighties and, twenty years later, had gone out of business, a casualty of trendier fast-food outlets that had sprung up around it. It may not have had any clientele or appeal to potential buyers but, for Pedro, its positioning was perfect. It was located just two buildings away from the Banco Estero. He only had enough money to cover the lease payments for twelve months, but knew he only needed eight to build the tunnel. Two weeks after he took it over, he plastered the two front windows with old newspaper so no one could see inside. A handwritten sign on the door simply said, *Café Torino is being renovated and will reopen soon.*

Once Pedro secured the café, he set about recruiting two associates. Although he had no personal background in crime, he knew exactly where to go. His first cousin, Sebastian Ramos, was a serial criminal whose signature crime was house robbery. He knew Sebastian had been caught and convicted on two occasions during the last thirty years but had successfully completed well over a hundred robberies. That gave him a ninety-eight per cent success rate, which was good enough for Pedro.

Ramos recruited the third member of the team, Ricardo Gonzales. He was a plasterer and small-time criminal who was literally built like an ox. And he worked like one too. Initially, for two months, the three men met up after work every Monday, Wednesday and Friday night. The meetings took place inside the deserted café, where they devoured Pedro's home-made chilli and planned every step of the heist. Using a fake account, Pedro bought all the equipment and materials they needed on eBay and the purchases were delivered to the rear entrance of the café. The single most expensive item he sourced was a second-hand earth drill boring kit, normally used for excavating driveways.

At precisely midnight on Monday, 23 May 2011, the drilling began and continued every weekday night and weekend for the following eight months. Once a week, in the early hours, the freshly excavated earth was placed into large cloth bags, loaded onto a lorry and driven south out of the city to the Pinar del Norte forest where it was carefully dumped. The mining work was draining and relentless, but the three men grew to love their daily routine and finally, after many gruelling months, the tunnel was complete.

Ricardo only needed about forty minutes to drill through the concrete floor and, when he had finished, he'd created a hole about four feet wide. Pedro peered up into the murky darkness that seeped through the newly created opening.

"Guys, time is our only enemy now. Let's get the lighting up there and then hit the shit out of those boxes. Remember, we only go for the ones on the list."

Sebastian switched on a huge LED torch and climbed on top of Ricardo's shoulders, a move they had practised dozens of times in the café. "Okay, big man, here we go."

Fifteen minutes later, all three men were standing inside the giant vault, now illuminated by six 800 watt HMI movie lights on stands, cabled back through the tunnel to a small generator, which sat on the floor of the café.

All of them wore plastic monkey masks due to the six CCTV

cameras inside the vault, which were now recording their every move. The cameras were only monitored live when the bank was open, so didn't pose an immediate threat. Pedro had memorised the camera positions from his monthly visits to his empty box. A box that *wasn't* on their hit list.

Over the next fifty-three hours, the three men worked tirelessly, without a break, meticulously drilling through the dual locks that protected every individual box. This was a tricky and tedious process, requiring finesse rather than brute force. Each time a box was opened, its contents were emptied into large, unmarked cloth bags. The haul was spectacular: government blue-chip bonds from over twenty countries and huge quantities of US dollars, euros, English pounds and Argentinian pesos. One box alone held twenty solid gold bars while others were crammed with jewellery, designer watches and hundreds of loose gemstones.

None of the men paid any attention to a battered black leather case that was tightly jammed inside Box 1321. Its contents included three large brown Manila files, two 8mm film cans and a small tobacco tin, containing a collection of ancient military medals.

Most of the time, they behaved exactly as they had re-hearsed for the last ten months. All three of them knew their job descriptions inside out, part of which meant no talking.

"Shit, Pedro, look at the size of these beauties!" Ricardo was the first to break the vow of silence. In the palm of one of his clawlike hands he held a loose pile of enormous uncut diamonds, the smallest of which weighed at least ten carats.

Sebastian was busy pouring massive wads of US dollars into one of the bags but stopped for a moment to look up. "That's a million dollars you're holding right there, Ricky.

Who are the bastards who own all this stuff?"

Pedro remained the calmest of the three. "It doesn't matter. We own it now. No more talking until we are out of here."

The deadline for leaving had been set for five in the morning, two hours before the bank was due to reopen.

At four forty-five, the three men stood beside the large hole in the floor of the dilapidated kitchen of the café. None of them had slept for two days and they were running on pure adrenalin. Pedro called time on the job.

"We've hit ninety of the one hundred and twenty boxes on our list. I'm guessing we've landed well over a hundred million dollars. The lorry is bulging, so I suggest we get the hell out of here."

Sebastian took a long drag on his Marlboro, the first cigarette he'd smoked in two days. "Cousin, we've filled our boots, so it's time to say goodbye to the Café Torino."

Pedro turned to Ricardo, who was holding the van keys in his right hand. "Let's go, and, Ricky, drive carefully. We don't want to get pulled over by the police."

Two hours after the bank raid was discovered, a phone call was placed on an encrypted line from an office in Buenos Aires to an impressive skyscraper block six thousand miles away in downtown San Francisco.

Richard Franklin, CEO of the Franklin Pharmaceutical Corporation, reached for the receiver of the red phone on his desk that hadn't rung for over two years. There was only one person in the world who had the number.

"What's up, Matias?"

There was a short pause on the line as the caller gathered his thoughts. Then, a cold, heavily accented voice broke the silence. "Señor Franklin, Box 1321 has been stolen in a bank heist that took place over the weekend. We will, of course, focus our entire resource into recovering it as soon as possible."

The line went dead.

Chapter Two

9 January 2012

Buenos Aires

Chief Inspector Nicolas Vargas of the Buenos Aires Police Department stood in the middle of the safe depository, surveying the wreckage. He had already made a return trip through the hundred-foot tunnel, connecting the bank to the café, so he knew exactly how the thieves had pulled off the most daring robbery of the decade. He bent down and carefully picked up one of the ninety broken boxes that were strewn across the floor of the vault.

At forty, Vargas was one of the youngest and brightest chief inspectors on the city force. He was an impressive looking man. His six-foot-two frame and boyish film-star looks were complemented by a natural charisma that matched his physical attributes. Three years earlier, his life had been brutally derailed by a personal tragedy and, ever since, his mental energies had been focused entirely on his work. This intriguing, high-profile robbery was a welcome new distraction. He placed the box back on the floor and turned to Marcelo Morales, the general manager of the bank.

"Interesting M.O. The drilling on each lock is remarkably neat and precise and, by the look of things, they only targeted the largest boxes. Do we know exactly how many they hit?"

Morales was clearly in shock, still taking in the enormity of what had happened and the severe implications for both the bank and his career. In contrast to Vargas, he was short and rotund, his expanding waistline a casualty of too many client lunches at some of the city's finest restaurants. It had taken him a lifetime to work his way up to the top of the tree, having started as a bank teller twenty-five years before, and he had no intention of being forced into early retirement. Morales nervously adjusted the waistcoat of his three-piece linen suit and slowly ran his hand through his thinning grey hair. His heavy jowls wobbled as he spoke. The man was a bag of nerves.

"We make it ninety and you are correct, inspector, they only went after the elite boxes."

Vargas was now peering down the black hole that had been gouged out of the concrete floor. "These guys ran this like a military operation. The tunnel must have taken months to complete and it seems they took the lease out on the café last March. This job was a long time in the making." Vargas paused for a few moments before continuing. "Señor Morales, I want the names and contacts for every box owner in the vault, regardless of whether their boxes were broken into or not. I'm particularly interested in anyone who rented one in the last twelve months. Also, we'll need the footage from the monitoring cameras in here."

Morales made copious notes in his diary before replying.

"Of course, inspector. All the cameras record onto a massive hard drive, so you can take it away today. Unfortunately, the interior vault cameras don't transmit through to our exterior monitoring operation and are only viewed internally when the bank is open. I'll email you the owner list in the next hour."

Vargas gestured to his colleague, Juan Torres, who'd been listening to the conversation between his boss and the bank manager. "Detective Torres will stay behind to collect the drive and I'd also like you to provide him with a list of any owners who have visited their boxes in the last year."

Morales acknowledged Torres and turned back to face Vargas. "Inspector, obviously there are some very notable people who use our service, so I would ask you to use extreme discretion if you decide to contact any of them directly."

Vargas nodded. "By the way, Señor Morales, did you ever frequent Café Torino?"

The bank manager gave a wry smile. "Regularly. I'm a creature of habit. Every morning, on my way to the bank, I would stop off for a cappuccino and a croissant. It was terribly run down but very authentic and I was quite upset when the owners went bust. It has a sign on the door saying it is being renovated and, ironically, I've been looking forward to it reopening."

Chapter Three

9 January 2012

Buenos Aires

Theodor Consultants was founded in 1981 and, thirty-one years on, had established itself as one of the most respected private security companies in Buenos Aires. Its sprawling offices were located in the heart of the city, directly opposite the famed Recoleta Cemetery, arguably the most beautiful burial ground in the world and the resting place of Eva Perón, as well as other prominent Argentinians.

The CEO and founder of the company was Matias Paz. A former mercenary and lifelong fascist, Paz cut a truly intimidating figure. Although he was in his late fifties, he didn't carry an ounce of fat on his body and his slicked back, dyed jet-black hair, with its Dracula-style widow's peak, helped create the striking appearance of a much younger man who always looked immaculate in his high-end black Italian suits, American Pima cotton shirts and hand-stitched leather brogues. His employees called him the "Black Scorpion" due to the intimidating contents of a large glass terrarium that sat prominently on his office desk. It housed two glossy black-skinned emperor scorpions, which thrived on a daily diet of live crickets, locusts and mealworms. It was a nickname Paz pretended to be unaware of, but secretly relished.

Paz often spent hours walking through the fourteen-acre grounds of the graveyard, especially when he needed time to think. Recoleta Cemetery contained over six thousand grandiose mausoleums in an eclectic mix of architectural styles, including art deco, neo-Gothic and baroque. He always ended his walk sitting on a stone bench opposite a vault containing the body of one of his country's greatest ever boxers, Luis Ángel Firpo. After the boxer's death in 1960, he was buried in a relatively modest mausoleum but a stunning full-sized bronze statue stood outside its entrance. Paz idolised Firpo, who was regarded as one of the greatest punchers of all time and was known by millions of boxing fans across Argentina, affectionately, as "The Wild Bull of the Pampas".

Today was one of those days when Paz needed some precious thinking time, as he urgently had to find a quick solution to placate the concerns of his most valuable client. Richard Franklin, the CEO of the Franklin Pharmaceutical Corporation, covertly owned seventy-five per cent of Theodor Consultants, having been instrumental in founding it thirty years earlier. Paz knew Franklin had the power to shut his beloved company down at any moment and wouldn't think twice about it, if he deemed it necessary.

Paz had to use every resource at his disposal to locate the contents of Box 1321 before they were discovered by the thieves. He knew they were potentially worth far more than the jewels, cash and gold contained in the other stolen boxes.

He flicked through the contacts on his iPhone and dialled his long-time assistant, Luciano Herrera. The phone answered after just one ring.

"Luci, I want you, Benjamín, Thiago and six of our best operatives in the boardroom in the next hour. We have an urgent problem to solve and, until we fix it, nobody rests, nobody sleeps."

The nine senior agents of Theodor Consultants sat around the large rectangular walnut table in total silence, waiting for their leader to speak. Paz was seated at one end, staring intently at the screen of his laptop, which was logged on to the home page of the *Buenos Aires Times*. The banner headline reported the sensational safe-deposit robbery at the Banco Estero. Paz slammed the laptop shut and broke into life. As ever, his tone was menacing.

"Gentlemen, the very survival of our company and possibly our lives depend on your ability to solve a very big problem. You all know about the robbery by now. One of the boxes broken into belongs to our most valued client, who also happens to be our principal investor. We need to retrieve its contents. Create whatever chaos is necessary but find the men who are behind this."

Paz paused and looked around the room at the grim faces of his senior men. He was staring directly at Luciano when he resumed speaking. "We are going to need to shake down every contact we have in the city to get a lead on who these guys are – jewellers, pawnshops, drug dealers and any other informants we have on the payroll. Someone must know something. Call in whatever favours you're owed but get me some names. I wanna know how these fuckers pulled it off. We also need a full list of the owners of all the boxes in the vault, in case one of them was involved."

Everyone around the table nodded as the Black Scorpion continued. "Luci, have we still got our source inside the City Police Department? We're going to need to know every single step they take in this investigation."

Luciano sat forward in his chair and rested his arms on the table. "Yes, boss, we do. We already know from them that the man running the case is a chief inspector named Vargas. He visited the bank earlier, where he met with the general manager and requested a great deal of information. He also took possession of a hard drive that holds camera coverage of the break-in. Our source says they can get sight of all emails that Vargas sends and receives so, hopefully, we can always stay one step ahead."

Paz picked up his laptop from the table. "Good. And I want a copy of that fucking hard drive as well."

He rose from his chair and nodded at Herrera, then turned to face the room. "And one last thing for now. Once we find the assholes who did this and we retrieve our client's materials, none of those fuckers are going to live to tell the tale."

Paz returned to his office, eased back into the black ergonomic Herman Miller chair and glared at the computer screen displaying his email inbox. He felt a familiar urge in his loins, which only occurred at times of extreme stress. He despised his lack of mental control at moments like this but knew his craving had to be satiated. He carefully moved the cursor down the side of the screen and clicked on a second inbox that had no mention of Theodor Consultants in its name. Paz began to type the word *Eros* into the header and a familiar email address popped up. He felt a twinge of self-loathing as he created a new message.

I require a representative from your company to attend my home at nine o'clock tonight. Keep to my usual specifications and send over your latest selection of photos.

He knew his predilection for rent boys was his only weakness and also his biggest secret, which neither his colleagues nor enemies knew anything about. A secret he would protect at all costs. Thirty seconds later a fresh email notification appeared and Paz immediately clicked on the attachment. He scrolled through the five naked shots and his mouth formed a slightly distorted smile. As usual, all the boys were blonde and blue-eyed and each image displayed a name graphic. It was a tough choice but he knew instantly who he wanted. He typed in a new message and hit reply.

Send Tomás. Tell him to bring the usual items. He will be required to stay the night.

Chapter Four

San Francisco

Senator John Franklin walked briskly through the open-plan office of his campaign headquarters, based on the twentieth floor of a high-rise overlooking the Golden Gate Bridge. Over fifty young volunteers were hammering the phones, enthusiastically campaigning for their candidate. The mood on the floor was euphoric as poll after poll rolled in, showing Franklin holding seemingly unassailable leads over his nearest rivals in the upcoming presidential primary elections.

Franklin was a remarkable candidate who ticked all the right boxes with the American public. He had been groomed from a young age for a political career. The son of one of the country's most successful and respected businessmen, his schooling included Harvard, where he completed a Bachelor of Arts Degree in Government and International Affairs, and Stanford, where he achieved an MBA. His academic path mirrored that of John F. Kennedy, one of the country's most revered presidents.

In 1995, aged twenty-five he'd joined the board of his father's pharmaceutical corporation as director of research and development. Founded in Argentina in 1946, the Franklin Pharmaceutical Corporation was ranked seventh in Forbes' America's Top Public Companies list and forty-fifth in its Global 2000. Its annual revenue sat at thirty billion dollars, making it one of the most powerful pharma companies in the Western world.

Four years after joining the board, John married socialite Caroline Bush in one of the most talked about weddings of the year. Twelve months later, she gave birth to their son, Bill, and, in the same year, at the age of thirty, he became the youngest mayor of San Francisco in over a century.

In 2009, he became a senator and now, just three years later, he was the runaway front runner for the presidential nomination of the Republican Party. John Franklin's growing momentum appeared to be taking him on an unstoppable ride straight into the White House.

He headed directly for his large glass-fronted office with its spectacular views of the bridge. Waiting for him was his campaign chief, Cathy Douglas. They had been friends for over twenty years, having been classmates at both Harvard and Stanford.

Cathy was staring out of the window, watching the rush-hour traffic struggle its way home across the bridge. She turned to face Franklin and smiled warmly as she handed him a stack of papers containing the latest poll data.

"Fourteen-point leads in Iowa and New Hampshire. Seventeen-points clear in Nevada and, wait for this one, twenty-one points clear in South Carolina. By the time we hit Super Tuesday, it will be a fucking coronation."

Franklin laughed as he studied the latest report. "Cathy, you've done an amazing job but let's keep our eye on the main prize. We're still a few points behind the man in the White House. Once we nail the nomination, we've got to move everything up a gear."

Franklin's mobile burst into life. He saw the identity of the caller and gestured to Cathy that he needed some privacy. As she left his office, he took the call from his father.

"Dad, the latest figures are insane. We are hitting forty per cent plus across the country. Every day we are climbing by two or three points. It's totally—"

Richard Franklin interrupted his son mid-sentence. "John, I'm in the car at the back of the building. I need to see you right now."

The black Rolls-Royce Ghost glided elegantly through the traffic in downtown San Francisco and for ten minutes neither man spoke. Eventually, it pulled up in a quiet residential street and Richard Franklin turned off the engine.

"John, there could be a problem. Over the weekend there was a robbery at the Banco Estero in Buenos Aires. They hit the safety-deposit boxes and one of them was mine."

John Franklin glared at his father, his skin slowly starting to turn puce. "You told me there was nothing left – no papers, no photos, no trail. So, what the fuck is inside that box"?

Richard Franklin stared straight-ahead, a million thoughts tumbling through his brain. "John, before he died, your uncle and I decided some specific items should be preserved for posterity and for the sake of political history. Maybe it was a mistake but we both believed it was the right call to make at the time. The men who stole those boxes were only looking for cash and jewellery."

"But, Dad, what if they stumble across what's in that box?"

Richard Franklin leaned across and rested his arm on his son's shoulder. "John, it's in hand. I really don't want you to worry about this. Matias Paz is all over it. He has all of Theodor's resources focused on finding the thieves. I know we should have destroyed everything but, once they recover the contents of our box, I promise you I won't make the same mistake again."

Chapter Five

30 April 1945

Berlin

At precisely four in the morning, Adolf Hitler left his infamous bunker for the final time. Erich Kempka, his loyal driver since 1934, escorted the Führer to an unmarked Mercedes, accompanied by his new bride Eva Braun and his private secretary, Martin Bormann. A few minutes earlier, Bormann had arranged for Hitler's barber, August Wollenhaupt, to be smuggled into the bunker with the express task of removing the Führer's trademark moustache. Hitler's fear of falling into the hands of the Red Army marginally outweighed his vanity and, at the last minute, he reluctantly agreed to Bormann's request.

Wollenhaupt cursed under his breath as he waited nervously in the corridor outside Hitler's study. He could feel his hands violently shaking; they were armed with a top grade cut-throat razor and a pair of black-handled stainless-steel scissors. He had been Hitler's barber since 1932, but this was by far the most bizarre visit he had ever made to attend to the

Führer's needs. He clearly recognised the huge implications of what he had been requested to do. His mind was buzzing with questions when he suddenly caught sight of Bormann emerging at the end of the corridor, and, as he approached, he managed a half-hearted salute.

"Obergruppenführer, are you sure this is what the Führer wants?"

As soon as he uttered the words, he instantly regretted opening his mouth.

Bormann's reply was laced with contempt. "Old man, it's part of my plan and, if you wish to see your family again, you will not question it, especially when you are with the Führer." Bormann's eyes momentarily flicked down to the implements in the barber's hands. "I just hope you can keep your hands steady enough to do the job."

A few seconds later the door creaked open and Hitler's valet poked his head out of the doorway, checking to see who was outside. "The Führer is ready for you now, Herr Wollenhaupt."

As the bemused barber walked forward, Bormann fired off a parting shot. "Old man, one last thing. This entire event never happened."

It took less than two minutes for the barber to complete the task, but, even with his moustache removed, Hitler's hypnotic steely-blue eyes and pronounced cheekbones still combined to make his face instantly recognisable.

The three fugitives were dressed discreetly in drab civilian attire, sourced by Hitler's valet, Heinz Linge. Only the Führer made a further cursory attempt to disguise his infamous features, wearing a brown cashmere fedora with the brim turned down across his forehead.

22

Bormann had actually planned the escape to take place ten days earlier, on 20 April, to coincide with Hitler's fifty-sixth birthday but, at the last minute, the Führer had changed his mind. The two men had become inseparable since first entering the bunker three months earlier and Bormann had no intention of them being captured by the Red Army. He would stay by his master's side, come what may. Now, as the bunker shuddered from the impact of Russian bombs landing directly above, Hitler had finally agreed to leave.

Berlin was being bombarded from all sides and the Russians were less than a mile away from the Führer's secret underground base. Stalin's troops, led by Marshal Georgy Zhukov, were approaching the city from the north and Bormann, who had planned the escape route, had no real idea of the Red Army's exact positions. In the immediate hours before they fled, he instructed his secretary, Else Krüger, to call random phone numbers of German civilians who lived on the northern outskirts. If a Russian voice answered, she knew the house and the street had been taken. It was a bizarre game of telephone roulette. Phones rang off the hook and, when they did occasionally answer, a German voice was never heard.

Despite the grim news from his secretary, Bormann knew they had no options left and the three most notorious figures in Nazi Germany began a hazardous five-hour drive through enemy lines, heading north-west towards the coastal city of Kiel. Their destination was the port which, throughout the war, had been one of the Nazis' prominent naval bases on the Baltic coast. It housed enormous shipyards that had been used by the German Reich to build state-of-the-art submarines and, during the previous six months, had been subjected to constant aerial attacks from the Allied forces who appreciated its strategic importance. However, the Allies had been careful not to totally destroy the harbour, as they planned to use it as a naval base of their own, once they gained control of it, which was only a matter of days away.

Kempka was a skilled driver and, for the majority of the journey, maintained a steady speed. He kept to B roads, most of which were badly bomb damaged and deserted. Nevertheless, as they reached the outskirts of Kiel he knew he had no choice but to switch to the main road, as it was the only way to gain entry to the port. It involved a precarious end to the journey and for a few minutes all was well but, as they entered the city suburbs, he spotted an impromptu roadblock a few hundred yards ahead. Two Russian soldiers were positioned in the middle of the road, standing in front of an armoured half-track vehicle that was parked sideways on, forming a temporary barricade. They had spotted the approaching car a few seconds earlier and their PPD-34 submachine guns were raised and pointed directly at it. A third soldier was sleeping on a makeshift bed of fallen logs by the side of the road. His gun lay a few feet away, resting by an empty bottle of Stolichnaya vodka.

Kempka immediately began to slow the Mercedes 770K and turned to Bormann, who was sitting alongside him in the front passenger seat. It was the first time he'd spoken on the journey. "Obergruppenführer, what are your instructions?"

Bormann reached inside his overcoat and retrieved his 6.5 calibre Mauser pistol. "Erich, drive slowly up to the guards and keep your best fake smile on show. Try and park alongside them."

Bormann glanced over his left shoulder to make eye contact with Hitler, who nodded to acknowledge that he had heard the conversation and was aware of the imminent threat. As the car drew to a halt, Bormann and Kempka maintained their beaming smiles while the wary guards approached the front passenger door. The senior guard lowered his machine gun and barked instructions to the inhabitants of the car in Russian.

"Get out! Get out of the car."

Bormann continued smiling and nodded his head repeatedly as he began slowly winding down the car window with his right hand. Without pausing, he raised his left hand and fired in one simultaneous movement. The round entered the guard's neck just above his Adam's apple and, as he slumped to the ground, Bormann fired another shot that struck the second guard directly between the eyes, creating a mini crater in the centre of his forehead. The gunshots had woken the sleeping soldier, who instinctively leapt across the logs in pursuit of his machine gun. As he reached it, two more shots rang out and he spun backwards as the rounds ripped open his chest. He rolled sideways into a shallow ditch and came to rest on his back. Blood seeped through his uniform as he struggled to breathe. The shadow of his attacker loomed over him.

Adolf Hitler raised his left hand and slowly removed the fedora from his head to reveal his features. His right hand held his favourite weapon, a 7.65 millimetre Walther PPK. He glared at the fallen guard, desperately wanting the dying man to know the identity of his killer. The Russian somehow managed to tilt his head upwards and stared back incredulously, focusing his bloodshot eyes on the face of the gunman. Hitler's words dripped with venom.

"You are part of Stalin's scum army and, like all your

countrymen, deserve to die a painful death for invading my country."

Hitler crouched down and leaned forward until he was only inches away from his victim's head. He launched a mouthful of phlegm onto his face and, moments later, fired a third shot that blew away most of the soldier's skull.

It took Kempka almost fifteen minutes to figure out the intricate workings of the armoured car's manual gearbox but, eventually, he managed to drive it to the side of the road. Half an hour later, the Mercedes entered the war-torn seaport of Kiel. Awaiting them in the harbour, squeezed between the U-boats and warships, was a small, unimposing cargo boat that Bormann had purchased for five hundred thousand dollars six months earlier. *Santa Cruz III* had been built in South America and was registered in the port of Río Gallegos on the south-east coast of Argentina. Its twelve-man crew had been paid handsomely to bring it across the Atlantic to moor up in the harbour where, for the previous few months, it had been hidden from sight in one of the huge submarine bunkers. At just over nineteen hundred tons, it was powered by two diesel engines that generated a top speed of ten knots.

A fortnight earlier, Bormann had put in place the final piece of his intricate escape plan. He had instructed one of the navy's highest-ranking captains to travel to Kiel to take the helm of the pitiful cargo boat. A top-secret assignment that had left Hans Küpper completely bemused. Küpper was one of the German Navy's most decorated officers and, more importantly, he spoke fluent Spanish: the reason Bormann had selected him for the task. Küpper was to take command of the *Santa Cruz III* and its South American crew.

In addition to Hitler, Braun and Bormann, there was a

fourth passenger.He had arrived separately and was smuggled on board a couple of hours before the three VIPs arrived.

Küpper was summoned to meet the illustrious trio inside one of the base's vast storage structures, especially built to house giant submarines while they were under repair. When he entered the small administrative office inside the bunker, he was astounded to discover the identity of his three passengers. Hitler and Braun were sitting against one of the walls on small metal office chairs while Bormann sat behind an improvised desk, making notes. Küpper had never seen any of them before in the flesh and felt like an extra on a movie set about to meet the lead actors. He immediately stopped and saluted the Führer and held his position just inside the doorway.

Bormann laid down his pen and looked up at the captain. "Küpper, the Führer will require your quarters for the duration of the voyage. Myself and his wife will be berthed close by. I have already arranged for certain food provisions to be stored on the ship and I will give you a breakdown of the meals that should be prepared for the Führer. There is another passenger who will need to requisition the medical cabin as well as a separate one to sleep in. He is a physician and his medical supplies are being brought on board right now. Do you have any questions?"

Küpper was clearly confused and uneasy about the whole operation but wise enough not to question Bormann. "Obergruppenführer, I understand and will action your requests immediately. However, there are some embarrassing problems I need to bring to your attention. Lack of hygiene on board may be an issue. The cabins are damp, poorly ventilated and have no running water or heating. The wooden bunk in my cabin has a makeshift mattress, which is nothing more than a cloth bag stuffed full of straw. There are only two toilets which are shared by the crew of twelve. One of them is situated next to my cabin so, of course, I will requisition it for the Führer but I'm afraid the interior of the boat is in poor condition and in my opinion not fit for purpose."

Bormann's eyes fixed firmly on the captain. He cursed under his breath as he reflected on his negotiation with the boat's owner, who had assured him *Santa Cruz III* was in pristine condition and a bargain at half a million dollars. He was normally meticulous when it came to detail but, on this occasion, had been forced to take the man at his word. A rare mistake that he had every intention of rectifying once he was safely ensconced in his new base.

"Captain, the boat is perfect for our requirements and you will find charts on board detailing our journey to South America."

Küpper was completely stunned but didn't reply. Dozens of questions came to mind but he knew to stay silent, so simply nodded.

Hitler and Braun sat listening impassively. Bormann was now evidently bored with the conversation and keen to continue with his paperwork. "Captain, I expect you and the crew to make the voyage as comfortable as possible for the Führer. We will be boarding in two hours."

With that, Bormann returned to his notes and Küpper realised the meeting was over.

Chapter Six

9 January 2012

Chascomús

The remote farm building Pedro had rented was located just outside the small city of Chascomús, seventy miles south of Buenos Aires. Situated on a quiet country lane, most of the property was shielded from passing cars by a large copse of jacaranda trees. The rental included a huge wooden barn, set behind the main house, accessed by a narrow stone drive. It was totally hidden from the road and backed onto twenty acres of unused farmland, which was the main reason Pedro had chosen it.

It took the thieves less than an hour to unpack the thirty large cloth bags from the back of the lorry, which they neatly laid out into three separate piles, each containing ten bags. Pedro stood behind the centre stack. For the first time in six months, he had a smile on his face.

"Sebastian, which one do you want, left or right?"

Ramos walked across to the pile situated to the right of Pedro. "I'll take this one."

Ricardo ran past both men and leapt on top of the remaining pile. One of the bags spilled open, revealing large wads of one-hundred-dollar bills. He grabbed a handful and threw them in the air. Moments later he was rolling on the ground, covering himself from head to toe with pristine US currency notes.

Sebastian shook his head, and a huge grin broke out on his face. "Ricky, you remind me of a giant pig, wallowing in a pile of green shit."

Pedro ignored Ricardo's antics, crossing the barn towards the three white vans parked against the far wall.

Six months earlier, each of them had sold their cars, or in Ricardo's case his motorbike, and bought cheap second-hand transits. A key part of Pedro's plan involved them stashing their own cut in a secret location and not touching the contents for twelve months. None of them would know where the others had hidden their share. The plan was to live normally for a year before going anywhere near their bounty. Pedro gestured for Ricardo and Sebastian to join him by the vans.

"Okay, let's load up and no offence, guys, but I hope we have no reason to speak to each other ever again."

Sebastian opened the rear doors of his van and threw the first of his ten bags inside. "Pedro, if we do have to talk, something will have gone badly wrong."

* * *

Vargas stood in front of the giant whiteboard positioned at the far end of the open-plan office. It was covered with printed imagery linked together by hand-drawn arrows. There were a number of photos showing the vault, the interior of the tunnel and six grabs taken from the CCTV footage showing still images of the three perpetrators. A second, smaller board held three lists of names. The longest one showed the names of the owners of all twelve hundred boxes. The second was a list of the ninety owners whose boxes had actually been raided, and the final list showed the names of any owners who had visited their boxes in the previous twelve months.

Vargas signalled to his assistant, Juan Torres, to call the assembled detectives in the office to order. In total, there were ten of them assigned to the case, including Vargas and Torres.

"So, here's what we know so far. This heist was carried out by three men wearing monkey masks and one of them is a fucking giant." Vargas pointed to one of the CCTV grabs, which showed the three thieves standing together near the tunnel entrance and one man's six-foot-six frame towered above the other two. "We also know the tunnel must have taken them months to excavate and the lease for the café was taken out under a fake name and profile. What else have we got, Juan?"

"We have the lab boys going over everything we found inside the café and the tunnel. They think we may have a lead on where the carpet came from, although it's quite old. Who the fuck worries about laying high-quality carpet in a hundred-foot tunnel?"

Vargas cut back in and pointed at the smaller board. "I want these three lists worked through and broken down. Look for anything unusual or suspicious about any of the owners and let's contact everyone who visited the vault in the last twelve months. I want them all interviewed in person."

Torres moved over to the board displaying the lists. "Chief, the list from the bank shows over two hundred of the owners made visits in 2011 and forty of those came on more than one occasion. It's going to take time but we will work our way through them."

Vargas nodded at his assistant. "Okay, Juan, let's start with any owners who visited their boxes more than once and see what we find. Somewhere down the line, our boys will have made a mistake. Our job is to find out what it was."

Chapter Seven

Buenos Aires

Prior to the robbery, the three thieves had plenty of time to plan and source their respective hiding places and, unknown to each other, they all came up with completely different ideas. The small lock-up garage Pedro had hired to stash his share was just under three miles away from his flat in the Villa Lugano district. It was positioned at the end of a run of ten garages located in a quiet cul-de-sac, which rarely saw any traffic. It was close to midnight when Pedro steered the white transit van into the garage and, as there were no street lamps, his only source of light came from the headlights. As he made the thirty-minute walk back to his flat, he mused he had sourced the most unremarkable location possible. The garage's owner had insisted on a year's rental upfront and Pedro had no intention of paying for a second year.

As a young man, Sebastian Ramos had worked as an apprentice carpenter before turning his attention to crime.

His skills proved very handy when it came to creating a novel hiding place for his share of the haul. Sebastian lived in a small one-bed basement flat in Barrio Soldati, a rundown neighbourhood located in the south-west of the city and, before the robbery took place, he began carefully lifting up the old pine floorboards in his living room. They rested on wooden joists that ran lengthways across the room and were about four feet apart. He calculated the gaps between them were wide enough, and just about deep enough, to provide a safe haven for the valuables he planned to steal.

Sebastian used twelve-inch-wide strips of chipboard to create a smooth base underneath the wooden floor so the cloth bags could rest on a clean surface. His estimates were spot on and, sure enough, two months later, the bags filled the gaps between the joists perfectly, just as he had planned. He replaced the floorboards and ensured he left no sign they had ever been tampered with. The interior of the flat looked exactly the same as it had before the robbery. The only difference was, his cheap apartment was now worth approximately thirty million dollars.

Ricardo Gonzales had given great thought to where he would hide his share of the raid. His tiny third-floor studio flat in Pompeya was less than five hundred square feet in dimension and had no hidden spaces. But he had another location in mind that he knew would be absolutely perfect. His father had suffered two major strokes in the last five years and was housebound. He still lived in their family home, a small three-bedroom detached house on the outskirts of the city.

Ricardo had no interest in visiting his father, whom he hadn't seen for over three years, since the passing of his beloved mother. However, he didn't need to visit the house to enact his plan. At the bottom of the garden was a substantial shed he had helped his father build some years earlier, when he was living at home. He knew it wasn't used any more and the wooden door was well secured by a mortice lock. A lock he had fitted himself and for which he still held a spare key. The shed was built from ten-inch rendered concrete blocks with a solid base and no windows, and so provided a perfect temporary home for his newly acquired assets.

At four in the morning, he parked the van outside the front of his father's house. The lights were off inside and the street was deserted. Ricardo made ten separate trips, carrying the bags one at a time from the back of the van to the shed at the bottom of the garden. As he expected, it was completely empty, except for a rusty old lawnmower and a couple of watering cans that were covered by a layer of cobwebs.

About an hour later, he relaxed back in the driver's seat of the van and turned the ignition. The engine burst into life and Ricardo resisted the usual instinct to flick on the headlights. He carefully placed the shed key back inside his jacket pocket and smiled to himself as he slowly steered the van away from the pavement. It had been a good night's work and he was feeling euphoric. Unfortunately, he was totally unaware of the small red velvet pouch that had spilled from one of the cloth bags and was now lying on the grass verge inside his father's garden, a few feet from the front door. The first mistake had been made.

Chapter Eight

10 January 2012

Buenos Aires

Maria Vidal was running late. As a carer, working for the city's social services, she had three housebound clients she visited five days a week. She was on her way to see Raúl Gonzales at his home in La Boca, one of the city's poorest districts, located in the southeast, near the old port. Her regular bus had broken down over a mile away from the house, so she had been forced to walk the rest of the journey laden with two heavy shopping bags full of groceries.

Life had not been kind to Maria. At sixty-three, she lived alone in a small rented apartment and struggled every week to try and make ends meet. She'd never married as, for thirty years, she'd looked after her mother, who'd suffered from a disastrous mix of Parkinson's and early dementia. Following her death, Maria lost the income of the monthly pension that used to keep them both going and the only work she could find was with social services. So, after a lifetime of looking after her mother, she was now caring for a small group of elderly citizens she didn't really give a damn about. They just helped pay the bills.

Maria was nearly an hour late and braced herself for the verbal abuse she knew she would receive from her ungrateful client. Raúl Gonzales was an arrogant, abusive old man whom she truly despised. She cursed under her breath as one of the shopping bags slipped from her grasp while she struggled to find the correct door key from her bulging key ring. As she bent down to pick up a couple of apples that had fallen from her bag, she noticed a small red velvet pouch lying on the grass. She grabbed it and quickly stuffed it inside her coat pocket before opening the front door.

She spent the following hour as usual, washing and feeding the old man, who was as ungrateful as ever for her company or help. Gonzales was a bear of a man. He was six feet tall and weighed over two hundred pounds. Maria speculated that, in his day, he must have been attractive, but now, well into his eighties, he was crippled with arthritis and confined to a wheelchair. His mind, however, was undiminished and, sure enough, she received a tongue-lashing for keeping him waiting for his lunch, a disgusting microwaved concoction of meat and pasta. As usual, she couldn't wait to finish her duties and leave his company as quickly as possible. Today, though, she had an extra incentive to get away as she had a nagging curiosity about the contents of the velvet pouch.

She bid Gonzales goodbye and made her way to the bus stop, which was a five-minute walk away. The street was quiet, and Maria sat down on the short wooden bench, breathing a heavy sigh. She felt inside her coat pocket and retrieved the velvet pouch, which was now screwed up into a tight ball. The gold drawstring opened easily and she poured the contents into her hand. Two rings tumbled out. One was a plain, thin gold band but the other was far more interesting: a solitaire diamond mounted on a simple open setting. The stone was enormous and was held in position by four platinum claws.

Maria knew absolutely nothing about diamonds, having never owned one, but she was stunned by the size of this gem. She assumed it must be a fake, but, even so, it would still have some commercial value, as would the gold ring. She wondered who might have dropped the pouch, as, to the best of her knowledge, Gonzales had no visitors other than her and the postman. She vowed to visit her local pawnshop early the next day, before she started work. Maybe she could get a couple of hundred dollars for her lucky find.

The following morning, she headed straight to her local pawnbroker and stood outside the front door waiting for it to open. Her first house visit wasn't due until ten thirty, so, if Señor Ortiz opened up at nine as usual, she would have time to do some business first. Since the death of her mother, she had made a number of visits to his shop, pawning a mixture of the household ornaments and costume jewellery she had inherited. But now the home cupboard was bare, so a few unexpected dollars for these two trinkets would be very welcome.

The shop had been under the same ownership for forty years, and Alexandro Ortiz knew all his regular customers by name. When he saw Maria waiting outside the shop, his heart sank as he knew she only ever brought in total crap, but things were quiet, so every customer still had to be welcomed to his premises.

"Maria, darling, how are you? What treasures are you

bringing me today?"

Maria was far too preoccupied with her own anxieties to pick up on the sarcasm in his voice. She had spent the previous evening at home preparing a suitable script.

"Good morning, Señor Ortiz. I have some of my mother's most precious jewellery that I was determined never to sell but needs must as bills have to be paid. Please be generous as they are of great sentimental value to me."

She took out the pouch and handed it across the counter to Ortiz. The first thing that caught his eye was a small gold Cartier logo stamped on the velvet at the bottom of the pouch, a marking Maria had completely missed. He opened it up and carefully retrieved the contents. His heart skipped a beat when he saw the solitaire. He knew the gem was at least ten carats in weight, and at first glance it looked genuine. He gathered his thoughts as he peered through his eyeglass at the pure white stone.

"This is a nice replica, Maria. Your mother obviously had very good taste. What were you looking to get for the two rings?"

Maria decided to go for broke. "I'm thinking five hundred dollars."

She held her breath.

"Maria, I think three hundred would be fairer, but, as it's you, how about we agree at four?"

Maria didn't hesitate. "Thank you, Señor Ortiz, I think that's very fair."

A couple of minutes after Maria left the pawnshop, clutching four one-hundred-dollar bills in her hand, the old pawnbroker made a phone call to Theodor Consultants.

Chapter Nine

22 May 1945

Atlantic Ocean

The crossing was proving to be laborious and miserable for the three VIP passengers. They had been at sea for more than three weeks and were only halfway through the journey.

The conditions were appalling; there was no way of showering or washing clothes and the boat stank of urine and faeces. As Küpper had predicted, the hot water and heating only worked intermittently and Hitler and Braun spent most of the time in their cabins, lying on their bunk beds, huddled under piles of blankets.

The Führer suffered from frequent bouts of seasickness and had lost nearly a stone in weight since they'd boarded the boat. The only time he'd left his cabin had been during the second week of the voyage when he spent three days in the medical area being worked on by Doctor Friedrich Hipke, the plastic surgeon, who had reluctantly joined them on board for the course of the voyage. Hitler had insisted Bormann be first to go under the knife a few days earlier, as he wanted to be sure Hipke could work safely in such a confined space.

The Berlin-based surgeon was a master of his craft, lauded by the rich and famous, who paid huge sums for his much sought-after handiwork. He specialised in facial implants, chin augmentation, rhinoplasty and eyelid surgery. Hipke enjoyed his celebrity status and was mortified when four Waffen-SS soldiers turned up unannounced at his private surgery. He was put under immediate arrest and, despite the obvious dangers of travelling through a war zone, was transported by car, under armed guard, to Kiel, where he boarded the *Santa Cruz III*, totally unaware of the task that lay ahead. The SS soldiers ransacked his surgery, collecting his surgical implements and medication, which were also transported onto the boat.

He was astounded when, on the second morning of the voyage, he discovered the identity of his two new clients. Without any notice, he was escorted by one of the crew members to the captain's cabin, where Bormann and Hitler were waiting. Bormann did all the talking, presenting Hipke with a series of detailed artist drawings, which were to be used as a guide for the reconstructive surgery. He was terrified by the unsolicited commission but could only be impressed by Bormann's extensive knowledge of plastic surgery; a level of comprehension he had never encountered before in a layman.

* * *

Eva Braun was getting restless. Bormann had rationed her visits to the Führer to twice a week, normally for no longer than an hour and, for the rest of the time, she languished in her tiny, filthy cabin. She resolved that something had to be done and made her way to Bormann's, prepared for a face-to-face confrontation with the man who was dictating events and controlling her life. A man she sincerely loathed.

The door to Bormann's cabin was slightly ajar and she knocked twice before entering. Unknown to Braun, he was up on deck, harassing the captain with his daily complaints about the lack of speed on the voyage. He repeatedly reminded Küpper they had a schedule that had to be kept to, no matter how unrealistic it may be, and failure was not an option. The German skipper was left under no illusions as to the consequences of a late arrival in Argentina.

The small wooden table in Bormann's cabin was covered with typed paperwork, arranged into a number of neat piles. Braun's curiosity got the better of her and she picked up a handful of papers from the closest one, which were clearly bank statements. The headers revealed the banks were based in South America and some of the bottom-line figures were absolutely staggering. Most of them contained millions of US dollars, and, in two cases, she spotted figures in excess of a hundred million. Her eyes flicked to another pile that contained complex architectural drawings of what she thought was likely to be her new home. She was holding the top sheet high in the air to get a better look when Bormann entered the cabin. He slammed the door and Braun jumped back in surprise, dropping the sheet onto the floor.

"Eva, I don't appreciate you searching my cabin. As far as I'm aware, we're not scheduled to meet today."

Braun could sense large streaks of redness breaking out on her milky complexion and was desperately searching her brain for a suitable reply when Bormann softened his tone.

"Anyway, I see you've been looking at the designs for the Führer's new residence."

She still hadn't regained her composure and blurted out a bland remark. "It looks amazing, Martin. Will it be ready in time?"

Bormann bent down and picked up the drawing. "My dear, it will indeed be ready. All part of the plan."

"Martin, all you and the Führer talk about is the plan. Yet neither of you ever discuss it with me. What is it and where do I fit in?"

Bormann pursed his lips and forced them into a crooked grin. "Eva, there is one essential part of the plan that you need to carry out and you cannot afford to fail."

Braun felt her heart race as she stared into Bormann's eyes and waited for him to continue. His voice dropped to a menacing whisper. "You need to deliver the Führer a healthy son and heir."

* * *

Every day of the journey, Bormann talked through his strategy for the future with the Führer and kept him informed of ongoing developments inside Germany. He would crouch next to Hitler's bunk to give him the latest update.

"Führer, the war has been lost. The traitor Dönitz ordered Alfred Jodl to sign an unconditional surrender on 7 May in Reims. You have been betrayed by your own military. The bastards have sold out the Fatherland."

Hitler's skin was badly bruised, his temple and part of his face were still wrapped in bandages. His chin was exposed and he stroked the growth that was now turning into an unkempt grey beard.

"Martin, only you and Goebbels stayed loyal to the Reich and now the weakness of the generals who led our brave soldiers has cost us dearly. They have betrayed me and the German people and must be punished."

"Führer, trust me, their time will come and, believe me, they will suffer. But I do have positive news from Argentina. The regime has confirmed they've received the latest transfer of funds, so our safety and security is guaranteed. Building work is well under way on your new home in Patagonia and, as you requested, it will be a sizeable residence, big enough to house all three of us."

Hitler shivered under the blankets and nodded his approval. "Will it be safe?"

"It is in the middle of nowhere. Trust me, Führer, no one will ever find us."

Chapter Ten

11 January 2012

Buenos Aires

Pedro was not surprised when he received a call from the City Police Department. As one of the box owners at the bank, he knew he would be summoned for an interview and he'd had plenty of time to prepare his story. Detective Alex Martin sat opposite him in the bare, windowless interview room, located in the basement of the station. Between them was a small metal table, on which sat a couple of polystyrene cups of water and a blue folder that the detective was flicking through.

"Thanks for coming in to see me, Señor García. We are interviewing all the owners of the security boxes kept at the Banco Estero, whether they were stolen or not. Turns out you were one of the lucky ones."

Pedro nodded and tried to stay relaxed. "Detective Martin, it's a sad state of affairs when a man's possessions aren't secure inside a safe-deposit bank. I was told that vault was impregnable. Seems not."

Martin was looking down at the file. "It appears you made regular visits to the bank. Can I ask you why you checked your box every month?"

Pedro moved smoothly into autopilot. "Since the 2001 crash I, like many of my fellow countrymen, decided it was pointless keeping cash in a current bank account. I always used to keep my savings at home but, as you know, in recent times, house break-ins have become a regular occurrence in the city, so a few years ago I decided to take out a box. I could only afford one of the smaller ones and, at the beginning of each month, I made cash withdrawals from it to top up my earnings. I'm self-employed and, to be honest, in the last year, work has been hard to find, so my savings have basically run out and my box is now empty. I was about to end the rental at the end of this month as I can't afford to keep it going."

Detective Martin appeared quite disinterested in the story, which was a great relief to Pedro, who had delivered his rehearsed lines perfectly.

"One last thing, Señor García. I believe you work as an air-conditioning engineer. How much do you know about underground ventilation?"

Pedro kept his composure. "Detective Martin, you flatter me. The truth is I'm nothing more than a glorified repairman."

* * *

Maria had a spring in her step as she walked down the street, heading for the bus station. Maybe her luck was changing. She planned to use some of her windfall to treat herself and buy the blue designer cardigan she had been eyeing for weeks, and which was now on special offer in her local department store.

She paid no attention to the blacked-out transit that was tracking her every move as she walked along. Without warning, it accelerated past her and screeched to a halt. Two figures wearing black balaclavas leapt out and grabbed Maria from behind, dragging her into the back of the van. The whole operation took less than ten seconds and, rather than resist, her body went limp, paralysed with shock. The van doors slammed shut and, moments later, she found herself sitting on a bench between her two kidnappers, facing a third man who was unmasked.

Luciano Herrera was holding the diamond ring in one hand and the red velvet pouch in the other. Maria felt her bladder give way, and she wet herself. He smelled the sudden whiff of urine and saw the terror in Maria's face.

"Hello, Maria. There is nothing to worry about as long as you are completely truthful with your answers to my questions."

Maria was transfixed by the diamond ring Luciano was holding in the palm of his hand. Her mind was racing, trying to work out what was happening. "I didn't steal the ring – it belonged to my late mother." She found herself blurting out the lie without really meaning to.

"Maria, please calm down. Let's not start on the wrong foot. Remember, I asked you to tell the truth. Your mother was a cleaner and the nearest she would ever have got to a ten carat Cartier ring would have been window shopping. Now, why don't you tell me where you got it, and everything will work out fine."

Maria was terrified but somehow her instincts told her she should carry on lying. How could they possibly know where she'd found the ring? "You are right. She was a cleaner and one of her customers left it to her in their will. I always thought it was costume jewellery, which is why I sold it for a few hundred dollars."

Luciano was an experienced interrogator and could tell Maria was lying. He nodded towards the man sitting to her right. A moment later, a large serrated knife was jammed against her neck. She screamed with terror and began to cry uncontrollably. "Now then, Maria. This is the last time I am going to ask you nicely. Where did you get the ring?"

"I swear, Señor, I didn't steal it. I found it. I found it in the garden of one of my clients."

Luciano leaned forward and indicated to his henchman to remove the knife from Maria's throat. "There we are, Maria. You see how easy it is to tell the truth? Now, I want you to tell me the name of your client and take us to their home."

"His name is Raúl Gonzales, and he lives in La Boca, close to the port."

The van's engine fired up and headed for the south-east of the city.

Raúl Gonzales was dressed in his cotton pyjamas, sitting in a wheelchair in the corner of his living room. Resting on his lap was a small bowl of cornflakes, drenched in cold milk. He was watching a daytime game show, part of his regular morning routine, while he awaited the arrival of his carer. The transit pulled to a halt outside the front of his small house. The journey had taken about thirty minutes and no one inside the van had spoken since Maria had given up the address. She had stopped crying and was rigid with terror. The driver turned off the ignition and turned to Luciano.

"We're here, boss."

Luciano turned to Maria and smiled reassuringly. "Thank you for your help, Maria. There's one last thing. Can you kindly give me the key to Señor Gonzales's residence?"

Maria fumbled inside her bag and pulled out a large bunch of keys. She handed them across to Luciano. "It's the one with the blue tape at the end."

"Now that wasn't very hard, was it, Maria? Thank you for all your invaluable help. I really appreciate it."

Luciano smiled malevolently at Maria and then, a moment later, his eyes flicked to the man sitting next to her, who was brandishing the knife. His head gave an almost imperceptible nod.

For a brief moment, Maria felt an intense pain as the knife ripped into her skin and lodged itself inside her heart. Everything went black. The killing had begun.

Luciano stood outside the front door with three of his men, who were awaiting instructions. He turned to the driver. "Thiago, looks like the garden runs all the way around the back. You check out the grounds. Boys, you two come in with me. We will have a chat with Señor Gonzales and then we will tear his fucking house apart."

As Maria had indicated, the key with the blue tape turned the lock, and, seconds later, all three men were inside the house. The TV was blaring out from the sitting room. Luciano and his two associates followed the noise. Raúl Gonzales was engrossed in the game show and didn't sense the intruders enter the room, but that all changed when Luciano yanked the plug powering the TV set out of the wall socket.

The old man turned in his chair and saw the three men standing in his living room. "What the fuck do you guys want with me? If you've come to burgle my home, help yourself. There is fuck all left in this house to steal, unless you are desperately in need of toilet rolls and soap."

"Calm down, old man. I just want to have a talk with you about this." Luciano walked across the room and held the diamond ring up in front of Gonzales's face. "I want to know where you got this bit of ice from and if you have anything else like it in your house."

Realising that Gonzales was an invalid and offered no physical threat, he sent his two men upstairs with instructions to start the search. He then turned back to the old man. "So, Señor Gonzales, while my friends have a look around, why don't you tell me about the diamond."

"Fuck you and fuck your diamond. Why don't you shove it up your arse? Look at me. Do you really think I'm a man who owns diamonds? Are you fucking mad? I can hardly afford to pay my weekly food bills and I live off benefits."

The sheer anger and contempt that Gonzales exuded seemed totally genuine and Luciano wasn't sure what to do next. That all changed a second later when his earpiece buzzed into life.

"Boss, I'm in the shed at the bottom of the garden. You won't believe it. It's a fucking Aladdin's cave."

The two men, who'd begun tearing the bedroom apart upstairs, also heard Thiago's message and came running down the stairs, joining Luciano in the sitting room.

Herrera barked out orders. "Antonio, you stay here with Señor Gonzales. Carlos, come with me."

By the time they reached the shed, Thiago was ripping open the last of the cloth bags and the floor was covered with an assortment of cash, jewellery and government bonds. It truly was a cave of wonders.

Luciano pulled out his iPhone and took a couple of photos, which he texted to his boss. A few seconds later, Paz was on the line.

"Boss, we've hit pay dirt. We've found the boxes."

"Great work, Luci. Now, remember what we are searching for – a black leather case containing two 8-millimetre film cans, an old tobacco tin and three Manila files. As soon as you have them, call me back. And, Luci, however tempting it is, don't touch anything else."

Two hours later, after carefully sifting through literally millions of dollars' worth of goods, Luciano was forced to acknowledge the items he was looking for were simply not present inside the shed.

He reluctantly called Paz back. "Boss, they are not here. I promise you we've been through everything really carefully. I don't understand it."

Paz had total trust in his assistant and thought for a moment. "Okay, Luci. Let's think for a moment. We know they broke into almost a hundred boxes. Does it look to you like the bags held that much?"

Luciano scanned the floor of the shed, which now had a number of piles containing different items neatly stacked, including ten cloth bags which were in one of the corners. "No, boss, it really doesn't. I'd say this is less than half of the haul."

"Think about it, Luci. We know from our friend at the police department there were three of them in the gang that pulled this off. The chances are this is just a third of what they got."

"Yes, boss, that makes sense. We need to find out who

stashed the bags here, as it certainly wasn't Gonzales. The old man doesn't look like he could go anywhere without his wheelchair."

It took two of Luciano's men to carry the old man down to the bottom of the garden. He was a dead weight who offered little resistance but also no help. When they dumped him on the floor, he looked totally stunned. He found himself sitting in the middle of a treasure trove that had suddenly manifested inside his garden shed. It was insane. Luciano could see the genuine look of bewilderment on the face of the old man and so he chose his next words carefully.

"Señor Gonzales, I have no doubt at all that you are just as surprised as me at seeing all this. Thiago, here, had to break open the lock to gain entrance, so let me ask you a question. Who else has a key to your garden shed?"

The old man hesitated before replying. "No one, except my son Ricardo but then he hasn't been here for years. We don't speak."

"I think you are mistaken, Señor Gonzales, and, what's more, I think you'll find he was here just a few days ago."

Chapter Eleven

11 January 2012

Buenos Aires

Matias Paz decided it was time to update Franklin on the investigation. He wished he had better news to report but at least they were making progress. Although his iPhone looked like a regular model, it was able to encrypt calls to certain dedicated numbers. He placed the call to San Francisco.

Richard Franklin picked up after just two rings.

"Señor Franklin, we have discovered the identity of one of the bank thieves, Ricardo Gonzales. It appears there were three in the gang and we have found what we think is one third of the haul. Unfortunately, it didn't contain the contents of your box."

Franklin snapped down the phone. "What about finding the names and whereabouts of the other two?"

"Very shortly, we plan to have an in-depth conversation with Señor Gonzales and I'm sure he will be very helpful in that matter."

* * *

Vargas was sitting at his desk, working his way through the latest reports when his number two, Juan Torres, burst through the office door.

"Sir, there's been a homicide in La Boca. A shooting of an eighty-two-year-old wheelchair user in his home."

Vargas looked up from the folder that contained the latest transcripts of interviews with a number of the safe-deposit-box holders. "Juan, why would the murder of an old man in his wheelchair be of interest to us?"

"Because, sir, he wasn't killed in his chair. His body was found by a council carer in his garden shed, along with millions of dollars' worth of stolen property."

By the time Vargas and Torres arrived at the small house in La Boca, the pathologist was already on-site, working in the shed. He was accompanied by a local policeman, Miguel Vega, who had received the initial call.

Vargas surveyed the surreal scene inside the shed. Gonzales's body was lying in the centre of the floor. Surrounding it were neatly stacked piles of cash, jewels, small paintings and paper bonds. The piles of cash were subdivided by currency and he estimated there must be at least a million dollars in a single pile stacked in one of the corners.

"What can you tell us, officer?"

Vega was kneeling on the floor, looking through a pile of government bonds. He stood up before addressing his superior.

"Well, sir, just after midday, we took a call from a woman named Elena Sanchez. She is a council carer who works in the La Boca district. Apparently, one of the other carers didn't turn up for work this morning and hadn't called in sick either, which is highly unusual. Sanchez was sent out to take over the rest of the daily visits and her first one was here. When she arrived, she found the front door open and no sign of Gonzales. She checked the entire house but it was empty, although his wheelchair was in the sitting room. The upstairs bedroom was a total mess, stuff thrown about everywhere. She was about to leave when she spotted the back door open, which led her to check out the shed."

"Where is she now?"

"After we took her statement, one of our cars took her home. I told her we would probably want to interview her again down the line."

Vargas tuned to the pathologist, Dr Hugo Fernández, who was busy taking photographs of the body. "What can you tell us, doctor?"

"It's early days but I can give you some headlines. Señor Gonzales, if that's who this is, was killed some time in the last few hours by a single gunshot to the head. Looking at the burns on the skin, I would say the gun was held very close to the forehead. There's an exit wound at the back of the skull, so the bullet may well be embedded in one of the concrete walls. There's no obvious signs of resistance on the body, so this feels like a cold-blooded execution."

Vargas turned back to Vega. "Officer, I want you to find that bullet. Don't touch anything else until the lab boys have given the shed a full dusting. Clearly, we will need to bag up all this stuff very carefully before taking it away." Vargas turned towards the door. "Juan, let's take a look inside."

Vargas and Torres toured the house before ending up in the small sitting room which, unlike the upstairs bedroom, appeared neat and tidy. The only things that seemed slightly off were the TV plug and lead lying in the middle of the floor next to the empty wheelchair and the upturned cereal bowl.

"So whoever did this was clearly looking for the deposit-box haul in the house and then discovered it was in the shed. But what does an old man like Gonzales have to do with the robbery? He was an invalid, for Christ's sake—"

Torres interrupted his boss. "Even more puzzling is why did they shoot him and leave millions of dollars behind?"

Vargas wasn't listening to his colleague. His attention had turned to a small framed family photograph sitting on the windowsill. He picked up the wooden frame and showed it to Torres. "What do you see here, Juan?"

Torres took the frame from his boss and studied the image that showed three figures.

"Gonzales from years gone by, together with his wife and their son, I guess."

Vargas nodded. "How tall would you say the corpse was?"

Torres's mind flashed back to the interior of the shed and the prone position of Raúl Gonzales.

"Quite tall. I would estimate about six feet." Torres continued to study the photograph showing a young man framed between his mother and father. He stood head and shoulders above both of them.

Vargas took the picture from his assistant. "Which means his son must be at least six foot six. A colossus of a man. He's got to be our fucking giant from inside the vault."

* * *

At exactly the same moment Vargas worked out the identity

of one of the three bank robbers, Matias Paz, Luciano Herrera and three of their men were in an apartment five miles away in the Pompeya district, about to begin an interrogation with the same man.

Ricardo Gonzales was stripped to the waist and slumped on a wooden chair. His arms were tied behind his back and his legs were held in place by thick black leather straps. His face was a rubbery mess of blood and cartilage and his right eye was almost shut.

Paz was truly in his element. Inflicting physical pain on his enemies always gave him a perverse buzz of pleasure. The man opposite him was obviously one of the thieves and had used his father's garden shed as a hiding place for his share of the robbery. But, more importantly, he would know the identities of the two other men involved in the crime, one of who was in possession of his client's property.

Gonzales had been caught by surprise when Paz and his henchmen broke into his apartment. One of the assailants had pistol-whipped his face, while another two held him in position. He had briefly lost consciousness and, when he awoke, he found himself tied to the chair, facing his torturer.

He figured that, somehow, a rival gang of villains had tracked him down and was after the safe-deposit pickings. He had no intention of giving away his own hiding place, let alone the names of his two friends. But then Paz spoke for the first time and everything changed.

"Ricardo, your father is lying on the floor of his garden shed with a bullet in his head. Before he died, he claimed he had no idea how the treasure trove got there, and you know what? I believe him. So I'm afraid you've already lost everything – your father and your cut of the money."

Ricardo's mind went into overdrive as it struggled to process the information he was hearing.

Paz was on a roll and relishing the inquisition.

"You will die a very painful and slow death unless you give me the names of your two associates, in which case I might spare you, although you will be under our supervision until we recover the rest of the haul."

Gonzales knew he was being lied to. His interrogator was clearly a psychopath and was not to be trusted. He made up his mind to hold out as long as possible in the vague hope that something miraculous might happen to save him. However, his plan for resistance instantly changed when Paz produced a small power drill and held it directly above his genitals.

Paz's face looked as if it were wearing a grotesque mask. His mouth was contorted with a fixed Joker-like grin. "Ricardo, I'm sure you used a far more powerful drill than this when you worked on the tunnel but I'm not planning to drill through solid earth."

Chapter Twelve

11 January 2012

Los Angeles

The Beverly Wilshire Hotel provided the perfect setting for John Franklin's latest fundraiser. Its magnificent Italian Renaissance facade exuded all the qualities he wished to portray to the American electorate: history, power and wealth, with a touch of glamour.

It was regularly visited by the likes of ex-presidents and high-profile celebrities. In a bygone era, some of its grandest, fifteen-hundred-dollar a night, suites had served as a permanent home for the likes of Elvis Presley, Warren Beatty and John Lennon. Franklin stood in the opulent Wintergarden reception room, alongside his campaign chief, Cathy Douglas, and surveyed the high-powered guests who were enjoying the champagne and canapé reception.

"John, there's a hell of a lot of money floating around in here. Some very big hitters. The team thinks we might raise thirty million tonight."

"Cathy, you've all done an amazing job getting these guys

together under one roof and the speech Leon's put together looks really good. I went through it with my father last night, who always comes up with some great one-liners, so we've added a few bits. Let's hope it plays well."

Cathy put her arm around her candidate. "They'll love it, John, they always do but, right now, it's time for you to mingle and do some one-on-one schmoozing."

Franklin nodded and headed off to hunt down some prospective donors.

John's father, Richard, was already in the thick of the fray, holding court in the centre of the room, entertaining three of California's highest-profile businessmen whom he figured were all good for at least one-million-dollar donations to his son's campaign.

"John's going to be the best thing that's happened for business in this country since Reagan was in the White House. He'll put American business first and impose new tariffs on foreign goods that threaten our domestic businesses. But he'll also sort out health care and welfare reform for the people, which makes him the perfect unifying candidate."

Franklin was in full flow when his phone buzzed. He looked at the screen and immediately recognised the Argentinian area code.

"Gentlemen, will you please excuse me, I need to take this."

The dedicated phone in his office had an automatic divert to his mobile if it didn't pick up after five rings. As he walked out of the reception room towards one of the vast lobbies, he took the call from Matias Paz.

"Señor Franklin, I have some encouraging news for you. We have made astonishing progress in a very short time."

"Paz, don't bullshit me. Have you got the contents of my

box back yet?"

"No, Señor, but we managed to persuade Gonzales to give us the names and locations of his two associates and, in the next few hours, we will be visiting both of them."

Franklin paused to think for a moment. "I assume Señor Gonzales is no longer a danger to us."

"That is correct. We took the appropriate action."

Paz could sense that Franklin was starting to calm down. "That's good work, Matias. Have there been any other casualties along the way?"

"Yes, Señor. There has been some collateral damage in the course of the investigation."

"How many?"

"Two."

"Okay. Where are the police on all this?"

Paz was hoping for this question and came back with his prepared response. "They are playing catch-up. We have a highly placed insider who keeps us constantly informed. They have no idea what we are up to. We'll have the materials back very soon and all three of the thieves will be taken care of, so the trail will go cold. The inspector running the case will look a hero because he will recover the stolen property but he'll have no way of knowing that the contents of one of the boxes is missing."

"Okay, Matias. Let me know the moment we have it."

Franklin ended the call and tucked his mobile inside his dinner jacket. His mind drifted back to the campaign and the hundred and fifty million dollars he personally had pumped into it so far. The American public had been bombarded by a relentless TV campaign that had driven his son to the top of the national polls. He had groomed John for this moment all his life and now he was just a few months away from being the father of the most powerful man on earth.

The dinner was a spectacular success and the affluent guests ate their way through a foie gras starter, a twenty-eight-day-aged rib of beef main and a delicious dessert of white chocolate and raspberry cheesecake, all washed down with some of California's finest wines. The waiters were serving coffee and liqueurs as the man of the moment made his way to the back of the stage in preparation for his rallying speech. Waiting for him behind the black drapes was his father. The two men hadn't managed to speak all evening, but now, for the first time, they were alone. They both could sense the elephant in the room. John spoke first.

"Dad, please tell me that Paz's guys have found the contents of the box."

"Not quite, but they are very close. They've got their hands on the thieves who carried out the robbery and expect to have everything in their possession in the next few hours. I told you it would all be okay, and it will be."

John let out a huge sigh.

"That's great news, Dad. Thank you. But until we actually have it in our grasp—"

"John, relax, it's all in hand. Now it's time for you to kill them out there with that motherfucker of a speech we worked on last night."

Richard turned away from his son, walked through the break in the drapes onto the small stage, and headed towards the podium where the microphone was set.

"Ladies and gentlemen, please welcome to the stage my son, the next president of the United States."

Chapter Thirteen

12 June 1945

Río Gallegos

On 12 June 1945, after forty-three days at sea, *Santa Cruz III* arrived at the small industrial port of Río Gallegos on the south-east coast of Argentina. Although seventeen people had boarded the small cargo boat in Kiel, only sixteen disembarked. Doctor Hipke had disappeared two days before the arrival. His cabin was empty and there was no sign of his makeshift operating theatre, which had been dismantled and scrubbed clean. The VIP party of three were transported by plane on a short thirty-minute flight to the Führer's new base: a large Argentinian-style farmhouse situated a few miles north of El Calafate, a small town on the southern border of Lake Argentino in the Santa Cruz province of Patagonia.

As Hitler's private secretary, Bormann had spent the previous few years making him an incredibly wealthy man. As well as his salaries as chancellor and president, he received massive royalties from both his book, *Mein Kampf*, and for the use of his image on postage stamps. Bormann had also set up the Adolf Hitler Fund of German Trade and Industry, which collected a special tax from major industrialists, all of which went straight into the Führer's personal account. He also supervised the secret warehouses scattered across the country, which were packed full of Nazi treasure, stolen mainly from Jews and wealthy businessmen who didn't support the Nazi regime.

By the summer of 1943, Bormann realised he and Hitler needed an escape route in case Germany ended up losing the war. He identified Argentine President General Edelmiro Julián Farrell and his vice president, Juan Perón, as passionate Nazi sympathisers; hence perfect bedfellows. So Bormann began to route millions of Reichsmarks into South American banks, as he looked to create an insurance policy against a possible defeat.

In the immediate months after the end of the war, the Argentines personally welcomed a number of senior Nazis to their country but with the prized cargo of Hitler, Bormann and Braun, they hit the jackpot. Bormann had arranged for the boat to be laden with large, unmarked wooden crates containing a potpourri of stolen treasures, including rare artworks, an array of gemstones and two tons of Nazi gold. A Führer's ransom worth over two hundred and fifty million dollars.

The fugitives arrived in style at their new home in El Calafate. Perón had arranged for one of the limos from his personal fleet to be on hand for the last leg of the journey. The long-wheelbase Fleetwood Sixty Special was Cadillac's most luxurious vehicle. It was parked up on the makeshift airstrip which had been hastily constructed in a field on the east side of the lake. They landed in a twenty-seater DC-3 aircraft and immediately switched to the chauffeur-driven limousine.

Ten years earlier, Bormann had been personally responsible for supervising the renovation of the Berghof, the Führer's beloved holiday home in Berchtesgaden, on a hilltop village in the Bavarian Alps. Hitler insisted the retreat should be totally private and had instructed Bormann to remove any neighbours who lived in the area. Nazi funds were used to purchase all the properties within a five-mile radius and those who refused to sell were shipped off to concentration camps. Two days after the work was completed, Hitler and Braun stayed at the new property for a weekend and the Führer complained that his view across the valley was ruined by a single farmhouse almost eight miles away. The following weekend, Bormann gave instructions for it to be razed to the ground. That episode was an early indicator to the Führer that his private secretary was totally ruthless when it came to carrying out his orders and was therefore an invaluable asset. An attack dog with unquestionable loyalty.

In January 1945, Bormann sent off detailed plans to the team of Argentine architects in charge of the new construction. Like its owners, the residence would conceal a secret of its own. The exterior resembled a traditional local farmhouse, so as not to stand out, but the interior included a few special furnishings and artworks that Bormann had shipped over from Hitler's beloved Berghof retreat.

The Cadillac pulled up outside the house where four heavily armed men were waiting to create a guard of honour for the Führer. A large name sign, *El Blondi*, hung directly above two wooden entrance gates at the front of the property. Braun was the first to react to it.

"Martin, you've given it the perfect name. It's a permanent memorial to the Führer's soulmate."

Bormann had chosen the name as he knew Hitler had loved his pet Alsatian far more than any human in his life. Bormann had surprised him with the puppy as a birthday present back in 1941 and the pair had become inseparable. Towards the end of the war, Blondi even moved into the bunker and slept in Hitler's bedroom. The day before the three of them fled Berlin, he gave instructions for his beloved pet to be given a cyanide capsule, rather than fall into the hands of Russian soldiers.

Bormann led them inside and, for the next couple of hours, they inspected their new residence. It had been specifically designed with three distinct living areas, as Bormann knew Hitler and Braun had never actually lived together. Even in the confines of the bunker, the Führer had insisted they have separate rooms and they never shared a bed. Despite the fact she was now Hitler's wife, Bormann knew the Führer would continue to treat her as a mistress.

The centrepiece of the ground floor was the grand entrance hall, furnished with ornate Teutonic furniture that had been shipped over from Europe a few months earlier. A gigantic black marble fireplace dominated the area and a number of silver-framed pictures, featuring the Führer in a variety of animated poses, were displayed on the mantel. Directly above the fireplace hung a watercolour, set in an ornate gold-leaf frame, that Hitler himself had painted. Two heavy oak doors led through to an enormous study that boasted light pine-panelled walls, broken up by rows of bookshelves. Bormann's meticulous eye for detail had ensured that Hitler's personal library had been replicated in the new surroundings. The Führer owned an impressive collection of first editions, and they had been carefully transported from Bavaria.

However, the showpiece in the study was the free-standing Zenith Console Radio Phonograph. It was Hitler's prize possession, as it allowed him to enjoy his favourite recordings. He was a huge opera fan and owned a large collection of vinyl records. The Führer was obsessed with Wagner's works and he claimed the composer's 1842 production of *Rienzi* was the inspiration for his politics. It featured a medieval Italian folk hero who led the people in a revolt against the nobility.

Another door off the hall led to a staircase that went straight down to a huge basement area that was home to a small group of live-in staff who Bormann had vetted remotely. They included a housekeeper, a cook and a maid who shared the accommodation along with the four guards. The cook had been sent recipes for some of the Führer's favourite meals, including a traditional Austrian broth with liver dumplings and an apple cake strewn with nuts and raisins, known as "Führer Cake". The industrial fridge in the basement was heavily stocked with imported bottles of Möet & Chandon champagne, Braun's favourite drink. The bottom two shelves housed fifty small bottles of Methamphetamine, the Führer's go-to recreational drug. Theodor Morell, Hitler's personal physician for the previous nine years, had shipped out the stimulants on Bormann's orders.

For years, Morell had personally injected Hitler with the drug on a daily basis, always immediately after breakfast. He knew that administering it intravenously produced an immediate rush that would go on to create an intense energy boost for at least eight hours. During the three months they were incarcerated in the bunker, Bormann instructed Morell to teach Hitler how to safely self-inject. As ever, the Führer's private secretary was obsessed with forward planning.

The huge fridge also contained a separate glass compartment stuffed with clear plastic bags of cocaine, sourced in Peru. Two years before the end of the war, Morell had begun treating Hitler with a bizarre eye-drop mixture. The concoction created by the Führer's personal physician contained a concentrated dose of diluted cocaine. By 1945, Hitler had moved on from applying the eye drops to snorting the powdered version directly into his nostrils. Bormann recognised the Führer was an addict and, in their new life, he knew the addiction would need continuous feeding.

El Blondi, like the Berghof, stood in its own grounds, five miles away from the nearest property. Hitler was clearly stunned by Bormann's incredible achievement in creating his new residence and, for the first time in many months, appeared happy and relaxed.

Bormann took advantage of Hitler's improved mood and joined him in the study to discuss a matter that was high on his list of priorities. He passed Hitler a solitary piece of typewritten paper across the desk. It contained five names.

"Führer, I know we discussed this on the crossing but, now we are here, we need to agree on a name. My three favourites are Johnson, Franklin and Wilson. We know that America is going to emerge from the war as the most powerful nation in the world and our plan for a future Reich means your new dynasty needs to be built there, so when Eva bears you a son he will be educated in English as his primary language, as well as Spanish and German. All these names belong to previous presidents and carry weight and credibility with the

American people. Which would you prefer?"

Hitler relaxed back into his chair and surveyed his new study. "You have done extremely well, Martin. Your loyalty is beyond question and your planning has been impeccable. I loathe the idea of choosing any of them but I know it's an essential part of our future plan, so I will leave the choice to you."

Bormann allowed himself the rare luxury of smiling back at the Führer. "Führer, I'm going to choose FDR. He was the only president in US history to serve four terms. Welcome to your new home, Señor Franklin."

Chapter Fourteen

11 January 2012

Buenos Aires

Vargas and Torres were driving to the address they'd sourced for Ricardo Gonzales. Behind them, riding in convoy, was a second police car containing four more officers. Torres was at the wheel, so when his mobile sparked into life he gestured to Vargas to take the call. It was from one of the other detectives working on the case, informing his boss that the body of a council carer, Maria Vidal, had been found on a rubbish dump a couple of miles from Raúl Gonzales's house. Vargas placed the phone down in the cupholder between the two front seats.

"They've just found the body of old man Gonzales's main carer, Maria Vidal."

"Let me guess … a single gunshot to the head?"

"No, a knife wound directly into her heart. Just as fatal."

Neither man spoke for a few seconds, then Torres broke the silence. "Jesus, sir. What have we stumbled into?"

Thirty minutes later, both men were standing in Ricardo

Gonzales's apartment. His body was slumped in the chair, his hands and legs still firmly bound. There was a single bullet hole between his eyes and his groin area was one of the most horrifying sights either detective had ever seen in their long careers. Vargas almost heaved as he looked at the badly mutilated corpse.

"That's three murders in quick succession. Gonzales was clearly brutally interrogated before he was killed. It's totally horrific. I've never come across anything like this before."

Torres had to look away from the body. "They obviously wanted the names of the other two men who did the job and, by the look of things, I'm sure they got them."

"Juan, if this was just some rival gang wanting to steal the haul, then it would make some kind of sense. But whoever did these murders left the entire stash in the old man's shed – millions of dollars in cash just ignored. So what is this really about? What do these guys really want?"

Torres looked back at the disfigured face of Ricardo Gonzales. "It's got to be about what's inside one of the stolen boxes. Whoever owns that box wants the contents back badly."

* * *

The boardroom at Theodor Consultants was set up for an extraordinary meeting. What made it unusual was the time of day. It had been set for midnight. Every seat was occupied and all eyes were on Matias Paz who sat at the head of the table with his number two, Luciano Herrera, sitting to his right.

"Okay, gentlemen, we are going to launch the raids at three in the morning. There will be two teams – one led by Luci and the other by me. The vital thing is to hit the two marks at exactly the same moment so they have no time to warn each other. My team are going after Sebastian Ramos, who has a flat in Barrio Soldati and Luci's team will hit Pedro García at his home in Villa Lugano, which is only a few kilometres away. Remember, before they die, we need to know exactly where they hid their share of the haul. Before this day is out, I want the contents of that box back in our hands."

The synchronised raids kicked off precisely on time. The locks at both apartments proved easy to pick, and within ten seconds of breaking in Paz and Herrera were standing in the respective bedrooms of their targets. Sebastian Ramos heard the front door crash open but didn't have time to reach his bedroom door before a Glock 17, complete with silencer, was jammed against his forehead. At exactly the same moment, Luciano Herrera and two of his men entered Pedro García's bedroom. The bed was neatly made and the room was empty. The cupboard was bare.

* * *

Pedro García had no idea his fishing trip with his younger brother, Aldo, had saved his life. Forty-eight hours earlier, the two men had driven north out of the city and headed for a small hunting lodge located on the Paraná River, which they had taken on a three-day rental. They planned to spend the trip fishing for golden dorado, the most prized catch for an angler. Both brothers were highly skilled at the art of fly-fishing, having been taught by their late father who used to love taking them on family fishing trips when they were young boys. Aldo had booked it over three months earlier and Pedro had always figured that, as the trip was organised for after the date of the robbery, he would either be free to enjoy it with his brother or else he would be languishing in a prison cell.

Pedro and Aldo sat next to each other on the riverbank for a last fishing session. Both men were enjoying an early morning coffee laced with brandy.

"I'm so glad we did this. I'm loving it. And I bet Dad is up there smiling down at us."

Pedro took a swig of his drink and grinned at his younger brother. "Me too, Aldo. I don't want this to end. One day soon I aim to buy you a lodge like this. You can bring your own boys out for regular trips."

Aldo burst into laughter. "Yeah, right, and why don't you buy us both a couple of brand-new Mercedes sports while you are at it."

"Aldo, I'm serious. In a year or so I hope to come into some money and, when I do, I'll make sure you and the family are well-looked-after."

Aldo could see that his brother was deadly serious and was puzzled. "Right, Pedro. What are you going to do, rob a bank?"

* * *

Sebastian Ramos stood with his back against the wall in his small living room facing Paz and two of his men, who were pointing Glocks directly at his head. Considering he'd only been awake for a few seconds, his senses were on full alert and his mind was working overtime.

Matias Paz broke the silence, his voice laden with menace.

"Sebastian, I can see you're wondering what's going on, so let me enlighten you. You see—"

A mobile rang out and Paz turned to see one of his men lower his gun to answer it.

"Boss, it's Luciano." He handed the phone to Paz.

"Yes, Luci. What news?"

"The news is not good. The flat is empty and it looks to me as if García has gone away, but not necessarily forever. Most of his clothes are still here, but the fridge is practically empty, which suggests he knew he wouldn't need it for a while. It just doesn't have the feel of a sudden escape. I'm sure he'll be back."

Paz was reeling from this unexpected setback, and he instantly dreaded his next call with Franklin. "Fuck it. Okay, Luci. Search every inch of the flat and then leave four men to run twenty-four-hour surveillance outside the apartment." Paz's eyes fixed intensely on his new captive. "This news makes my talk with Señor Ramos even more important."

Paz handed the phone back to his henchman and reached inside his jacket for his own mobile. He flicked through the menu to his photo album and selected a picture. He held the phone directly in front of Ramos's face. The image displayed the pulverised body of Ricardo Gonzales. His face was a mushy, bloody pulp with a bullet hole directly in the middle of his forehead. Ramos felt the bile rise in the back of his throat and couldn't stop himself retching. Galvanised by a mixture of shock and fury, he lashed out at the phone, knocking it from Paz's grip. It smashed against the wall before falling onto the wooden floor.

Paz lunged forward and assaulted Ramos with a flurry of punches. For the next few seconds, he gave him a savage beating, before his mind cleared and he remembered he needed the man to be compos mentis, at least until he gave up the information they needed. He stepped back and picked up the mobile. The screen was cobwebbed where the glass had shattered from the impact with the wall. Paz cursed as he put the broken iPhone down onto the wooden dining table. Next to it was a small black toolbox that one of his men had brought into the flat. A few seconds later, he was armed with his current favourite instrument of torture. He held the power drill high in the air above Ramos's head.

"Señor Ramos, I have only three questions for you. Firstly, where have you hidden your share of the haul? Secondly, where has your friend Pedro García hidden his cut? And thirdly, where is he right now? Where has he gone?"

During the following few minutes, despite enduring unimaginable pain, Ramos was only able to answer the first of the three questions and, just before Paz shot him in the head, he knew the thief was telling the truth.

Ramos had given up his own hiding place and Paz's men set about hacking up the wooden floorboards in the apartment. Before long, the cloth bags came into view. One by one they were carefully emptied onto the floor to be scrutinised. It seemed perverse to the men that they weren't allowed to stuff their pockets full of cash and gemstones. Instead, the hunt for the contents of Box 1321 was all that mattered to their obsessed boss. In truth, they were far too scared of the Black Scorpion to even consider risking disobeying his instructions.

Occasionally, they would come across some loose documents or folders that would immediately be handed over to their boss for scrutiny. He was the only person in the room who knew specifically what they were searching for and his frustration grew as, yet again, they were facing another failure.

His men worked tirelessly and, after two hours, there was only one bag left to sort through. It was awkwardly jammed underneath the far corner of the kitchen floor by a couple of stubborn pine floorboards. Using a large carpentry hammer from Ramos's own toolbox, one of Paz's men began ruthlessly smashing through the wooden barrier and, after a brief attack, he managed to free the final cloth bag.

The persistent banging noises eventually woke up the old lady who lived directly above Ramos's basement flat. Martina Soto was an elderly widow who had lived in the housing development for over thirty years. She kept herself to herself and had very little to do with her neighbours. Ramos had lived beneath her for almost a decade and, in all that time, they had only spoken twice. She leaned across the bed and glanced at the clock on her bedside table. It was five in the morning and something was clearly wrong. As well as the banging, she was sure she could detect a number of different male voices emanating from the flat below. She reached for the phone and dialled 101.

Paz was kneeling on the floor, desperately clawing through the final bag. Yet again he was thwarted, as there was no sign of the contents of Franklin's box. He was about to ask his men to recheck everything one more time when his earpiece broke into life.

"Boss, a police car has just pulled up outside. Two cops are heading your way."

One of Paz's men, Thiago Rivas, was positioned outside the front of the building in a black transit and he watched as two police officers made their way towards the front entrance of the housing estate. Ramos's flat had a tiny backyard that was accessed from the kitchen door.

Paz and his men headed for the only exit left to them and climbed over the wall, which led directly on to a small side street. He screamed down his wrist mic, "Thiago, swing the transit around to the back of the estate."

At the same moment the two officers entered Ramos's flat, Paz and his men were clambering into the back of a blacked-out van. Héctor Santos was the senior of the two patrol cops and had worked the same beat for nearly twenty years, but he'd never seen a sight like this before. The entire floor of the apartment had been savagely ripped apart and was covered with what he figured must be millions of dollars' worth of items. In the corner of the room lay the prone body of Sebastian Ramos. His green eyes were wide open and appeared to be staring directly back at him. The blood surrounding the bullet wound in his forehead had started to congeal into a grotesque crust.

The rookie cop turned to his superior. "Héctor, what the fuck has gone on here?"

Santos flicked down the switch on his chest-mounted radio. "This is Officer Santos. We are in apartment 1B at the main housing estate on Avenida da Lacarra. We have a murder scene and we urgently need senior backup."

There was little traffic on the road and the black transit made its way swiftly back towards the offices of Theodor Consultants. No one had spoken since the sudden retreat from Ramos's apartment and the men on board knew better than to attempt to break the awkward silence as their boss was evidently seething with anger.

Paz decided to call Luciano to bring him up to speed and

reached inside his jacket pocket for his mobile. In an instant he remembered he had left the broken phone behind in the flat on the dining table. At that moment, he let out a terrifying cry which sounded more like a howl than a scream.

* * *

Vargas and Torres stood over the slain body of Sebastian Ramos. He had patently suffered at the hands of the same torturer as his friend, Ricardo Gonzales, and now two of the three bank robbers were dead.

Torres looked away from the corpse and turned to his boss. "Identical M.O. as before. Interrogation and then a single gunshot to the head. I'm betting ballistics will confirm that Ramos was shot with the same gun that killed both members of the Gonzales family. Ramos obviously hid his share under the floor while Gonzales used his father's shed but, otherwise, the story is the same."

Vargas nodded in agreement as he stared grimly at the outlandish crime scene. "Once again, the haul is left behind, but what we don't know is whether they found what they were looking for this time. Yet again, these bastards have a head start on us. Get the team to check out the immediate families and close friends of both our victims and see if anyone jumps out as a possible suspect. It's vital we locate his whereabouts before they do."

Vargas was turning to leave when he spotted the broken mobile on the dining table. Torres handed him a pair of transparent latex gloves to slip on before picking it up.

"Must be Ramos's phone, sir. I'll get the boys to bag it up and bring it back to the station."

Vargas didn't reply. He continued to stare at the horrific image frozen underneath the broken glass of the mobile. Despite the cracks on the screen, he could clearly make out the corpse of Ricardo Gonzales. He angled the screen for Torres to see.

"No, Juan. This phone doesn't belong to Sebastian Ramos. It belongs to his murderer."

Chapter Fifteen

September 1946

El Calafate

I n September 1946, three highly significant events took place within two weeks of each other. Ronald Franklin, aka Martin Bormann, founded a new business based in Buenos Aires. Emilia Franklin, aka Eva Braun, gave birth to a son, and the Nuremberg trials issued their verdicts on 199 high-ranking Nazis, who were being tried for war crimes.

Bormann was a genius of finance and administration and, in the fifteen months following his arrival in Argentina, had deployed some of the massive sums he had secretly invested in South American banks to create a brand-new enterprise: the Franklin Pharmaceutical Corporation. He recognised that, in the post-war era, the pharma industry would flourish and that drug manufacturers would be intrinsically linked to the economic well-being of developing nations. His long-term plan was to migrate the company to the United States and build it into the biggest pharmaceutical corporation in the world.

He greatly admired American giants such as Johnson & Johnson, Merck and Pfizer, viewing them as a template for his new enterprise. Bormann diverted over fifty million dollars into setting it up from scratch, recruiting the very best talent. He sought out research scientists, biotech specialists, industrial pharmacists and experienced senior management. He also funded the purchase of a major new office development in a prime location and kitted out three floors of the building with purpose-built labs, stacked full of state-of-the-art equipment.

There was a significant German population living in Argentina, with over forty thousand based in the capital alone. Many of them wielded great economic influence inside the country and controlled a considerable part of the nation's industrial, chemical and electrical goods production. A number of them were Nazi sympathisers who revered Ronald Franklin as, despite his altered physical features, they were aware of his true identity and were in total awe of him.

In December 1945, six months after their secret arrival into the country, Bormann invited a hand-picked group of businessmen for a weekend stay at El Blondi, where they were granted a brief audience with the Führer. Rumours had been circulating for months among pro-Nazi elite circles that Hitler and Bormann had escaped from Berlin and set up a home somewhere in the Santa Cruz area. Once the businessmen had seen Hitler for themselves and confirmed the rumours were true, Bormann became the most powerful and significant figure in Buenos Aires. Financially, he had access to seemingly unlimited funds and, politically, he had the support and protection of the Perón regime. For the second time in his life, he found himself at the centre of a country's economic and political power base.

Three years earlier, in 1943, Bormann had started to learn Spanish and English: essential skills he knew he'd require in order to pull off his long-term plan. Two female tutors, specialising in the respective languages, came to his house every day at separate times. The lessons only stopped when he was forced to move into the bunker. Within a week of relocating to El Calafate, he'd recruited a local schoolteacher who was fluent in both, a huge bonus for Bormann as it saved him precious time. He was a dedicated student, and when he chaired the first ever board meeting of Franklin Pharmaceuticals on 17 September 1946 his English was getting there but he was fluent in Spanish, albeit with an unmistakable German accent.

He glanced around the impressive boardroom at the assembled directors, some of whom were meeting for the first time. He had poached most of them from rival pharmaceutical companies located throughout South America. An easy task as he had tripled their salaries and offered generous sign-on bonuses in order to entice them away from their jobs.

"Gentlemen, welcome to the birth of a new enterprise. Today, we begin life as a virgin company with zero status. In five years, we will be the largest pharma company in South America and, in twenty years, the Franklin Corporation will be the biggest pharmaceutical company in the world."

No one in the boardroom who heard Ronald Franklin's opening words had any doubt he would achieve his aim.

* * *

Ten days later, at three o'clock in the morning, Eva Braun gave birth to an eight-pound baby boy. Hitler and the Third Reich had gained an heir. Richard George Franklin entered the world at precisely three fifteen in the morning, after Braun had gone through two days of difficult labour. Hitler insisted on the choice of the baby's middle name as a tribute to his paternal grandfather, Johann Georg Hiedler.

It had been a complicated pregnancy and, on two occasions, Braun had nearly miscarried, so Bormann had arranged for a local midwife to live at the house for the last three months, just in case the baby was premature but, in the end, Richard was born only two days early.

Such was Bormann's deference towards the Führer, he let five hours pass before informing him of the overnight birth, waiting until the maid had taken him his breakfast tray. Hitler was sitting up in bed, scooping out some yolk from a boiled egg, when Bormann knocked and entered.

"Führer, I have excellent news. Eva has delivered you a healthy son and both are well. She has fulfilled her duty. When you are ready, I'll ask the midwife to bring the baby to you."

Hitler smiled and rested his spoon on the silver tray. "Martin, tell me, how should I feel? You've experienced this so many times. I feel absolutely nothing. Why do I have no desire to see the baby?"

Bormann was not surprised by Hitler's indifference and had expected the low-key reaction.

"Yes, as a father of ten, I can tell you they only become interesting once they can converse. But, Führer, this baby is special as he will eventually take forward your legacy and continue your bloodline."

Hitler rarely joked but he laughed out loud at what he was

about to say.

"Martin, my sources tell me you have spread your genes far and wide and that you have fathered many more children than those you refer to with your wife, or should I say the ten you admit to."

This was the first time in their entire working relationship that Hitler had ever shown any interest in Bormann's personal life and he relished the moment.

"I'm proud to say I take every opportunity to extend *my* pure bloodline and to the best of my knowledge, I have fathered another ten at least."

Bormann was known to be a serial womaniser and, in his previous existence, had made no secret of his relationship with a famous theatre actress, whom he openly referred to as his second wife. He also regularly engaged in other extramarital affairs and both his spouse and mistress had little choice but to accept the public humiliation.

Bormann was not a handsome man. He was short and stocky and possessed little charisma or charm. However, he was an unstoppable force of nature who was happy to exploit the power and influence of his position to seduce women.

Hitler downed his glass of orange juice and continued to smile at Bormann.

"Martin, it seems that, in the matter of paternity, I am no match for you. Inform the midwife to bring the baby to my room. I am ready to meet my son."

"Yes, Führer."

Bormann left the room feeling totally ecstatic. Braun had produced an heir for the Führer and the next part of his plan had been successfully executed.

* * *

In late September, the infamous Nuremberg trials drew to a close and sentences were handed down to senior representatives of the Nazi regime. Bormann had been following events closely through local radio and newspaper coverage. In addition, he was constantly updated on his telex machine by pro-Nazi allies, still based inside Germany. Throughout the trials, Hitler's mood swings heightened as he became increasingly agitated. Bormann noted that the Führer's daily cocaine intake almost doubled overnight. He met with Hitler in his study once a week to give him an update on developments. On 1 October, just four days after Braun gave birth, Bormann briefed the Führer on the grim details of the sentences.

"Göring, Streicher and Ribbentrop have all been sentenced to death."

Hitler's hands were trembling and he glared at Bormann as he digested the information. He eventually nodded and then carefully wrote the names down on a pad in front of him. Despite his best efforts, the writing was an illegible scrawl.

"What about Albert?"

Bormann knew that Albert Speer, the renowned architect, was one of the Führer's oldest friends and a close ally. In 1942, Hitler had appointed him minister of armaments and, in that capacity, he had been responsible for supervising the use of slave labour from the occupied territories in the production of munitions.

"Speer has been sentenced to twenty years."

Hitler grimaced and added to his unreadable notes. "What about the traitor, Hess?"

"Führer, he escaped the death penalty but has been sentenced to life imprisonment."

Hitler was clearly distressed to hear his former deputy had escaped the hangman's rope. He burst into life, smashing his fists on the desktop. This brief flash of rage instantly reminded Bormann of the psychotic, unstable nature of the man who had once been the most powerful leader in the Western world.

"Martin, we need to find a way to end his life inside prison. It is an outrage he has been spared. He must die ..." there was a long pause before the Führer completed the sentence "... and he must suffer first."

Bormann knew this was an impossible request to fulfil, but was happy to humour the Führer.

"Of course. I will issue instructions."

Bormann stood up to leave but Hitler had one final question.

"Martin, what about you?"

Bormann's face broke into a devilish grin. "Führer, this very day I have been sentenced to death by hanging."

Chapter Sixteen

12 January 2012

Buenos Aires

Paz sat in the cemetery at his usual spot. He stared at the imposing statue of Firpo, desperately hoping to find some inspiration to help determine his next move. He had two important phone calls to make and opted to make the easier one first. He pulled out his newly acquired burner and punched in Luciano's number from memory.

"Luci, it's been a shitstorm of a morning. Can you believe that bastard Ramos hid his cut under the fucking floorboards of his flat? We went through everything but no sign of our stuff."

Herrera could sense the desperation in Paz's voice. "Boss, did he give up anything that can help us find out where the hell García is and what he did with his share?"

"He knew fuck all, Luci. He said the three of them made a pact not to make any contact with each other for twelve months and they all did their own thing with their share of the boxes. I worked the bastard over and there's no way he was lying. Did you find anything at García's flat?"

"Boss, we ripped it apart but found nada. Also, unlike Ramos, his apartment floor is solid concrete, so that wasn't an option for him. It doesn't feel to me like he has done a runner. I think the rat will return and we'll be waiting for him."

There was a short pause before Paz continued the conversation. "Luci, I've fucked up big time. I left my phone at Ramos's flat. The bastard smashed it up. When the police suddenly turned up, I left without it."

Luciano was clearly stunned by this news but tried to sound positive. "Boss, that phone is secure. They won't get anything from it."

A cynical smile broke out on Paz's face. "For all our sakes, Luci, I hope you're right. If not, we're all fucked."

Paz took a deep breath before making the second of his planned calls. He'd already made a decision on whether to tell his employer the grim news about the lost mobile. Richard Franklin was working at his office desk and reached for the red phone, knowing that Paz would be on the other end.

"Paz, I hope this time you are calling with some better news."

"Yes, Señor. We continue to make progress. This morning we located the second of the three thieves and his stash from the break-in."

Paz heard the sharp intake of breath from the other end of the line.

"Unfortunately, he didn't have the contents of your box."

Franklin grimaced before replying. "For Christ's sake, Paz, I thought you had some good news for me. My patience is running out fast."

"Señor, we have the name and address of the third thief and

right now my men are staking out his apartment. As soon as he returns, I can guarantee we will find your box. It has to be in his share of the haul."

"What do you mean *returns*? Where the fuck is he?"

Paz moved the phone away from his ear as he felt the sheer force of Franklin's unbridled anger. "We don't yet know, but we believe he'll be back sometime soon."

"Have you got any other bad news for me?"

Paz thought about his mobile, which he guessed was now in the hands of the police. "No, Señor. Everything else is good."

He glared at the unsecure burner phone he was now forced to use and sat for a moment reflecting on the raging hatred he felt towards Franklin – the only figure in his life who wielded total power over him. He knew it was an inevitable consequence of doing a deal with the devil. Then a subconscious switch in his brain automatically flicked into action and his thoughts turned towards Tomás. He wondered if the boy was available, and, a few moments later, he reached for the phone and began typing an email to the Eros agency.

Chapter Seventeen

12 January 2012

Buenos Aires

Vargas was back in his office, discussing the latest developments with Torres. They had passed the mobile to their IT specialists, whose initial diagnosis had not been encouraging. It appeared this was not a regular iPhone. It was encrypted with an inbuilt firewall that required a set of passwords to open it up.

"Juan, we've had four executions in the last twenty-four hours and we badly need a break if we are going to prevent a fifth. We've got to find out who the third man is. And pronto."

"I'm backing our tech boys to break into the mobile and then at least we might find out who we are up against."

"What about prints?"

"A lovely clear set, chief, but no match on our servers."

Vargas moved towards the office door. "It's time to rally the troops."

Flanked by Torres, he made his way through to the open-plan area where the bulk of the detective team were based.

He stood in front of the main crime board and addressed his men.

"Listen up, everyone. If we are lucky, we've maybe got a few hours before the third of our thieves is tortured and executed. Everyone needs to step up to the plate. Keep looking for a common denominator between Gonzales and Ramos that might help us identify our man."

Vargas turned to walk back to his office, signalling to Torres to follow him, when Detective Alex Martin stood up from his desk.

"Sir, I think I may have something."

Martin handed the chief inspector a report containing details of his interview with Pedro García. Vargas read through the notes and looked at the detective.

"Okay, Alex, so this guy García rented one of the boxes that wasn't broken into – as did hundreds of other people. I can't see anything suspicious here."

"To be honest, sir, neither did I when I first interviewed him. He appeared to be a pretty regular guy who decided to keep his cash in a safe-deposit box. In fact, he seemed a bit pathetic and I remember feeling sorry for him—"

Torres jumped in. "Detective Martin, what's your point?"

"Well, sir, as you know we've been running checks on Gonzales's and Ramos's friends and family."

Vargas was getting impatient and stepped forward to interrupt the detective.

"And what have you discovered?"

"It appears that Ramos and García are first cousins."

* * *

Pedro packed the fishing gear into the back of Aldo's ten-year-old red Focus Estate. He took a last glance at the spot on the riverbank where he had fished for the last few days and walked back into the lodge. His brother was just finishing breakfast.

"Aldo, this has been our best trip yet. Twenty dorado and six tararira as a bonus. Not bad for a couple of city fishermen."

Aldo took a final spoonful of muesli before walking across to the sink to wash out his bowl.

"Brother, I've loved it too. I could easily stay for a few more days but I guess we both need to get back to the real world."

Pedro knew that, following the robbery, he was now one of the richest men in the country and was determined to use some of his new-found wealth to look after his younger brother and his family. As Aldo drove them back towards the city, he flicked on the car radio, which was tuned to a local news station. Pedro leaned across and hit the off button.

"Brother, please let's enjoy the peace and tranquillity for a little bit longer."

Had Pedro left the radio on for a few more seconds, he would have heard the breaking rolling news story reporting the grisly murders of his two associates.

* * *

Two of Paz's men were stationed inside García's apartment while, outside the front of the building, the black transit contained another four, including Herrera. It was a waiting game, as Luciano was convinced García would return to his apartment sooner or later. However, there was a potential new problem on the horizon. The TV and newspapers had just broken the news of the slaying of Gonzales and Ramos. The story claimed both men had been involved in the safe-deposit robbery and had been killed by a rival gang who were intent on stealing the haul that was estimated to be over ninety million dollars. Herrera decided to call his boss, who was back in the office.

"Boss, have you seen the breaking news?"

Paz didn't appreciate being interrupted while feeding his beloved scorpions and let rip. "Of course I've seen the fucking news. As will have Franklin. We have to pray that Pedro García hasn't."

* * *

Vargas stood in front of the six detectives who were about to set off with him to García's apartment.

"The reason we are going in unmarked cars is we don't know the status of the suspect or his apartment. For all we know, our unknown enemy may already be on-site, so we have to be very careful. These people have already executed two of the thieves. We need to keep García alive and find his share of the robbery as, somehow, the answer to this case lies in the contents of one of those boxes."

Torres picked up from his boss. "García's apartment is on the second floor. Those of you with me will enter the building from the front and the other group, who will be with the chief, will enter through the rear of the building. Any questions?"

None of the officers replied.

"Okay, then, let's go."

The two white Peugeot 508s made their way in convoy across the city and came to a stop a few hundred yards away from García's apartment in the Villa Lugano district. Vargas was sitting in the front passenger seat in the lead vehicle. He clicked on his radio.

"Juan, give us time to get set at the rear of the building and then, when I give the signal, we all go in together. Remember, for all we know some very highly trained criminals may be inside the apartment right now interrogating Pedro, or just waiting for him to come home, so use caution at all times and be ready to defend yourselves."

"Okay, chief, we will hold our position out front and wait for you to action the entry."

Vargas nodded to the driver and the Peugeot set off for the rear of the housing estate. The detectives were fully kitted out with body armour as Vargas was expecting the worst. All he knew about his unknown enemy was they were cold-blooded torturers and professional killers and therefore dangerous adversaries.

Vargas's Peugeot parked up on the quiet backstreet with a clear line of sight to the rear of the building. The rusted iron fire escape was the only way in or out of the back of the apartments and he signalled to the other detectives to exit the car. The four men drew their standard Beretta 92 semi-automatic pistols and stealthily made their way across the large, open concrete parking area behind the building. Vargas was in front and stopped about fifteen metres from the bottom of the fire escape. He reached for his chest radio.

"Okay, Juan. It's a go. Tell me when you are entering the front of the building."

Torres and the two detectives with him heard the message and left the car in unison. Luciano Herrera was sitting in the front of the black transit parked directly opposite the front of the apartment block. He was listening to some American eighties pop on the radio when he caught sight of the police approaching the building in his wing mirror. He snarled into his wrist mic to warn his two men inside the flat.

"Jesus Christ, there are three cops coming your way. Get the hell out of there right now. Use the fire exit."

Herrera's men wasted no time in making their escape and, within seconds, they had clambered out of the back-bedroom window onto the iron platform, only to discover Vargas and his team waiting down below.

"Hold your positions and raise your hands slowly above your heads."

Vargas and his men trained their weapons on Herrera's two henchmen. They were both professional killers; hardened mercenaries who had served in Africa alongside Paz. They had no interest in surrendering to City Police.

Without appearing to flinch, they gave a subtle nod to each other and then, acting perfectly in sync, dived onto the floor, while at the same time reaching for their Glocks. Gunfire rained down on Vargas and his men, who instantly returned fire. One of the detectives was taken out in the opening exchange, catching a bullet clean through the neck. The entry wound sat just above the top of his Kevlar vest.

Vargas reeled around in horror as he saw his colleague fall and signalled to his other two men to take cover behind some giant metal rubbish bins positioned near the base of the fire exit. One of the officers held his crouched position for a few more seconds as he had a clear line of sight of one of the escaping gunmen. He let off two shots, both of which hit their target. The bullets ripped almost simultaneously into the right lung and heart of Benjamín Benítez. The mercenary was dead before his body tumbled down the steps of the fire escape.

His colleague, Ángel López, was now kneeling behind a narrow concrete pillar located on the iron platform just outside the first floor of the building. He only had two rounds left and, as there were three cops below him, he figured he was screwed. At that moment, Torres, along with his two men, climbed through García's back window onto the fire exit platform, one floor above, and yelled down to López to drop his weapon, as he was now an open target. He was trapped at both ends and knew there was no way out.

"Okay, don't shoot." He stood up warily and held his pistol high in the air, with the barrel clenched between his thumb and forefinger.

Moments earlier, Luciano had heard the gunfire and had signalled to his driver to make their way around to the rear of the building. As they entered the street, he gave his instructions in a calm, matter-of-fact manner.

"Franco, nice and easy. Just keep it at ten. Let's see what's going down."

It only took him a few seconds to take in the scene, and then he knew instantly what he had to do next.

"Okay, pull over right here."

The transit eased to a complete stop. The electric passenger window slid down and the barrel of an AS50 sniper rifle poked out. Luciano took careful aim and the single incendiary round took off the majority of López's head. For a brief moment, Vargas and his men froze on the spot at the sight of the headless corpse. Most of them were close enough to be hit by the blood spray that filled the air. Torres was the first to react and shouted to his fellow detectives below him.

"The shot came from the black transit behind you!"

Vargas and his men spun around just in time to hear the screeching tyres of the van as it sped away. Within seconds, it had turned the first corner and was gone.

* * *

Paz and Herrera took their usual places in the cemetery opposite the statue of their favourite boxer. Paz sat in silence on the stone bench as he listened to his lieutenant's grim report. Herrera took him through the whole sorry episode that ended with the killing of one of his own men.

"Boss, I figured we couldn't risk López being taken in for questioning. He was tough but you never know."

Paz put his arm around Herrera. "Luci, you had no choice. You took the only possible option. But how did those fuckers find out about García and where the fuck is he?"

"I don't know, boss, but it looked to me like our boys had nailed one of them before I got there, so they're going to be pretty pissed. Plus, they'll stake the flat out until García returns. What are we going to do?"

Paz stood up and walked over to the statue of Luis Ángel Firpo. He carefully studied the carved features of the boxer's rugged but strikingly handsome face.

"I wonder what The Wild Bull of the Pampas would do."

Chapter Eighteen

12 January 2012

Buenos Aires

Vargas left Torres and the rest of the men behind at the flat, as his immediate thoughts turned to the family of the fallen officer. He faced the unenviable job of visiting Miguel Pastor's wife to break the dreadful news that her husband was dead. Moments like this were by far the worst aspect of his job and, as the patrol car weaved its way across the city, he pounded the steering wheel, desperately trying to find the right words for the task in hand.

He spent over an hour consoling Valentina Pastor and left her in the safe hands of two female family liaison officers. This was only the second time in his career he'd had to perform this part of his duties and the emotional impact cut through him like a knife. He knew how painful it was to face the death of the person you loved most in your life.

Vargas climbed wearily into his car, fully intending to drive back to García's apartment to meet up with Torres. Instead, he found himself heading out towards the outskirts of the city, tears streaming down his face. Forty minutes later he arrived at La Tablada Cemetery, the largest Jewish burial ground in South America, containing over a hundred thousand graves. One of which belonged to his wife.

He trudged, unseeing, through the grounds, following a route he knew all too well. He'd lost Sophia three years before to a savage and rampant brain tumour. His life had fallen apart then, all their dreams and plans cruelly ripped away from him so quickly. His future lost. Vargas knelt down next to his wife's grave, his body heaving with gut-wrenching sobs. Watching over him like a guardian angel, Sophia's headstone displayed her picture with her name etched underneath, Sophia Koppel-Vargas, in both Spanish and Hebrew.

Sophia's paternal grandfather was one of hundreds of thousands of like-minded Jews who fled Nazi Germany in the mid-thirties and headed for South America to begin a new life. Most of them settled in Buenos Aires and, by 1939, half the small manufacturing factories in the city were owned by Jewish immigrants.

Sophia was not orthodox and didn't practise Judaism but, nevertheless, she was incredibly proud of her heritage. Once a year, on Yom Kippur, she would take Vargas to their local synagogue, where he'd spend the day fasting with her parents and younger sister. He had been born and brought up as a Catholic, but fully embraced the cultural aspects of her religion. She had worked in the city centre as a nursery teacher and he used to love hearing about the small children she cared for. They had planned to have a family of their own but then the tumour came to light and their lives were shattered.

Vargas spent most of the next hour sitting on the ground

in front of her grave, weeping like a baby.

* * *

Torres and Martin went back inside the flat and two other officers stayed in one of the Peugeots opposite the front entrance to the block.

"Alex, you spoke to García. What's he like?"

Martin's thoughts flashed back to their brief interview at the station.

"The thing is, sir, he was one of about twenty box owners I met after the raid. He was pretty unremarkable. He claimed he regularly visited his box to take out cash to live on and—"

Both men heard their radios buzz at the same time.

"Inspector Torres, a red estate car has just pulled up outside. Two men got out and are busy collecting stuff from the boot. One of them fits the description of our man."

Torres gestured to Martin to shut the front door, which was currently ajar. "Okay, don't make a move, but let us know as soon as García goes inside the building. Detective Martin will be able to confirm his identity as soon as he enters the apartment. Keep your eyes open for any trouble in case those goons from before return to the scene. Once he enters the block, give it a few seconds and follow him in."

Pedro placed his fishing gear and a small overnight bag onto the pavement and gave his younger brother a long bear hug.

"Aldo, say hello to those boys of yours and tell them their Uncle Pedro will be over to see them very soon. Also, thanks for sorting out the trip. I promise I will pay for the next one."

"Will do. And, brother, don't worry. I know things are tight for you and there's not been much work about during the last few months."

The two men broke off their embrace and Pedro smiled at his younger brother, who represented the only family he had left. In that moment, he decided he would break his own golden rule. He would take some cash from the hidden stash in the lock-up to pay for their next fishing trip. He would also buy some special gifts for his young nephews.

"Thanks, Aldo, but next time it's my turn and I promise we'll do it in style."

Aldo turned away and opened the door on the driver's side of the Focus. "Until then, take care of yourself, Pedro."

Pedro nodded to Aldo, collected his belongings and walked away from the car towards the entrance of the block. Torres's radio buzzed into life.

"The subject is on his way into the building. He should be entering the apartment in the next minute. All quiet out here, so we'll follow him in."

Torres and Martin were standing in the middle of the open-plan living room, their guns drawn.

"Understood. We are in position and ready for his arrival."

Pedro was still planning the details for his next fishing trip as he opened the front door. His flat looked like a war zone and, instantly, his mind lurched back to reality as he found himself face to face with two armed men. He felt a sudden pain in his stomach that almost made him want to vomit as he recognised one of them as the detective who'd interviewed him at the police station. His brain froze but he knew he needed to unscramble his thoughts and compose himself for this confrontation. Detective Martin broke the silence. He took in the fishing rods that Pedro had now dropped onto the floor.

"Hello, Señor García. It's good to see you again. How was your fishing trip?"

Pedro surprised himself by remembering the young detective's name. He tried to maintain a poker face, even though inside he was squirming.

"Detective Martin, the trip was good. The dorado were biting. I was down at the Paraná River with my brother at a small lodge. But I don't think you are here to discuss my hobby. How can I help you and why are your guns pointing at me?"

Torres lowered his weapon and indicated to Martin to follow suit.

"Señor García, I am Inspector Torres. You need to accompany us to the station headquarters. We have a great deal to discuss with you."

Pedro continued to exude a calm persona and made his way over to the kitchen table, where he grabbed one of the wooden chairs and sat down. Torres moved across the room and perched himself at the end of the table so he was directly facing García.

"Señor García, you are an extremely fortunate man."

"Why so, inspector?"

"Because it is Detective Martin and me waiting here to greet you, and not somebody else."

Chapter Nineteen

20 April 1949

El Calafate

The guest list for Adolf Hitler's sixtieth birthday party was truly astonishing. The headliners were undoubtedly the president and first lady of Argentina, Juan and Eva Perón. They were joined by a number of senior government officials and politicians, as well as elite figures from the worlds of industry and commerce. Bormann had chartered a private plane to transport the guests in style from Buenos Aires to Santa Cruz, where a fleet of limos was on hand to complete the journey to El Calafate. In addition to Argentina's finest, Bormann had invited three prominent Nazis who'd also fled Germany in the last weeks of the war. All of them were on the Israeli government's priority search list and faced the death penalty if they were ever captured and extradited.

Adolf Eichmann was one of the notorious architects of the final solution and a valued member of Hitler's inner circle. The infamous SS Lieutenant Colonel had masterminded the transportation of millions of Jews to the death camps in German-occupied Poland. He now lived in Buenos Aires, where he worked at a car factory under the false identity of Ricardo Klement.

Josef Schwammberger was a sadistic SS commandant who also ran a number of death camps inside Poland. He had personally executed hundreds of Jews by shooting them in the back of the head. He was another Nazi butcher, with the blood of thousands of inmates on his hands. He presently lived in La Plata, a small town thirty miles south of Buenos Aires, where he worked at a petrochemical plant. Incredibly, his inherent arrogance meant he was the only one of the three who kept his original name, refusing to hide under a false identity.

The final member of the infamous three was the notorious "Angel of Death", Doctor Josef Mengele. He'd earned his grotesque nickname as he was personally responsible for carrying out thousands of gruesome experiments on pregnant women and children at the infamous Auschwitz concentration camp. He'd used them as human guinea pigs for his medical research. Like Eichmann, he also now lived in a quiet suburb in Buenos Aires, under the alias of Gerhard Wolfgang, where he ran a small mechanical equipment shop. The two men had become friends and often met up socially.

Bormann had requested the three prominent Nazis stay overnight at El Blondi to attend a private audience with the Führer the following morning. In total, there were fifty guests who mingled together on the sprawling manicured lawns at the rear of the house. Dozens of white-suited staff hovered around the distinguished visitors, holding silver trays carrying champagne bellinis and assorted canapés.

Circular wooden tables, dressed with immaculately pressed white tablecloths, were dotted around the lawns, surrounded by red velvet-backed chairs. A twenty-piece orchestra played classical tunes on a large temporary stage, built especially for the party, in the centre of the main lawn.

Hitler sat observing it all from a small oblong table positioned on the raised decking running along the back of the house. Juan and Eva Perón sat either side of him and the remaining three chairs behind the table were occupied by Braun, her two-year-old son, Richard, and a female interpreter who spoke fluent German and Spanish. Everyone wanted an audience with Hitler and, Bormann, in his role of host, was constantly on the move, chaperoning small select groups of guests to and from the Führer's table, where they were greeted with a limp handshake and a fake smile.

Other than Eva Perón, that is, with whom the Führer was clearly besotted. He greatly admired her rise from poverty and obscurity to her current standing as one of the world's most loved political figures and he felt a true affinity with Argentina's first lady. Knowing he was due to meet her for the first time, he had read up extensively on her background and one of her most famous quotes had resonated with him. Giving a speech in front of thousands of her supporters she had proclaimed, "One cannot accomplish anything without fanaticism."

He was fascinated that a woman could achieve the same level of hero-worship from the masses that he had personally experienced in the Fatherland. It was the first time in his life he had spent time with a woman who he felt shared his intellectual and political instincts and he found her incredibly stimulating. In the days leading up to his birthday, he doubled his drug intake and was on a massive high, bursting with artificial energy. He totally ignored her husband and spent the entire afternoon monopolising her, via the interpreter.

"First lady, it is an honour to meet you. I believe we share many values and objectives. We are both greatly loved by our own people, who respect strong and patriotic leadership. In the future, as we look to build a Fourth Reich, we can work together to create a superior regime."

Eva Perón maintained eye contact with Hitler as she listened to the interpreter. Despite the facial surgery he'd undergone four years earlier, his piercing blue eyes were still unmistakable and, in recent months, he had reinstated his trademark moustache, which was now iron grey.

"Führer, you are a true legend and a personal inspiration to me. We share the same philosophy and beliefs, and I and my husband will do everything possible to support your return to power. Your generous donations to our cause will never be forgotten."

Hitler and Perón continued to be locked in animated conversation for the following two hours, much to the annoyance of their respective partners. They were finally interrupted by Bormann, whose unmistakable voice boomed out across the garden. He was using the stand microphone on the stage and called for a moment of quiet.

"President and first lady, distinguished guests, please join me in wishing our beloved Führer a happy sixtieth birthday."

The orchestra struck up and guests took their cue, joining in with a rousing chorus of "Happy Birthday" sang in a mix of Spanish and German. Hitler stood throughout and relished the tumultuous applause that followed. Bormann left the stage and, a few moments later, a stunning figure appeared.

A young woman, dressed from head to toe in a Christian Dior couture black evening gown, made her way elegantly to the microphone. Her olive skin and rich red lips were perfectly framed by long, flowing black hair, and her eyes shone like diamonds. Silence fell across the garden and even Eva Perón sensed she was in the presence of a true diva. The orchestra began playing and Hitler instantly recognised the opening chords to one of his favourite arias. The soprano began to sing "Liebestod", the final dramatic sequence from Wagner's 1859 classic, *Tristan und Isolde*. Her remarkable voice was almost celestial and overwhelming in the purity of its register.

Every guest was transfixed by the performance and, as she delivered the final note, she was greeted by a spontaneous standing ovation. Bormann led her offstage and escorted her across the lawn to Hitler's table. The Führer stood up to greet them. She offered him her hand, and he took it in his own and then, to the amazement of the assembled guests, he lowered his head and gently kissed it.

"What is your name?"

She instinctively turned to Bormann for assistance, as she didn't understand German. He stepped forward to join them.

"Führer, allow me to introduce you to Maria Callas."

* * *

The garden party was a great success, and, at eight in the evening, the limos returned to ferry the guests back to the private plane for the return flight to Buenos Aires. Hitler and Braun immediately retired to their respective bedrooms, leaving Bormann to entertain the three house guests. It was a balmy evening and the four men sat around one of the circular tables drinking the exquisite German cognac that Bormann had shipped over from the Fatherland. He took them through the agenda for the upcoming meeting with Hitler, making sure they were fully briefed and on his side. Although they were still respectful of the Führer, by the time Bormann had finished, it was absolutely clear to all of them who was really pulling the strings.

The following morning, they assembled in Hitler's study, where four chairs had been laid out in a semicircle facing his imposing desk. Bormann sensed the Führer was far more energised and alert than normal. The adrenalin from the party was evidently still coursing through his veins, as was his latest intake of cocaine and, when he spoke, his voice was stronger than ever.

"Gentlemen, there is much to discuss. We and the German people were betrayed by our own military, who bent their knee to the communists and the Western powers. My generals ignored specific orders and couldn't wait to surrender. Even Hess betrayed me."

Despite the fact he was in exile and had lost the war, Hitler was still able to conjure up feelings of fear and trepidation when he addressed the three former prominent Nazis.

"Martin and I have been working together for many years, developing a long-term plan to build a Fourth Reich. There is no question that America is emerging as the strongest nation in the world and we plan, in time, to take control of its political structures, just as we did with the Weimar regime. We believe the major pharma companies will become the most powerful institutions in the world, which is why we are pouring millions of dollars into creating our own vehicle.

The Franklin Corporation will eventually migrate to America, as will Martin and my son, Richard. In time, it will grow to become one of the biggest and most formidable companies in the world. At the same time, it's vital that my grandson is born a US citizen. He will be groomed from birth for the role of president and, when he achieves that goal, my lineage will be secured. The new Reich will enjoy political, financial and institutional power on an unparalleled level."

Mengele was the first of the three to speak. He was as obsequious as ever.

"Führer, the work you and Martin have carried out is truly remarkable. How can we help to secure this new Reich? What can we offer?"

Hitler acknowledged the interruption and continued. "Josef, you are all great men and have always been loyal to me and our cause. Most of you have sons and, from this day forward, Martin will ensure that, when they reach the appropriate age, senior positions in the Franklin Corporation will be made available for them and then, in time, for their children. Our descendants will carry forward our master plan and bring it to fruition."

Mengele glanced across at Bormann. "What about your sons, Martin?"

Bormann's reply was instant. "The day I left the bunker with the Führer, my family became dead to me."

Hitler totally ignored the brief exchange. "Gentlemen, the Franklin Corporation will be run by the Nazi Party and, when the time is right, it will spawn a future president of the United States."

Chapter Twenty

13 January 2012

Buenos Aires

Early on Friday morning, Vargas and Torres stood in the hallway outside the interview room. The chief inspector was holding a thick blue file containing case notes and photos of García's two dead accomplices.

"Okay, Juan, let's see what García's got to say for himself. Hopefully a night's sleep courtesy of our five star facilities has oiled his brain cells."

Pedro looked up as the two detectives entered the room. Vargas sat directly opposite him, with Torres flanking him to the left. The only other person present was a young, newly graduated pro bono lawyer, appointed by the district, who sat alongside the accused man.

Vargas flicked on the tape recorder, the only object sitting on the table, and placed the folder down in front of the suspect.

"Good morning, Señor García. I'm Chief Inspector Vargas and I believe you've already met Inspector Torres?"

Pedro nodded.

"Señor García, we have good reason to believe that between the sixth and eighth of January you took part in a safe-deposit robbery at the Banco Estero, aided by Ricardo Gonzales and your cousin, Sebastian Ramos."

Pedro tried his best to look unimpressed but couldn't prevent his pupils slightly dilating. Vargas saw the telltale sign and continued.

"We believe the three of you split the haul and hid your respective shares in different places. Am I correct so far?"

Pedro couldn't think of a decent reply so kept silent.

"Would you like to know where your associates decided to stash their shares?"

Pedro stared straight-ahead at the digital wall clock and remained silent. Vargas was only just warming up. He knew the best was still to come as, clearly, García had no idea his friends were dead.

"Ricardo decided to hide his share in a shed at the bottom of his father's garden. He knew his old man was confined to a wheelchair, so figured it was a pretty safe location. Sebastian, on the other hand, decided to keep his share much closer to home. As you know, he was an accomplished carpenter and he hid it all under the floorboards in his flat."

Pedro wondered if, right now, his two associates were somewhere inside the station being interviewed in separate rooms. But, at the same time, he had a nagging feeling that something wasn't quite right. He knew both men well and was convinced neither of them would have named him or handed over their share of the take.

"Now, Señor García, would you care to tell us where your stash is hidden?"

111

Pedro still refused to speak. Vargas knew it was time to play his ace card and slowly opened the blue folder. He retrieved two A4-size photos that showed the mutilated bodies of Gonzales and Ramos. He slid them across the table so they fell directly under the gaze of his suspect. Pedro reeled back in his seat but couldn't take his eyes off the photos of his friends. Torres spoke for the first time.

"Now you understand why I told you earlier you are a very lucky man. Unfortunately for your friends, we were not waiting for them when they returned to their homes. But somebody else was."

Pedro's face was now frozen with fear. He looked up from the pictures and glared at his two interrogators before speaking for the first time.

"Who did this and why?"

Vargas picked up the photos and placed them back in the folder.

"Two very good questions, Pedro. Questions we don't yet have an answer to. But we do know one thing – you and your friends have seriously pissed off some very powerful people who appear as if they will stop at nothing to retrieve whatever's in their stolen box. It seems that whatever they are looking for must be in your share of the haul. So, I'll ask you again, where have you hidden it?"

Pedro was clearly stunned by the revelations but decided that for now his best chance of survival was to say nothing. He needed some thinking time and, at least for the moment, he was safe from whoever was out there looking for him. After two minutes of total silence, Vargas collected the folder and stood up from the table.

"Señor Pedro García, you leave us with no choice but to

charge you with the unlawful entry and robbery of the safe depository at the Banco Estero on Avenida Cabildo in the Belgrano district. As it's Friday, you will remain in custody over the weekend and then, on Monday, you will be taken to the federal courthouse in Morón, where you will be formally charged."

Vargas and Torres made their way to the door while Pedro sat quietly in his chair, contemplating his fate. The chief inspector turned to look back at García.

"You seem an intelligent man, Señor García. Hopefully, a couple of nights' sleep in a cell will help you to remember what you did with your cut."

Chapter Twenty-One

13 January 2012

Buenos Aires

Matias Paz had summoned his key men to another emergency board meeting. He sensed the sombre mood in the room and chose his opening words carefully.

"Gentlemen, sadly we've lost two of our brothers and, while we mourn them, we all know the risks involved in what we do. The success of this operation is key to the survival of our company and, right now, we are failing badly. I can't accept that. Failure is not a fucking option."

After Paz and Herrera, Hugo Otero was the longest-serving employee in the company, holding the title head of operations. Like most of the men in the room, in a previous life, he had served with Paz as a mercenary and knew the prospect of an untimely death came with the territory.

"Boss, we've just heard from our contact inside the police department. As far as they know, García hasn't yet given up the location of his hiding place and he's going to be formally charged on Monday at the federal court in Morón. From there, we think he'll be taken to Devoto Prison where they will no doubt keep him in the high-security wing. Once he's inside, it's going to be impossible to get our hands on him."

Herrera cut in. "Boss, we may not be able to extract him, but I think we can silence him. I know the plan has always been to find the contents of the box, but if García dies before he talks, then no one gets them, and the secrets remain secret."

Nobody spoke for a moment, and then Paz nodded to his trusted number two. "What exactly are you thinking, Luci?"

* * *

The walls of Richard Franklin's study were covered with animal trophies. All the victims had died at his own hand. He had a passion for big-game hunting and one of his prize possessions, mounted behind his desk, was the head of a rare South African white male lion he had killed on one of his many illegal hunting trips. Despite his passion for killing animals, the one true love of his life, his German shepherd, Mucki, lay curled up on the carpeted floor at his master's feet, awaiting his next command.

Franklin sat at his desk, reading the single-column story buried on page sixteen of the *San Francisco Chronicle* for a third time. The small headline had caught his eye a few minutes earlier. It referred to rival gangland killings that had taken place in Buenos Aires earlier in the week. The story covered the torture and execution of two men who were suspected of being involved in a recent safe-deposit robbery. The police had recovered a significant amount of the stolen property and were reportedly tracking down a third robber.

Franklin grimaced and reached for the red phone on his desk. He had no idea the police now had Paz's mobile. Instead, Franklin's call was diverted from Paz's landline to his new burner phone.

A few moments later, Paz was on the line. He stayed silent as the owner of his company let rip. He knew the man on the other end of the phone could wipe him and his business out at a moment's notice. Franklin's high-level connections throughout South America made him an extremely dangerous adversary.

"Paz, you've not exactly been discreet in your methods. The exploits of your men have now made the news over here. How close are you to finding the third man?"

Paz knew he had no choice but to update Franklin on the disastrous events of the last twenty-four hours. He finished his report by explaining his hastily put together plan of taking García out on the steps of the courthouse where he was due to appear in a few days' time.

He repeated Luciano's line that he'd heard in the boardroom an hour earlier. "García dies and your secrets remain secret."

Paz fully expected to be on the receiving end of one of Franklin's trademark rants but it wasn't forthcoming. Instead, his reply was calm and reasoned.

"Okay, I can see the wisdom in that approach. But, let's be frank, your men have just had their arses whipped in a firefight with the police. I honestly don't rate their chances of taking García out next Monday when he'll be surrounded by officers as he enters the federal court. If we miss him then, we're all fucked."

"Sir, I promise you that this time—"

Franklin ignored the interruption and carried on talking.

"However, I know of a man who might be able to help us solve our problem. In the past five years I've had need of his services on two occasions and both times he was successful."

Paz jumped in. "A hitman?"

"Paz, I'm talking about a contract killer who, to the best of my knowledge, has never failed to deliver on an assignment. He's based in Rio but operates all over South America. No one knows his true identity but he is rumoured to be an ex-colonel who served in an elite Spetsnaz unit operated by Russian Special Forces. He is known as The Ghost and charges two million dollars per hit."

Paz let out an audible gasp.

"He uses a sporting memorabilia website as a means of contact. It purports to sell old programmes from classic South American soccer and rugby matches from days gone by. You need to go on the live chat option and enquire whether they can source an authentic medal from the 1958 Brazil World Cup winning team. After that, you wait to see if he engages. I hope for your sake he does. I'm about to leave the office, so text me if this is a go and I'll transfer the necessary funds to the special account."

The line went dead and Paz got straight to work. The website was SA-Futbulsports.rio and looked completely genuine. The home page was peppered with colour images of classic sports programmes as well as old leather footballs, complete with laces and ancient-looking rugby boots. Paz hovered the cursor over the live chat button, clicked the mouse and entered the question, exactly as he'd been instructed by Franklin. The underscore icon pulsated in the box for what felt to Paz like an eternity, before suddenly breaking into life.

When would you need the medal by?

117

Paz thought for a second and then hit the keys. *Three days' time.*

Again, there was a long delay before the next reply came.

Highly unlikely. Where would it need to be delivered to?

Buenos Aires.

Where specifically?

Outside the front of the federal courthouse in Morón.

The next reply didn't come for fifteen minutes, and Paz feared his job offer was about to be declined.

The time frame is highly irregular, as is the delivery location. Therefore the cost of the medal will be twice as high as usual.

Paz winced as he read the demand.

Give me ten minutes.

Paz reached for his burner phone and sent off a short text to Franklin: *we're on, but due to the short notice it will cost double.*

The reply was almost instant.

Proceed. I'll make the appropriate arrangements.

Two minutes later, Franklin wired four million dollars to Theodor Consultants and Paz immediately transferred fifty per cent to a numbered account in Liechtenstein.

During the ten-minute gap in the exchange with Paz, the man known as The Ghost looked up from his Mac and stared out through the windows of his penthouse. Below him, stretched the glorious sands of Copacabana Beach. A stunning view he never tired of. He played his usual game of spotting and then scoring some of the bikini-clad Brazilian beauties playing volleyball on the beach.

He returned to his laptop and used the mouse to zoom in on the map grid displaying the street layout within a one-mile radius of the federal courthouse in Morón. He took his time clicking through the little red balloons representing various city landmarks. He was only interested in those that had a direct line of sight to the courthouse and were at least ten floors high. It didn't take him long to identify the perfect location. The government hospital was just under a thousand metres away from the courthouse and stood fifteen storeys high.

He flicked onto Google Earth and, within seconds, he was surveying the layout of the hospital roof. Other than housing a number of huge air-con units, it was a wide open space and he identified a white metal door that was obviously the access point from the fifteenth floor. Looking to the west, there was a clear line of sight to the front steps of the courthouse. The Ghost was a master of disguise but had never played the part of a doctor before. However, there was a first time for everything. He smiled to himself as he clicked on the mouse and saw the money land in his covert account.

Chapter Twenty-Two

14 January 2012

Buenos Aires

Pedro was woken early and taken from his basement cell back to the interview room where Vargas was waiting for him. A white polystyrene cup of steaming black coffee was positioned on the table in front of his chair. Next to it sat a second cup containing white sugar, and Pedro helped himself to a heaped spoonful.

Vargas flicked on the tape machine as he began their second interview. "I trust you had another good night's sleep?"

Pedro took a large swig of hot coffee before replying. "What do you think? It's my first experience of sleeping on a steel bedstead with a cockroach-infested mattress. I'm an innocent man and, as you must know by now, I don't have a criminal record, so this is my first experience of being incarcerated in a police institution. And where is my lawyer?"

Vargas turned off the recorder and glared at his suspect. "Pedro, you don't seem to have grasped the gravity of your situation. Not only do we know you took part in the robbery, but so does another party, who is clearly desperate to retrieve the contents of their box."

Pedro had done a great deal of thinking during a sleepless night and had decided on his strategy. "Chief inspector, as far as I can see, you have absolutely no evidence against me, other than the fact that I, like hundreds of other citizens, rented a box at the Banco Estero and that my cousin, who I wasn't particularly close to, took part in the heist. Both facts are purely circumstantial."

Vargas was surprised by the resilience displayed by the unemployed air-con engineer. "To be honest, Pedro. I think you were actually the brains behind this whole operation and that you recruited your cousin and Gonzales to help pull it off. Your extensive knowledge of air conditioning would have been vital in the design of the tunnel, and I'm convinced you rented the Café Torino and turned it into your base."

"I've never even heard of the Café Torino and, as I just said, you don't have any hard evidence against me. You need to release me."

"Señor García, we have more than enough evidence to charge you and, believe me, that will happen on Monday."

Vargas could see he was getting nowhere, so decided to end the exchange. "One last thing, Pedro. If I were you, bearing in mind the fate that befell your two accomplices, the very last thing I'd want right now is to be released."

Leaving that thought to permeate inside García's mind, the chief inspector stood up and left the room.

* * *

The Ghost closed his eyes and eased back into the business

class seat on board the TAM Airbus 319, which was about to leave Galeão International Airport in Rio on the three-hour flight to Buenos Aires. He reflected on what he'd achieved in the few hours since the two million dollars had hit his numbered account.

He was travelling with the aid of one of his many fake passports, posing as a Brazilian national, using the alias Felipe Sousa. He always travelled light when he was on an assignment, as he had a number of local contacts placed throughout South America whom he would call upon as and when he needed them. He had already received a confirmation text from his man in Buenos Aires that a suitcase containing every item on his list had been dropped off at the Park Hyatt Hotel, located in the north-east of the city. On receiving the text, he had wired the contact an instant payment of seventy-five thousand dollars, five times the cost of the actual purchases.

Before boarding the flight, he had studied dozens of images of the hospital and the exterior of the federal courthouse. He planned to check out both locations in person the following day. As the Airbus climbed towards its cruising height of thirty-nine thousand feet, he opened his iPad, switched on his Bluetooth headphones and settled down to watch a couple of episodes of his favourite Netflix drama.

* * *

Paz had moved into his office full-time and planned to stay there until the crisis was over. His burner phone was running red hot, and he was busy filling Herrera in about The Ghost, when he saw an incoming call flash up on the screen from

Hugo Otero.

"Hugo, what news from our friend?"

Otero knew his boss was referring to their informant inside the police department. "That's why I'm calling, boss. We've just heard from them, and it seems that García is still pleading his innocence. Vargas is proceeding with the charge and García is due in court for a preliminary hearing at eleven thirty on Monday morning. The word is, he definitely won't make bail so, if we want to hit him, it has to happen outside the courthouse."

Paz thought about the two-million-dollar transfer he had made the night before. "Don't worry, Hugo. It's in hand."

* * *

The yellow taxi pulled to a halt outside the magnificent neoclassical facade of the Park Hyatt Hotel which, in a former life, had been known as the Palacio Duhau. The palace had been built back in the 1930s and, in 2002, the Hyatt Hotel Group had taken it over. It was now recognised as one of the city's leading hotels.

Felipe Sousa drank in the surroundings. As the leading artist in his field, he knew he deserved the very best of everything. He strolled through the spectacular marble-floored lobby and made his way directly to the check-in desk. The enthusiastic blonde receptionist confirmed his booking and, after the usual paperwork, handed across the key card to one of the hotel's most expensive suites.

"Señor Sousa, I believe there is an item of luggage waiting for you at the concierge desk. Would you like it brought up to your suite?"

Sousa shook his head and smiled back at the receptionist. "No, thank you. I'd rather take it up myself."

* * *

Paz logged back on to the sporting website, clicked on the live chat icon and typed in a short message. *I can confirm the medal needs to be ready for collection at precisely eleven thirty on Monday morning.*

This time he didn't have to wait long for a reply.

Understood.

Paz logged off his computer and poured himself a straight scotch. He wondered if the hitman was already in the city.

* * *

Having replied to his anonymous employer, The Ghost switched off his iPad and turned his attention to the large black suitcase sitting at the bottom of his four-poster bed. He entered three numbers into the combination lock and flipped open the lid. Inside were some neatly folded cotton shirts, along with a pair of cream chinos and some Hugo Boss underwear. Sousa carefully removed the items and placed them on the bed, alongside the case. It only took him a few moments to locate the small catch that released the false bottom. Inside the secret compartment was a neatly folded white medical jacket, a steel stethoscope and a plastic lanyard displaying false credentials.

For now, none of that was of interest. His eyes were firmly fixed on the four neatly packaged components, the parts of a long-range sniper rifle. The SAKO TRG 42 was manufactured in Finland and regarded by most experts as the finest in the world. This particular version had a sound suppressor and an effective range of eleven hundred metres, giving him a cushion of one hundred metres more than he needed. It had a manually operated bolt action and chambered Lapua Magnum cartridges that could comfortably penetrate a solid concrete wall. One round would be more than enough to take a human life.

Chapter Twenty-Three

15 January 2012

Buenos Aires

The next morning, The Ghost got up early and jumped in a taxi that took him straight to the Federal Courthouse for Crime and Correction. Being a Sunday, it was closed, and he was the only person standing at the top of the ten stone steps that led to the front entrance. He made his way to the spot on the pavement where he expected the police van to drop García off and then timed how long it would take to climb to the entrance. He made the same journey three times, all at slightly different speeds, until he was happy that he had the correct range of timings. He calculated that, from leaving the van, García would reach the top step in somewhere between twelve and fifteen seconds.

Next, he took a leisurely ten-minute walk through the local neighbourhood that led him directly to the hospital. He paused outside the Emergency Department entrance and reached inside his jacket to retrieve the lanyard that gave him the status of a heart consultant. He then entered the building through the automatic glass doors. As soon as he was inside, he headed for a bank of lifts that he knew included a service elevator that would take him directly to the fifteenth floor.

Two minutes later, he walked up a small set of winding metal steps that gave direct access to the roof. He made his way across to the west aspect and removed a small telescopic gunsight from the inside pocket of his jacket. He adjusted the focus and zoomed into the top step at the front of the courthouse, then waited patiently for something to happen. After about ten minutes, he spotted a teenager casually walk up the steps and make his way to the front doors, where he stopped to read the signage giving the weekly opening times of the court. As the young man turned and walked away, he had no idea a gunsight was tracking his every step.

* * *

Twenty four hours later, Pedro battled his way through a paltry breakfast of cold scrambled eggs mixed with chilli peppers and a sausage that he was sure had never been anywhere near a real pig. At least the coffee was hot, and it helped wake up his senses. He'd only slept intermittently and was feeling physically and mentally exhausted. He'd had plenty of time to think and yet couldn't work out how this unknown enemy had tracked down Gonzales and Ramos.

While Pedro sat and contemplated what the hell was going on, The Ghost was already set up on the hospital roof, having checked out of his hotel at dawn. His aluminium precision rifle was resting on a titanium bipod, which kept the weapon totally stable. Pedro's court appearance was still two hours away and that gave him plenty of time to practise, as he lined up dozens of unsuspecting bystanders in his telescopic sight.

At precisely ten o'clock in the morning, Vargas and Torres entered García's cell. He was perched on the edge of his bed.

"Pedro, last chance before we head off to court. Where have you stashed your share?"

"Share of what, chief inspector?"

Vargas let out a frustrated sigh. "Okay, García. Let's go."

* * *

The Ghost glanced down at the display on his black digital watch. It showed 11.26, meaning García was due to arrive in the next four minutes. He leaned forward and peered through the telescopic sight. It was perfectly focused on a press photographer standing at the top of the steps. He could feel pure adrenalin coursing through his veins. It was moments like this he lived for. No nerves, no guilt, just pure excitement.

In fact, the police van containing García was running about five minutes late due to unexpected traffic. A large crowd had gathered outside the front of the courthouse and, hidden among the news reporters, camera operators and press photographers stood an interested observer, Matias Paz. A few yards away from him, another figure, who also shared a special interest in García's arrival, surveyed the scene. Vargas looked around for any sign of obvious danger as he waited for the police van to arrive.

Inside the back of the transit, Pedro sat on a raised ledge above the rear wheel arch, facing the two armed officers who had escorted him from his cell a few minutes earlier. His hands were cuffed, resting on his thighs, and he kept his head bowed to avoid eye contact with the policemen. He was deep in thought, contemplating his options, which were narrowing by the minute. Pedro figured there was probably enough evidence to convict him for the robbery, which meant he faced a minimum of ten years in Devoto Prison. That was bad enough, but even worse was the thought of being cleared, released and then being tracked down by the relentless psychopaths who had tortured and killed his friends. He concluded that the only rational option left open to him was to cut a deal, give up his share of the heist and hopefully source a new identity, courtesy of the police. There and then he vowed he would speak with his pro bono lawyer to request a pretrial meeting with Vargas. His life had spectacularly imploded, so it was time to make the best of a bad situation.

A roar went up as the black Ford Transit came to a stop by the front of the courthouse steps. The Ghost sensed a slight increase in his heart rate as he waited for the appearance of his prey. It seemed an eternity before the side door of the van slid open and García emerged, flanked on either side by a uniformed police officer. At that exact moment, all hell seemed to break loose. A cacophony of noise erupted among the hysterical crowd and, as the trio moved slowly forward, reporters screamed out questions, digital cameras beeped, and news cameramen jostled for position. Chaos reigned, and, for a brief moment, time seemed to stand still for Pedro. A random thought flashed into his mind: this must be what it's like to be a celebrity. It was the last thought he ever formed. A thousand metres away, an elite contract killer calmly counted to himself.

"... ten, eleven, twelve ..."

The Ghost's index finger gently began to apply pressure on the trigger. The movement was strangely elegant and perfectly controlled. It appeared as if everything was moving in slow motion. His body refused to flinch as he felt the sensation of the round leave the barrel of the rifle. The bullet took just over a second to reach its target. It ripped into García's back just to the left of his spine and exited through the right atrium of his heart. His body slumped to the ground like a rag doll. Mayhem broke out and two of the onlookers in the crowd reacted in completely different ways. Vargas ran towards García's stricken body while Paz moved in the opposite direction.

The man known as The Ghost collected the spent cartridge, broke down the sniper rifle and packed it neatly back into the suitcase. He dumped his white medical coat and stethoscope down one of the air-conditioning vents on the roof of the hospital and five minutes later was in a taxi heading for the central train station.

Pandemonium broke out on the steps of the courthouse. The large crowd scattered in all directions, although a number of news cameramen held their positions to film Vargas and the two officers who surrounded García's body as if they were trying to protect the corpse from further punishment. As he stared at the large gaping hole in García's chest, Vargas suddenly noticed a second body prone on the ground about ten feet away. The round had gone straight through Pedro and struck a female news reporter in the abdomen. The centre of her blue cotton dress was covered with a large red stain and she continued to leak a pool of blood onto the stone steps.

A screaming siren cut through the manic hubbub, and Vargas knew that meant the paramedics were close by. All they needed was a pair of body bags.

Within thirty minutes of the shooting, Paz was back in his office giving Herrera a blow-by-blow account. He could hardly contain his delight as he regaled his number two with the gory details of the sensational assassination.

"Luci, this ghost guy is a fucking genius. No one heard the shot, and there was no sign of a gunman. Straight through the fucking heart. He could have been a mile away for all I know."

Herrera laughed as his boss continued his ecstatic rant.

"No one will ever know where that bastard, García, hid his share. That secret is buried with him. For once, I can't wait to talk to old man Franklin. He's been kicking my arse since this whole mess blew up. Tell the boys, tonight we are going to hit the casino. I'm feeling lucky."

The Ghost left Retiro railway station, part of the central travel hub for Buenos Aires, and took his reserved first-class seat on the fast train to Rosario. It was the third largest city in Argentina and, essentially for The Ghost, it had an international airport. He knew he faced an onerous five-hour journey ahead but he always followed the same rules on a foreign assignment: never use the same airport or airline for entry and exit, and always use a different alias.

He slept for most of the journey and, a few minutes before arriving at Rosario station, he retrieved a small, soft travel bag from inside the black suitcase that still contained the rifle. As the train slowed to a halt, he placed the case in the rack directly above his seat number and walked through the carriages to the very front compartment. When he stepped onto the platform, his local contact, who had made the same journey in standard coach, walked along the aisle and entered the first-class compartment, making his way to seat 5A, where he promptly collected the black case stowed above it.

Fifty minutes later, Italian businessman Marco Rossi waited in line at the Aerolíneas first-class check-in desk for his one-way flight to Rio. He sensed his mobile buzz and, when he glanced at the screen, he saw an alert from his bank confirming he was two million dollars richer.

* * *

The red phone burst into life. Franklin deliberately let it ring for a good few seconds before taking the call from Paz.

"Sir, I have very good news – García is dead. Your ghost pulled off an incredible hit. I was right there when it happened, just a few yards away when the round cut him down."

Franklin's reply was not exactly what Paz was expecting. "I know you were there, you cretin. I spotted you lurking in the crowd outside the courthouse. The shooting is currently the fucking lead story on CNN rolling news."

"Shit, what are they saying?"

"At the moment they are speculating that it's all part of a gangland war that involves the three dead bank robbers. Let's hope it stays like that."

Paz picked up his remote and aimed it at the giant eighty-inch TV screen on the wall opposite his desk. He flicked the channel on to CNN and, sure enough, the shooting was being shown from multiple angles. He kept the sound muted and continued with his act of deference towards Franklin.

"What do you want me to do now, Señor?"

"I still want you to find the contents of our fucking box.

Work on García's friends, workmates, relatives, anyone with a connection to him. Someone must know something. I suspect the cops won't stop looking for the stash, so neither should we. And, Paz, try and be a bit more subtle with your methods. We really don't want any more killings unless they're absolutely essential. Later tonight John is taking part in a live TV debate with four other nominees. He is creaming it in the polls and a strong performance will almost guarantee the nomination. In a few months' time, I'll be the father of the next president of the United States. That's why I won't feel safe until I know everything has been destroyed."

* * *

Vargas was holding court in the open-plan office at police headquarters, debriefing his team on the morning's events. The safe-deposit robbery, which had occurred ten days before in Buenos Aires, was now leading the world news. He was the man in charge of the investigation and yet he didn't actually have a clue about what was really happening.

"García was taken out by a highly trained sniper. A completely different M.O. to the other four killings. We need to check out every building within a mile radius that has a direct line of sight to the courthouse."

Torres interrupted his boss. "Chief, we're already on it. We've been looking at Google Earth and it seems there are four contenders. As soon as we finish here, the guys will check them all out."

Vargas nodded and continued. "The reality is, whoever did the hit is probably already out of the country. But there's a much bigger picture to consider here, and, right now, we haven't got a handle on what's actually going on. This case is not really about a bank robbery any more. We're facing a highly skilled and motivated organisation that wants its property back at all costs. They've walked away from millions of dollars in pursuit of whatever was in their box and they've ruthlessly killed nine people along the way, including one of our own. Now it looks like they brought in an outside contract killer to take out García, which tells us they are extremely well funded."

Vargas paused and Torres cut in again. "It feels like we are up against a secret army that is always one step ahead of us."

"And that, Juan, is possibly the most worrying aspect of this entire case."

Vargas moved towards his office and signalled for Torres to join him.

As they walked together, Vargas suddenly stopped dead in his tracks. At the opposite side of the open-plan office, two senior detectives were deep in conversation with a female, also dressed in civilian clothes. She had her back to Vargas, but, for a brief moment, he believed for all the world that he was looking at his wife. Her particular stance, her petite frame and her long black hair were so much like Sophia, Vargas was convinced it was her and was transfixed. Torres followed his superior's eyeline and smiled.

"She's a hot one, chief, but I've heard she is a bit of a ballbreaker. She's the deputy head of HR and works out of the commander's office."

Torres's voice brought Vargas back to earth but his hands trembled as he wiped his brow and he swallowed hard. Slowly he gathered himself together and led Torres into his office. Once the two detectives were alone, Vargas finally managed to pick up the thread of his thoughts.

"Juan, I think they must have someone on the inside. It's uncanny how they always seem to be one step ahead of us. From now on, any major operational decisions need to be kept between you and me until the very last possible moment. We don't know who we can trust."

"Understood, chief. By the way, what you said out there about a hitman, do you really believe that?"

"Yep. And, as I said, I think he is probably long gone and—"

Vargas was interrupted by Detective Martin, who knocked and opened the office door in one simultaneous movement. He strode in, accompanied by another man who neither Vargas nor Torres recognised. He was casually dressed in a black T-shirt and a pair of washed-out Levi's.

"I'm sorry to crash in, sir. This is Daniel Colombo from IT. He's been working on the mobile that you found at Ramos's flat."

Vargas smiled at the young tech expert and gestured for him to take the chair in front of his desk. "Daniel, we could really do with some good news. What have you got for us?"

Colombo placed the iPhone down on Vargas's desk. "Chief inspector, the data on this phone has been encoded and encrypted to a level that I've never seen before. Plus, everything has a triple-lock password, which makes it almost impenetrable."

"Daniel, what do you mean by *almost*?"

"Well, we did get a small break, sir. For some reason, the very last call made by this mobile didn't get fully encrypted."

Vargas almost leapt out of his chair. "So we have a lead?"

"Sort of, sir. The number we retrieved doesn't belong to anyone in Argentina. The last call made on this phone was to an international number in America, placed to area code 415."

"And what state might that be?"

Daniel grinned like a cat that had got the cream. "California, sir. San Francisco, to be precise."

Chapter Twenty-Four

16 January 2012

Los Angeles

Studio City on Radford Avenue in Los Angeles was the setting for the first live television debate between the five remaining Republican presidential nominees. Inside Studio 7, a partisan audience bayed for blood as the contenders savaged each other's policies and personal values. At times, it was hard to believe they were all members of the same party. Some of the exchanges were particularly brutal but it was obvious to those watching at home that one of them was enjoying the overwhelming support of the live crowd. Every time John Franklin went on the attack, he was backed by huge bursts of applause and raucous cheers and his four opponents were usually greeted with a cacophony of boos whenever they took him on directly.

His father stood in the corner of the green room, glued to one of the live monitor feeds. He loved the gladiatorial tone of the debate, and the crazy amount of money his team had spent on vetting the studio audience was evidently worth every dollar. As the host wound up the broadcast, Franklin made his way to his son's dressing room. Ten minutes later, the two men were enjoying a cold glass of Dom Pérignon as they relived the best moments of the debate.

"John, you absolutely smashed it out of the park. I smell at least three dropouts in the morning. Trust me, they'll all be angling to support you in the hope of a VP post down the line. And, because you're so far ahead in the polls, my sources tell me the party grandees are working behind the scenes to orchestrate a coronation and bypass the primaries. They want to take advantage of your momentum and give you a clear run at the Oval Office."

John was busy refilling his champagne glass. "Dad, that would be incredible. As we predicted, all the international stuff went down a storm – Iran, North Korea and China. That crowd hates the ayatollah more than we do. Plus, I was the only candidate out there arguing for reforming healthcare."

Richard Franklin gave his son an enormous hug. As they separated, his voice dropped to a chilling whisper. "Remember, John, you're the unifying candidate. We're playing the long game here. For now, you offer everything to everybody. Just keep repeating the same message. Goebbels was a master politician and he created the golden rule, 'If you tell a lie big enough and keep repeating it, people will eventually come to believe it.'"

Franklin paused for a moment of reverential reflection before draining his glass in one long swallow. His pencil-thin lips formed a poisonous smirk. "John, we know the right of the party and the white supremacists are already on board and they'll prove to be useful allies down the road but, right now, we need to shore up the regular conservative voters, especially the soft ones, and not scare the horses. The polls are telling us that swing voters can't get enough of the healthcare initiative, as well as the tough stance on law and order. They love strong, charismatic leaders, who they foolishly believe are on their side. Look at Putin – the thug's a dictator, yet the Russian people believe he runs a democratic government. The truth is, once he achieved absolute power, there was no way he was ever going to give it up through democratic means. So, remember, keep your grandfather's strategy in mind. When he first took control of the Weimar Republic, no one really knew what was coming down the line. Just like people today don't realise that reuniting the Americas is our ultimate goal. All those failed states in South America are absolutely ripe for takeover. We'll create our own Lebensraum, a massive living space that gives us the largest and most powerful country in the world."

John smiled as he poured them both another glass of champagne, downing his in one. "Yes, and eventually Mexico will become our massive dumping ground for dissidents and enemies of the state. One gigantic prison."

Richard nodded his approval and toasted his son. "John, Martin would be so proud of you. As you know, he planned everything meticulously and now we're almost there. I can taste it. And, while we're celebrating, I have some more good news."

"You've got the box back?"

"Not quite, but the men who stole it are all dead, so no one knows where it is hidden and the trail for the police has gone cold. Cold as ice."

John sat his glass down on the make-up table. "But, Dad, it's still out there."

"Yes, it is, and don't worry, our guys are on it. If it's findable, believe me, they will find it. If it's not, then the secrets stay with us."

Chapter Twenty-Five

1 May 1960

El Calafate

Bormann was feeling agitated. He had been sitting in Hitler's study for over an hour waiting for the Führer to join him for their scheduled weekly afternoon meeting. In recent months, Hitler had drifted into a routine that included an afternoon nap in his bedroom, and sometimes he didn't surface again for the rest of the day. Even his daily drug intake seemed to be having little effect, and his behaviour was becoming increasingly erratic.

Just as Bormann was concluding this would be another one of those days, the study door opened and Hitler appeared. He was clean-shaven and smartly dressed in a grey double-breasted suit, a white cotton shirt and a grey tie. Bormann was delighted to see he was ready for business and hoped his mind was as sharp as his appearance. He stood to greet the Führer, who nodded to him as he slowly shuffled across the room to his desk. These days he relied on a brass-handled chestnut walking stick for support and it took him some time to reach the chair, which was situated at the far end of the room. Once he was seated, he cleared his throat and fixed his gaze on Bormann as a signal he was ready for the briefing to begin.

"Führer, it's wonderful to see you looking so sprightly today. We have much to discuss, and, as ever, I am in need of your wisdom and guidance."

Although Bormann had been pulling all the strings since they'd arrived in Patagonia, he still displayed an instinctive deference to the Führer who, on days like this, somehow managed to conjure up an aura of power and authority.

Hitler leaned forward and rested his arms on the desk. "What matters do you wish to discuss, Martin?"

"Führer, for some months now, our contacts in Buenos Aires have been reporting concerns that Mossad and that despicable Austrian Jew, Wiesenthal, have been combining their resources to step up their search for some of our most important friends. I'm particularly worried about Eichmann and Mengele, and I wondered if we should think about relocating them and their families from Buenos Aires to join us in El Calafate."

Hitler instantly shook his head. "Martin, I won't sanction any action that endangers my security and our plans for the future. Go and see them both and offer whatever financial resources they require in order to move to a more remote location. It concerns me they both know where we are based, and, if they are subjected to interrogation from the Israelis, we may become compromised."

Unbeknown to Hitler, Bormann had already booked himself on the morning flight to Buenos Aires and had arranged meetings with both of the notorious Nazi exiles.

"I share your concern, Führer, and will meet with them as soon as possible."

"Very good. Give them both my regards."

Bormann stood to leave just as Hitler fired off a parting shot. "Martin, can you imagine what fun Josef would have had with Wiesenthal if he had been an inmate at Auschwitz?"

* * *

Three of the most wanted war criminals in the world sat huddled together at a small table in the corner of a deserted bar in Buenos Aires. It was located a few hundred yards away from Eichmann's house on Garibaldi Street, on the outskirts of the city. Bormann had called an emergency meeting with the two Mossad targets and Mengele had arrived exactly on time, whereas Eichmann kept them both waiting for the better part of an hour.

Bormann was aware the two Nazis held very different mindsets. Mengele was an extremely cautious man who lived in constant fear of exposure and capture and looked to Bormann for help and guidance. Eichmann was the complete opposite. He had total contempt for Bormann, whom he viewed as a talentless, over-promoted party official who had somehow managed to win the ear of the Führer during the last few months of the war. His instinctive self-importance and inbuilt arrogance meant he didn't bother to hide his total disregard for Bormann and he clearly resented being summoned to a last-minute meeting by the man he considered to be his inferior.

On the table stood a cheap bottle of whisky and a jug of water. Bormann poured out three scotches and called for a toast to the Führer. The three of them clinked glasses and drained them in one shot.

"Josef, Adolf, I bring the regards of the Führer who is aware of today's meeting."

Unlike Eichmann, Mengele still had huge respect for Hitler and was the first to reply. "How is the Führer's health these days?"

"His mind is as brilliant as ever. It's just his body that is beginning to let him down."

Eichmann was much more matter of fact. "So why the sudden panic for a meeting? It was very inconvenient for me to have to change my work schedule at such short notice."

Bormann refused to rise to the bait and ignored the obvious taunt from Eichmann. "Gentlemen, I am seriously concerned for your welfare. I understand that, right now, Mossad have agents sniffing around the city, trying to locate your whereabouts. You need to relocate as soon as possible and find a safe haven. I will transfer suitable funds into your accounts to enable you to make the move. Time is of the essence and this is not a request. It's an instruction from your Führer."

Eichmann snapped back immediately. "Bormann, fuck you and fuck the Führer. I am not a pawn of yours to be moved around on one of your fucking chessboards. I have built a good life here and my family is settled. Besides, everyone knows the government would never agree to extradite us back to Germany or Israel, so Mossad are fucked."

Mengele ignored Eichmann's rant and turned to Bormann. "Martin, I will speak to Martha tonight. If you and the Führer believe we are truly under threat from the Israelis, then we will look to move out of the city and disappear into the countryside."

Bormann reached into his pocket and retrieved two small ring-sized boxes.

"Eichmann, as always, you will make your own decision, but my intelligence is good, and my advice is sound. The city is not a safe place for you at the present time and you need to disappear, even if it's only for a few months."

Bormann leaned forward, placed the boxes on the table and opened the lids to reveal two tiny glass capsules.

"Above all, it is your sworn duty to serve the Führer at all times. Both of you know the whereabouts of his sanctuary and, should either of you fall into the hands of the Jews, I expect you to take the appropriate action."

Eichmann stood up and picked up one of the boxes containing a cyanide ampoule.

"Don't worry, Bormann. You and the Führer are perfectly safe in your beautiful country estate. Millions of people believe the bullshit story that Hitler and Braun committed suicide in the bunker – not even the Israelis are looking for them, so I won't be needing this."

He threw the box back onto the table and left the bar.

* * *

The following day, Bormann was back in Hitler's study, giving a full debrief of the meeting.

"Führer, to be frank, Eichmann's total lack of respect towards you leaves us with a big problem. If he were to be taken by the Israelis, there's no guarantee that, under interrogation, he won't divulge our location."

"Martin, what are you suggesting?"

Bormann knew that Hitler still held huge respect for one of the architects of the final solution, and the Führer continued to defend him.

"Yes, Eichmann was always an arrogant bastard, but I never doubted his loyalty and I don't believe he would ever betray me."

Bormann protested, trying again to convince Hitler that Eichmann was indeed a live threat. "Führer, he is not the same man you remember. I believe he is a danger to us and we need to take care of him. We have people in Buenos Aires—"

Hitler raised his left arm, forcing Bormann to stop mid-sentence. His voice quivered with undisguised anger. "Eichmann will not be touched."

* * *

Eight days later, on 11 May 1960, Adolf Eichmann was seized by three Mossad agents, less than a mile from his home, as he made his way back from work. They took him to a safe house in Buenos Aires, where he was held for nine days while the Israeli agents double-checked his identity and began an initial interrogation. Bormann leaned heavily on his government contacts to sanction a massive manhunt of the city and use the full force of the military regime to try to locate him..

On 20 May, Mossad pulled off a sensational escape plan that involved smuggling Eichmann onto a scheduled El Al passenger plane heading for Dakar in Senegal. From there, he was transferred onto a direct flight to Tel Aviv. Eichmann was one of the world's most wanted war criminals, and his kidnapping in Argentina and arrival in Israel created one of the biggest and most sensational news events of the year.

Three days later Hitler and Bormann sat in front of the small television set in the living room at El Blondi watching the grainy black-and-white footage of the live news conference where Eichmann was put on show to the media. They watched in horror as Israeli Prime Minister David Ben-Gurion addressed the worldwide audience.

"Eichmann is a Nazi war criminal who was in charge of the final solution, who will now stand trial in Israel for war crimes."

Ben-Gurion went on to make a solemn promise that he wouldn't rest until Mossad had located all the high-ranking Nazis who had escaped justice and were believed to be hiding in South America.

Hitler slumped in his chair and closed his eyes, leaving Bormann still glued to the live transmission.

"Martin, I suddenly feel old. My judgement is betraying me and I regret not listening to your advice. I hope my mistake doesn't prove to be fatal."

Chapter Twenty-Six

16 January 2012

Buenos Aires

L os Angeles local time was four hours behind Buenos Aires, so Vargas waited until just before midnight before placing his call to Lieutenant Troy Hembury of the Los Angeles Police Department. He figured Troy should be home and off duty, so they would have plenty of time to talk. Despite living thousands of miles apart, the two men had started an unlikely friendship four years earlier when they'd attended a five-day Law Enforcement Conference at The Venetian Hotel in Las Vegas.

The rationale behind the event had been for the brightest and most promising detectives from North and South America to have the opportunity to meet up and explore the latest technological innovations that were reshaping law enforcement around the globe. In reality, the two men had gone through the motions of attending the boring lectures and tedious workshops during the day and, at night, they'd explored the live shows, bars and casinos on the infamous strip. On one memorable occasion, they'd stayed up all night and attended the breakfast lecture the following morning wearing the same clothes they'd partied in the night before.

Both men were habitual winners, whether it came to hunting down criminals or beating the house blackjack dealers. Remarkably, they shared the same birthdate, the twenty-fourth of February, although Hembury was ten years older. This fact came to light when they played roulette together on the opening night of the conference and both men placed their respective chips on black 24. During the four intense days that followed, a strong friendship developed. On the morning the conference wrapped, they shared a taxi to the airport and vowed to keep in touch but, other than a few texts in the following weeks, they hadn't spoken since.

Hembury had been looking forward to a quiet night in, watching the game and ploughing through a Chinese take-away, accompanied by a few cold Buds. He'd supported the Clippers since he was a young boy, and tonight they were taking on their local rivals, the Lakers, in one of the most anticipated basketball games of the season. Hembury was a fifty-year old muscle-bound African American who maintained fitness levels that were truly age-defying. Although he was only six foot two, during his college days he had excelled at basketball and had not been far off turning pro, so was pumped up for the game. However, his well-laid plans for the evening suddenly changed when he saw the ID flash up on his mobile.

"Nic, how the hell are you? Can't believe it's been four years since that insane conference. Every birthday I raise a glass to you and mean to call. I feel really lousy about not keeping in touch."

"No need for guilt, Troy. I've been just as bad. But, right now, I really need to talk to you about a case I'm working. In fact, I badly need your help and wisdom."

Hembury sensed the serious change of tone in his friend's voice and slipped straight into work mode, hitting the remote to mute the sound on the TV.

"Go on, I'm all yours."

"Okay, I'm guessing you saw the news about the shooting outside the courthouse in Buenos Aires?"

Hembury's voice rose an octave with excitement and anticipation. "Jesus, are you involved in that case? That footage is everywhere. They say it was a revenge gang killing connected to a bank robbery. I've been following it, but, weirdly, it didn't cross my mind that it might be your investigation—"

Vargas cut in. "Troy, the gang-killing theory is total shit. This case involves a level of criminal power and ruthlessness that's off the scale. What started as an audacious but pretty regular robbery has morphed into a catalogue of torture and murder, the like of which I've never experienced before."

During the next hour, Hembury listened intently as Vargas took him through the intricate details of the case, starting with the safe-deposit raid and finishing with the sniper shooting on the courthouse steps. Troy nibbled on some cold prawn toast and downed it with a large swig of beer.

"Nic, clearly this is all about whatever's inside one of those boxes. The torture, the executions, the contract killer are all part of the pursuit of that one objective. What kind of criminal walks away from millions of dollars when it's handed to him on a plate? This case is a total head fuck."

"Exactly, and right now my only lead is a San Francisco

phone number, which is why I need your help."

"Nic, it's *our* only lead. Give me five minutes to check it out."

Hembury ended the call and logged on to his work laptop. Using the police database, it took him less than two minutes to discover the address and owner of the number. Unfortunately, he didn't think the information was going to be of much help to his fellow detective. He hit the last number on his mobile and Vargas picked up after just one ring.

"Okay, Nic, here's what we've got – the number is registered to a high-rise office block on California Street, which is located in downtown San Francisco. The entire building is owned by the Franklin Pharmaceutical Corporation, which is one of the ten largest companies in the States. They're a huge outfit. That building alone must house over five thousand employees, and that number is a direct line that could belong to any of them. They are an incredibly well-respected company. In fact, the son of the CEO, John Franklin, is running for the Republican nomination and looks odds-on to win—"

Vargas cut in. "Yes, they're enormous over here as well. They have offices in Buenos Aires and Córdoba. I think the company originated in Argentina."

He paused for a moment of thought. "Troy, my old man used to say that every good barrel can have one bad apple."

"Okay, Nic, if we are going to play the metaphor game … we are looking for a needle in a giant haystack."

Chapter Twenty-Seven

17 January 2012

Buenos Aires

The mood in the boardroom at Theodor Consultants was considerably lighter than it had been since the robbery. Paz had treated all the staff to a night out on a floating casino, a replica of a Mississippi riverboat, moored in Puerto Madero in the south of the city. He'd given all his men a thousand dollars each to play the slots and tables so, as Paz entered the room, his operatives broke into a spontaneous round of applause. Herrera was the first to speak.

"Boss, on behalf of the men, I want to thank you for a fucking amazing night. It's been a rough time, and we all needed to unwind. No one should forget this job cost Ángel and Benjy their lives and we need to sort out their families."

Paz took his usual seat at the top of the table and nodded to Herrera. "Well said, Luci. But now we need to talk about the next phase of the operation."

Herrera gave his boss a slightly startled look.

"Now that García is dead, the immediate pressure may be

off, but we still need to find the contents of Box 1321. We need to speak with García's family, friends and work colleagues. Somebody must know something that will help reveal his hiding place. Avoid violence and intimidation where possible. Offer money, lots of it. In fact, as an incentive to loosen tongues, offer a hundred thousand for any information that may help lead us to it."

Paz then turned his attention to Hugo Otero. "Hugo, I'm sure the cops are going to be thinking exactly the same way as us. So, more than ever, we are going to need our friend at the station to keep us fully informed."

Otero had been secretly hoping there would be no mention of his police informant. "Boss, there might be a problem there. They contacted us this morning to say that, following a meeting with one of the IT guys, the chief inspector suddenly appears to be keeping things on a need-to-know basis and so they're in the dark as to what's going on right now."

Paz's mood changed in a flash. "An IT guy? What the fuck would any IT guy know that might be relevant?"

That was the question Hugo had really been dreading. He couldn't hold eye contact with his boss as he murmured his reply. "Apparently, he was reporting back on the mobile that was left behind at Ramos's apartment."

Paz felt as if an electric shock had just surged through his veins.

* * *

Vargas sat in his office, staring at a torn piece of notepaper displaying a handwritten ten-digit phone number. It was the only lead he had. He was desperate to call it but wasn't quite ready. Instead, he made an internal call to one of his team.

"Alex, can you bring me the list showing the owners of the boxes that were actually stolen in the raid?"

Two minutes later, Detective Alex Martin entered Vargas's office and handed over a single piece of paper listing the details of ninety safe-deposit boxes.

Vargas had read it before, but this time he scrutinised it, looking for one particular name. "Jesus fucking Christ!" He leapt out of his chair, ran around his desk and grabbed the young detective in a crushing bear hug. "Alex, we have a match. One of the stolen boxes is owned by the Franklin Pharmaceutical Corporation. This whole fucking case has been about Box 1321."

Vargas summoned Torres and brought him up to speed while he placed a call to the manager of the Banco Estero. Within a few seconds, the bank switchboard operator had Marcelo Morales on the line.

"Señor Morales, I want you to tell me everything you know about Box 1321."

Morales was slightly taken aback by the bluntness of the request. "Chief inspector, you have to understand that—"

He was cut short by Vargas. "Let me explain something to you, Señor Morales. Nine people have been brutally murdered in the last two weeks, including one of my men. And they've all died as a direct result of whatever is inside that box. So, let me ask you again, what do you know about Box 1321?"

Morales felt the sheer wrath coming his way and changed his tone. "Chief inspector, please give me a few moments to find the paperwork."

Vargas tried his best to stay calm while he waited for the

manager of the bank to come back on the line. It was nearly five minutes before Morales returned. He sat back at his desk and opened a thin grey folder.

"The box was first rented on 7 July 1981. It was taken out by the Franklin Pharmaceutical Corporation and is registered to their head office in Buenos Aires."

Vargas jumped in with a question and held his breath as he awaited the reply. "Can you give me the names and exact dates of every person who has ever visited the bank to check on the box?"

"That's the strange thing about Box 1321. It hasn't been visited since the day it was opened thirty-one years ago."

Vargas shook his head in disbelief as he ended the call and glanced down at the American phone number. "The mystery surrounding this box gets weirder by the minute. Let's see where this takes us."

Vargas put his office phone on speaker, enabling Torres to listen in. Then he switched on the recording device for the upcoming call. It was midday in San Francisco and Richard Franklin was sitting at his desk going through the latest polls, which showed his son's position looking almost unstoppable. Since the live TV debate, three of his opponents had ended their campaigns, leaving a senator from Wisconsin as his only rival for the Republican nomination. However, the latest numbers showed she was twelve points behind Franklin, and even more encouraging were the overnight head-to-head polls that looked at a straight shoot-out between Franklin and the incumbent of the White House. For the first time, his son held a three-point lead over the Democratic president. Richard made a mental note to step up the national TV advertising budget, as it was clearly delivering.

155

Vargas dialled the number that had been retrieved from Paz's mobile and, almost six and a half thousand miles away, the red phone on Franklin's desk burst into life. He grabbed the receiver, hoping to hear some good news.

"Have you found it?"

The voice that greeted Vargas and Torres was educated and self-assured, but more than anything it was threatening. The chief inspector hesitated for a moment before replying. "You're referring to Box 1321?"

Franklin felt his entire body stiffen as a giant alarm bell invaded his brain. "Who is this?"

Again, Vargas took his time before answering. "This is Chief Inspector Vargas from the Buenos Aires City Police Department. Who am I speaking with?"

Franklin couldn't contain his inner rage. He slammed down the receiver and wildly yanked the phone cord from its floor connection. He glared at the red phone as if it were a disloyal traitor before launching it across the office where it smashed into pieces as it hit the wall.

Vargas turned off the recording device and replaced the phone.

Torres was the first to speak. "What did you make of that, chief?"

Vargas's face revealed a slight hint of a smile. "I think it's fair to say we rattled someone's cage."

Chapter Twenty-Eight

17 January 2012

San Francisco

It had been just over an hour since the car-crash phone call and Franklin had left the office for a cooling-off drive. The remnants of his red phone were now stashed in a black plastic bag in the boot of the Rolls. His white-hot temper had galvanised into a cold, clinical fury. He'd driven out to Potrero Hill, a quiet neighbourhood on the outskirts of the city, and pulled onto a small side street that ran alongside McKinley Square, one of the landmark parks in the area.

He reached for his mobile, which was resting on the console next to the gear lever, and dialled the CEO of Theodor Consultants. Paz was working out on a cross trainer in his study at home. It was the first time he'd been there in a couple of weeks, as he'd been sleeping at the office throughout the crisis. He was slightly surprised to see Franklin's ID flash up but jumped off the machine and grabbed his mobile.

"Sir, I've passed on your instructions to the men and—"

"I've just taken a call on our private line from a chief

inspector working for the Buenos Aires Police Department."

Paz felt a giant knot in his stomach start to tighten as Franklin began to rant.

"He asked me about Box 1321. Can you fucking believe that? How the fuck did he get my number and how does he know about the box?"

Paz felt the beads of sweat that he had worked up on the machine begin to turn into small rivers. "Sir, did he address you by name?"

"No, thank fuck. But he knows about the fucking box and, somehow, he gained access to our private line. It's a number that only you and I have, so, the question is, how the fuck did he get it and how has he managed to connect the Franklin Corporation to the robbery?"

Franklin's questions had given Paz the breathing space he needed to fabricate a story. If it meant hanging Luciano out to dry, so be it. He had to save his own skin.

"Sir, I think I know how he got the number. During the firefight at Ramos's house, the guys had to make a quick exit and the man in charge left his mobile behind."

"Why the fuck didn't you tell me at the time, and why did he have my direct line on his contacts?"

The lie from Paz grew a life of its own. "He told me it got badly damaged in the chaos and, like mine, it was heavily encrypted, so wouldn't offer up any secrets."

"But why would my direct line be on his mobile?"

Paz was now almost believing this newly invented narrative. "He is my number two, and I gave him the number just in case anything happened to me and you needed a point of contact. Otherwise, you'd have been out of the loop."

Franklin took a moment to digest this new information

before coming back. "Okay, I can see the sense in that decision. What's the name of this man?"

Paz breathed an audible sigh of relief. "Luciano Herrera. He has worked with the company for the last ten years. He is a good man and a great soldier."

Franklin had the final word before ending the call. "I don't care. The guy fucked up. He's a dead man walking. Do you understand me?"

Paz heard the dial tone cut in and lowered his mobile. He glared across at the blonde youth who was lying seductively on a blue leather sofa, clad only in a pair of white Calvin Kleins. "Get out of my fucking house, you pathetic piece of shit."

The terrified rent boy sprung from the sofa like a startled cat and darted into the bedroom to retrieve his clothes. Seconds later, he emerged and ran across the living room towards the front door. As he reached for the handle, Paz spoke again. This time his voice dropped to a sinister whisper.

"Tomás, don't go. I need your services once again."

* * *

Hembury had just got back to his apartment when Vargas called to bring him up to speed on all the latest developments. There was now a clear link between the Franklin Corporation and one of the stolen security boxes. It was apparent that Box 1321 was the key to unlocking the whole investigation.

"Nic, it's pretty clear that the Franklin Corporation are up to their necks in this. Their box was stolen and someone in the California office has been coordinating the operation to get it back."

Vargas knew he had no option but to ask his friend to get further involved in the investigation.

"Troy, whoever was on the end of that line got totally spooked as soon as I mentioned Box 1321. I'm going to need your help on the ground over there to move this case forward."

"No problem, I'm in. If for no other reason than I need to know what's so interesting about the contents of a box that hasn't been looked at for over thirty years."

Vargas could sense Hembury was now fully on board. "That, my friend, is the fifty-million-dollar question."

* * *

Paz knew he was left with little choice but to take out his loyal henchman. He had set Herrera up as the fall guy and now he would have to suffer the consequences. Luciano had to die and Franklin would demand proof of his death. Paz decided it would be a compassionate killing as, ironically, he didn't want his old friend to suffer. That was the least he could offer, after all his years of loyal service. He invited him over to his apartment for dinner, a rare honour which was viewed by Herrera as an acknowledgement of his status within the organisation.

The two men gorged their way through a massive takeaway banquet, sourced from the city's premier Indian restaurant. Paz knew it was Luciano's favourite food, and it was being washed down by two bottles of Châteauneuf-du-Pape, a fruity red wine Paz had shipped over every month from a vineyard in France.

Herrera downed his fifth glass of the evening and munched on a spicy poppadom. "Boss, it's a special honour to celebrate with you at your own home. You know I love you like an older brother."

Paz smiled and nodded towards the two empty wine bottles on the walnut dining table. "We need some more wine, brother."

Paz disappeared into the kitchen, and when he returned a few moments later he wasn't holding a fresh bottle of wine. Herrera was busy sorting through the remnants of his prawn curry and never saw his boss lift his arm and fire two rounds from his Glock, which shattered his skull. Paz placed the weapon down on the table and retrieved his phone from his back trouser pocket. He clicked on the camera and took a couple of different-sized shots of Herrera's slumped corpse. A few seconds later Franklin's mobile received two text images.

Chapter Twenty-Nine

18 January 2012

San Francisco

Mary Hutchinson, Richard Franklin's personal assistant, ran through the daily itinerary with her boss at their usual 8 a.m. briefing. Just before they wrapped, she brought up a slightly embarrassing matter that she'd deliberately left until last.

"Sir, I took a call last night from a Lieutenant Hembury of the LA Police Department. He would like to see you to discuss what he referred to as a delicate matter concerning someone on the senior management team. I told him you were incredibly busy and suggested he meet with the head of HR, but he was insistent he meet with you."

Franklin was clearly irritated by the request. "Go back and say I need to know the specific name of the employee before I agree to see him."

"I'm afraid I tried that angle, sir, but he wouldn't back down. He said he had to meet with the CEO of the corporation."

Troy Hembury took the short flight from LA to San

Francisco. He had no luggage, so exited the airport ten minutes after landing and jumped into a yellow taxi that took him downtown to the prestigious offices of the Franklin Pharmaceutical Corporation. Franklin's personal assistant had booked him for an end-of-day meeting on the proviso that he would only have a maximum of fifteen minutes with the company's CEO.

At six o'clock precisely, Mary Hutchinson ushered the lieutenant into Franklin's imposing office. The maple wood-panel walls housed some spectacular artwork. An eclectic mix of modern and Renaissance, which included a Picasso and a Raphael hanging side by side. The cream tumbled marble floor was partially covered by a midnight blue Chinese silk rug. Everything about the office screamed wealth, power and influence. Franklin rose from behind his massive designer Italian desk, coated with a white ebony veneer. He greeted Hembury with a firm handshake and gestured for him to take a seat on one of the two black leather sofas that faced each other.

His opening gambit told Hembury this wasn't a man who did small talk.

"Lieutenant, as I'm sure my PA already told you, I really haven't got much time, so I'd appreciate it if you'd get straight to the point and tell me which member of my management team is causing you some concern."

"That's my problem, Mr Franklin. At this point I don't know, and that's why I need your help."

Franklin felt a strange feeling of unease and didn't enjoy the unusual sensation of not being in total control of events. "Lieutenant, how can I help you?"

Hembury produced a small black notebook from his inside

jacket pocket and flicked it open.

"One of your employees uses a direct phone line that bypasses the switchboard system. The number is 742-9898. I'm assuming that only senior management staff would have the facility of a direct line?"

Even though he was completely stunned by Hembury's question, Franklin kept a totally straight face. "And why would that be of concern to the LAPD?"

"I'm assisting the Buenos Aires Police Department on a complex, high-profile case that involves robbery and murder. They believe that whoever uses that private line is somehow involved, and I'd like to speak to them. I assume it would be easy for you to check who the number is assigned to?"

Franklin answered the question with one of his own. "Lieutenant, is this an official Los Angeles Police Department enquiry?"

"Not at this time, sir. As I said, I'm assisting a fellow detective, Chief Inspector Vargas, who is working the case in Argentina."

Hembury studied Franklin's reaction to his deliberate mention of his colleague's name but there wasn't even a flicker of recognition on his face. Franklin suddenly stood up, and it was apparent to Hembury that their meeting was over.

"Lieutenant, this is clearly an unofficial enquiry and is of no interest to me whatsoever as, when I last checked, we are not answerable to the Buenos Aires Police Department. They have no jurisdiction here. Also, I refuse to believe that any member of my management team would be involved in the sort of behaviour you refer to. We are one of the most respected companies in the country and, it may have escaped your notice, my son is currently running for the presidential nomination, which means, lieutenant, I'm a very busy man and I'm afraid you are wasting my time."

Chapter Thirty

18 January 2012

San Francisco

John Franklin held two dark secrets. The one concerning his true lineage he kept from the American people, and the second one he kept from his wife. Just like his father and his beloved uncle, beneath the public veneer of respectability, he was innately immoral. He was a deep-rooted misogynist and, throughout his married life, had kept a string of mistresses in a discreet downtown apartment. He had just enjoyed an afternoon tryst with his latest fling, who was already beginning to bore him. Her name was Annabelle Johnson; a twenty-something fashion model who was hooked on cocaine and the presidential candidate. They had met backstage after one of Franklin's many TV appearances, and, for the last four months, she had been ensconced in the apartment. As he walked out of the bedroom, he paused in the doorway. He had already decided she'd overstayed her welcome. Annabelle had just finished showering and was drying her hair by the side of the bed.

"Annie, I want you gone by Friday as I'm redecorating the apartment. It's been fun, but it's time to move on."

She switched off the dryer and her eyes immediately began to well up. "John, what the fuck do you want me to do? I've got nowhere to go."

"Today I transferred thirty thousand dollars into your personal account. So just fuck off."

He slammed the door and walked into the hallway.

She screamed after him. "You fucking bastard. That dick of yours will cost you the White House."

He smiled as he reached the front door and murmured under his breath. "You stupid bitch. That's the least of my problems."

An hour later, he was enjoying dinner at home with his wife, Caroline, and their twelve-year-old son, Bill. In the last few months, he had rarely been home as he had visited over thirty different states in his relentless pursuit to win the Republican presidential nomination. Achieving that goal would bring him one step closer to the ultimate prize, which was now within touching distance.

He was deep in conversation with Bill, who was entertaining his father with an in-depth account of a school visit, earlier that day, from his football idol, David Beckham. Bill was a huge LA Galaxy fan and was telling his father about his favourite Beckham tattoo and how he wanted one exactly the same. The particular piece of body ink that Bill was besotted with featured a Gothic-style cross joined to a set of angel wings that were positioned above the name of his son, Romeo.

The debate on the merits of a twelve-year-old boy having a neck tattoo was cut short as Franklin's phone buzzed. Caroline gave him a slightly disapproving look, but he still took the call. It was from Cathy Douglas, who was heading up his campaign.

"John, I know you are having a family night off but switch the TV on right now and then call me back."

Franklin hit the remote and Fox News popped up on the wall-mounted LED screen. Nina Brewer, his last remaining rival for the nomination, was making a concession speech at a rally in Wisconsin. Franklin was glued to the live transmission. Brewer signed off with a rousing message to her disconsolate supporters.

"So, at this point, I want you all to get behind our party's nominated candidate and the next president of the United States, Senator John Franklin."

Caroline Franklin draped her arms around her husband's neck and pulled him into a tight embrace. The intimate moment was instantly broken as Bill shouted across from the kitchen table.

"Dad, does this mean that you are going to be the next president?"

Franklin looked at his wife and smiled. "Yep, it does, Bill, and it also means your mom is going to be the first lady, so no more talk of tattoos."

Franklin called Cathy back. She was enjoying her third glass of champagne and he could make out the sound of raucous celebrations kicking off in the background at the campaign headquarters.

"We made it, John. It's hard to believe but we fucking well did it. You've made history already. We haven't even hit Iowa and you're the last man standing. Tomorrow, the party will confirm you as their presidential candidate."

Franklin could sense she was slightly tipsy, as it was rare for her to swear conversationally. She was a brilliant strategist and he wanted her to enjoy the moment.

"We did and now just one more step to go before you become chief of staff at the White House."

Franklin's next call was to his father.

"Did you see it, Dad? Brewer just dropped out of the race."

"Of course I saw it and, as predicted, that bitch is now going to be all over you looking for a job."

"Dad, this is getting real now. All those years of planning are about to pay off. I owe you and the family so much."

Richard Franklin was a deeply troubled man but, as ever, showed no sign of it to his jubilant son. "Keep your eyes on the main prize, John. We don't celebrate until you are sitting behind that desk in the Oval Office. By the way, I've been thinking, with the presidency in touching distance, now is the right time for you to shut down the apartment and everything that goes with it. We can't take any chances."

"Sure, Dad, I was thinking exactly the same thing."

John allowed himself a wry smile. He knew this was one of the rare occasions when he was prepared to blatantly lie to his father, as he already had designs on the apartment's next occupant.

* * *

Richard Franklin sat in the study of his Pacific Heights mansion and downed a bourbon. Mucki was busy gnawing his way through a giant bone on the Persian rug in front of the huge marble fireplace. His master clapped his hands together and the Alsatian instantly stopped eating and took the "sit" position. Franklin waited a few seconds, nodded his head and

Mucki resumed his decimation of the lamb leg. For Hitler's son, total control was everything.

He reflected on how far he had come since his childhood days in Argentina. The intricate and improbable master plan hatched by his "uncle" over sixty years ago was now only a few months away from becoming a reality. But, suddenly, it was all in danger of unravelling, due to the actions of three insignificant men who had decided to rob a bank. He consoled himself with the thought they had all been executed on his orders and had died without ever knowing the reason why.

Now, there was a policeman six thousand miles away in Buenos Aires who was threatening to destroy everything and change the entire course of history. He couldn't be allowed to do that. It was time for another conversation with Matias Paz.

Paz hadn't heard from Franklin since he'd sent the images of Luciano's demise. His heart sank when he saw the incoming call from San Francisco.

"Paz, I've just had a visit from a lieutenant in the Los Angeles Police Department. He claimed he was working with the Buenos Aires police and mentioned Vargas by name. He asked a number of questions about the direct phone line coming into our offices. I shut him down and he shouldn't be a problem any more but I'm afraid Chief Inspector Vargas has become a threat that needs to be taken care of."

"Sir, with respect, taking out a senior police officer may not be a wise move as it could lead to far more scrutiny from the authorities." He normally knew better than to challenge Franklin's instructions but he thought this suggestion was madness. However, Franklin was in no mood for a debate.

"Paz, don't even think about questioning my orders. Just carry them out."

Chapter Thirty-One

31 January 2012

Los Angeles

Lieutenant Troy Hembury had never actually met the Los Angeles police chief but that was about to change as he had been summoned to a face-to-face meeting in his office on West First Street. John McDonnell was midway through his second term and had held the post for the last seven years, following his appointment by the mayor. McDonnell was, by nature, a very cautious political player; a stickler for process who had worked his way to the top of the tree after thirty years of service. Although Hembury hadn't been briefed on what the meeting was about, he had a pretty good idea. He was led into the office by a young secretary who then immediately left the room and shut the door.

"Take a seat, lieutenant."

McDonnell gestured towards a black leather chair and Hembury sat down opposite him. Troy noticed a file on the desk which undoubtedly contained his entire career history.

"Good to meet you, sir. How can I be of service?"

The chief sat slowly back in his chair before replying. "Lieutenant, we've got a bit of a problem that we need to talk through. Yesterday I received a call from the mayor who was pretty pissed, to say the least. Apparently you took it upon yourself to initiate a meeting with probably the single most important man in the state without clearing it with anyone."

McDonnell paused and shook his head. "What the hell were you thinking and what's all this crap about working with the Buenos Aires Police. Who is this Vargas guy?"

Hembury jumped straight in. "He's a good guy, sir, and a great detective. He's working on a complex case in Buenos Aires, which seems to have tentacles stretching as far as San Francisco. It involves a number of organised killings and—"

McDonnell shut him down in no uncertain terms.

"Lieutenant, listen very carefully as I will say this only once. As of yesterday, John Franklin has a clear pass to the presidential election in November, and I'd bet my pension on him winning. However, everybody knows that his father is the real brains behind the whole campaign. The man is the true personification of the American dream – an immigrant who became a self-made billionaire and built one of the biggest corporations in the country. And now his son is about to become president of the United States. So, Lieutenant, if you know what's good for your career, I suggest you stay away from him."

McDonnell sat back in his chair and waved his right arm in the air, pointing it towards the door, making it abundantly clear to Hembury the conversation had come to an end.

* * *

"Gentlemen, I apologise for the short notice in calling this meeting. There's only one topic on the agenda."

Richard Franklin eased forward in his upholstered chair and glanced around the room, making eye contact with each of the seven men present. The covert meeting for senior management of the Franklin Corporation normally took place once a year on 20 April, to mark the Führer's birthdate. It was always held in a different setting and no minutes were ever taken. This year, it had been called three months early and, on this occasion, the venue was a private suite at the eminent Fairmont Hotel, which was perched at the top of Nob Hill in San Francisco.

Along with Richard's son, John, the other six directors were also direct descendants of prominent Nazis who had escaped justice and created new lives in South America, under the cover of fresh identities. They all knew Franklin's secret but, equally, had secrets of their own when it came to their lineage. The small group of men who formed this clandestine board were the real power base of the Franklin Corporation and understood the true narrative of the organisation. All of them held the title senior vice president and had flown in from around the world as soon as they received the summons from Franklin.

"Unfortunately some sensitive documents are in circulation that could seriously compromise the corporation and all of us personally. Of course, I've taken extreme measures to retrieve them, but, until they are back in my hands, if any of you are contacted by a lieutenant from the LAPD called Hembury, or a Chief Inspector Vargas from the Buenos Aires Police Department, don't take the call and inform me immediately."

For a few seconds the men digested the information and

174

then one of them broke the silence. Patrick Strauss, aka Hans Schroeder, was the oldest man in the room, son of the infamous "Executioner of the Jews", Klaus Schroeder, who once held the ominous title in the Third Reich of head of concentration camp operations.

"Richard, how the hell did you let this happen and what do these documents reveal?"

Franklin's face turned claret and the veins on the left side of his forehead began to twitch. He slowly stood from his chair and glared directly at Strauss. "Remember who you are talking to, Patrick. Many years ago, Martin decided to preserve certain items that he believed should be kept for posterity."

He paused to achieve maximum impact with his next statement. His voice dropped to a whisper, forcing everyone in the room to lean forward and focus on his every word. "None of you are fit to question his reasoning and if a mistake has been made, it's mine. The materials in question came to light in Argentina following a safe-deposit bank raid and Matias Paz and his team are tracking them down."

For a few seconds no one spoke and then the awkward silence was broken by William Ames who ran the New York office and was one of Franklin's closest allies. His father, Kurt Fuchs, had been in charge of the final solution in Bulgaria, the Balkans and Hungary. Other than Richard Franklin, he was undoubtedly the shrewdest man in the room and the most obsequious.

"Richard, of course we would never question your judgement, but it concerns me you mentioned an LAPD detective. That feels a bit too close to home."

"William, I can assure you he is on a fishing trip and knows nothing. But, should he become a real problem, he will be dealt with."

Franklin turned away from Ames and addressed the whole room. "Gentlemen, I just hope none of you have been stupid or vain enough to have kept any compromising souvenirs of your own."

The six directors shook their heads in unison.

Franklin's mood noticeably softened, and he nodded his approval, allowing a sinister smile to break out on his face. "Good. Now, before you return home, I've arranged a private dinner for us in the Crown Room. The Maine lobster and Dungeness crab are the best in the bay. I'll meet you downstairs at eight."

He glanced at John, who had been sitting quietly on his right, relishing his father's impressive demonstration of total power.

"John, let's go back to my suite. I want to run through the latest campaign marketing plan."

The presidential candidate stood to join his father and the two men exited the room in stony silence.

In the following thirty-six hours, across the globe, in Paris, London, Berlin, Rome, Tokyo and New York, a number of treasured personal mementos were destroyed by their perturbed owners.

Chapter Thirty-Two

28 March 1969

El Calafate

Adolf Hitler was dying. He was only three weeks away from his eightieth birthday but those closest to him knew it was a milestone he was never going to reach. For months, he had been languishing in his bed, a mere shadow of his former self. His bowel, stomach and liver were riddled with cancer and his mind was showing clear signs of dementia and cognitive deterioration, indicating a strand of Huntington's disease. The only food he could keep down was Leberknödel, a traditional Austrian liver-flavoured broth he had loved since childhood. He was incapable of maintaining a coherent conversation and had not spoken with his wife or son for over four months. The only person allowed into his bedroom, other than his maid and physician, was Bormann.

Braun spent hours every day in the small cinema room watching old newsreel footage of the Nuremberg rallies, showing Hitler in his prime. She had always been obsessed with his charisma as a public speaker and had fallen in love with the Führer, rather than the man. However, she felt intellectually inferior to her husband and never really understood what he saw in her. Their relationship had been hidden from the German people as Hitler believed a public girlfriend would be a disaster for his image, so only a few people in his inner circle knew of their affair. When they began their new lives in South America, Braun had hoped their relationship would blossom, but nothing really changed. She often went days, sometimes even weeks, without seeing him, waiting to be summoned to his side. Nevertheless, she continued to idolise him and felt honoured he had chosen her to be the only woman in his life. She had also borne him a son, ensuring his bloodline would live on, long after the death of the Third Reich.

Their son, Richard Franklin, who was now twenty-two, was living and working in San Francisco. As a child, Bormann had insisted he be home tutored in English as well as Spanish and German, so he was fluent in all three languages. A few months earlier, the Franklin Corporation had opened its first office and laboratory base in the United States as, under Bormann's stewardship, it continued to expand at an exponential rate. Bormann commuted regularly to and from Argentina although, since Richard had moved there, he spent the majority of his time in San Francisco, building the business and grooming Richard in his new role as a company director.

Richard was in the boardroom, holding a meeting with a couple of his new colleagues when he was summoned to his uncle's office. As he arrived, Bormann was completing a phone call but signalled for him to take a seat. He quickly finished up and turned to Richard.

"I've just booked us on the night flight home. It's a matter of days."

* * *

Hitler's last few hours were spent in a medically-induced coma. Bormann, Richard and Braun kept vigil in the bedroom and, every few minutes, she would check to see if he was still breathing. At ten minutes to midnight, the Führer drew his final breath and was gone.

The following few days were spent planning the funeral. Bormann insisted the body should be cremated and the ashes safely hidden until the day they could be scattered in his birthplace of Braunau am Inn, a small riverside town that lay on the Austria–Germany border.

The funeral would be discreet and, besides themselves, only two of the infamous three and their immediate families would be present. The small Catholic church Bormann selected for the service was the oldest in the Santa Cruz district. Hitler had been raised by a practising Catholic mother and was baptised and later confirmed in the Roman Catholic Cathedral in Linz. He told Bormann he found the whole experience truly repulsive, and, as soon as he left home, he vowed never again to visit the inside of a church.

However, Hitler was also a pragmatist, and, in his book, *Mein Kampf*, he described himself as a Christian, encouraging followers of the Nazi Party to embrace his notion of "Positive Christianity". This concept rejected the divinity of Christ and talked instead of the racial purity of the German people, combined with the Christian philosophy of the Nazi Party. In the dark days of their confinement in the Führerbunker in 1945, Hitler confided to Bormann that he loathed the Christian movement but he knew he had to maintain a public association with them for tactical reasons. Bormann was the only person close enough to the Führer to fully understand the roots of his atheist views, but, nevertheless, he felt he had little option but to hold the service in a church.

The night before the funeral, Bormann and Richard met in Hitler's study to discuss the new future that lay ahead now the Führer was dead. They relaxed next to each other on a black Chesterfield style leather sofa and shared a bottle of Chivas Regal whisky, another cherished privilege that Bormann imported, this time from Scotland. He poured them both a large drink from the antique crystal decanter.

"Richard, as you well know, your father and I spent many years planning for the future and, now he has passed, it's important you become familiar with some of the finer details."

"I've always been aware how important it was to both of you to build the corporation into the biggest pharmaceutical company in the world and for its base to be located in a major city in the United States."

Bormann downed his scotch and poured them both another. "Indeed, but we have far more ambitious plans than that." Richard nodded and Bormann continued. "We moved you to America as soon as we thought prudent for another reason. Richard, you need to marry in the next few years and father a son. Your choice of the mother is vital to the success of the plan. She needs to fit the Aryan archetype – blonde, blue-eyed, long legs and broad hips for childbearing.

"We have mapped out your son's education path to replicate JFK's. That means a Bachelor of Arts in Government at Harvard, concentrating on international affairs, followed by a year at Stanford Graduate School of Business. By then, you will be running one of the most respected and powerful corporations in America, giving you the perfect platform to fund your son's political career all the way to the White House."

"Uncle, I've always known my life was predestined, and now it seems my son's will be too. I will do everything in my power to fulfil it."

Bormann, the arch manipulator, hadn't quite finished. "There's one more thing you need to fully understand. The woman who bears your son cannot live. Her existence would pose a potential threat to the plan. Do you understand?"

Richard drained his glass and set it down on the glass coffee table. "Yes, I understand. But it will be fun searching for the perfect candidate."

The Führer's funeral service took place inside the Santa Teresita del Niño Jesús Church in El Calafate, in the presence of a handful of people who stood in front of the open coffin. Although the local priest was present, no prayers or eulogies were offered. Bormann had installed a large speaker at the rear of the church and, for an hour, the mourners sat and listened to some of Hitler's prized Wagner recordings. No one spoke, and the only other sounds echoing around the church came from Braun, who cried intermittently throughout. As the final bars of the *Rienzi* overture tailed off, Braun and Richard stood and led the mourners outside to a small group of chauffeur-driven cars that were waiting to take them back to El Blondi.

Bormann was the only mourner not to travel back to the house. Instead, he sat in the front seat of the hearse on its fifty-mile journey to the nearest crematorium. He wanted to be absolutely sure the process was carried out to his exact specifications. Three hours later, he walked out of the front door of the crematorium, clutching a matt black urn containing the ashes of the most notorious dictator of the twentieth century.

Chapter Thirty-Three

19 January 2012

Buenos Aires

Troy Hembury sat at home in front of his laptop and placed a Skype call to Vargas. A few moments later, the two detectives were staring at each other courtesy of Wi-Fi.

"Good to see you, Troy. How's it going?"

"Not good. I've just had my arse kicked by the chief of police who, it seems, had his arse kicked by the mayor of Los Angeles."

Vargas cut in. "Jesus, Troy. What the hell have you been up to?"

Hembury took his friend through the meeting with Franklin and then gave him a line-by-line account of his dressing-down from the chief of police.

"So when you mentioned my name to Franklin, there was no reaction?"

"Zilch. The guy's either a fantastic actor or, more likely, he didn't know what I was talking about. But the bottom line is,

I've been well and truly closed down."

"Troy, don't beat yourself up. I really appreciate you trying to help. I'll keep working away at this end and see what breaks."

"Look, Nic, I've been on the force for twenty-three years and I've only got two more to go, so I don't really give a shit. If you need me, I'll be there for you."

* * *

Vargas finished the daily team briefing and returned to his office along with Torres. The hunt for García's hiding place and his killers was not progressing well. It had been four days since the discovery of the San Francisco phone number, which had offered a glimmer of light before being snuffed out. Torres could tell his boss was rapidly descending into a dark place.

"Chief, I think I'll pay another visit to García's flat. I feel we may have missed something."

"Okay. Take Alex with you. But, before you go, can you ask one of the team to bring me the García evidence bag?"

"Sure thing, chief, but there's not a lot in there."

Thirty minutes later, Vargas emptied a small pile of random objects from a transparent plastic bag onto his desk. They were the possessions García had on his person at the time of his arrest. The tiny collection included a battered brown leather wallet containing a small amount of pesos and dollars, a set of flat keys, a squashed pack of Marlboro Red containing four cigarettes and a disposable plastic lighter.

Vargas had seen everything before but found it strangely cathartic to check every item again. He flicked open the wallet, desperately hoping to find something he might have missed. But there was nothing. All the items were regular, run-of-the-mill belongings that anyone might own. His focus moved on to the small brass ring holding the keys to García's flat. Something seemed wrong. He grabbed his mobile and speed-dialled Torres, who answered after a couple of rings.

"Juan, are you guys at the flat yet?"

"Yes, chief, we got here ten minutes ago."

Vargas picked up the key ring and held it tightly in the palm of his left hand. "Go to the front door and tell me how many locks it has."

Vargas held his breath as he waited for Torres to come back on the line.

"Two, chief. It's got two locks."

Vargas leapt to his feet in triumph. "Then why are there three keys on García's key ring?"

Vargas jumped in his car and drove over to García's apartment, where he met up with Torres. It only took a few seconds for them to establish which two keys matched the locks on the front door. Vargas prised the mystery key off the brass key ring and held it up in the air.

"What are the odds that this baby fits the lock to García's secret hiding place?"

An hour later, the two detectives were back in Vargas's office where they were joined by a local locksmith who was scrutinising the key. Vargas began the questioning.

"Señor Rivas, it would be incredibly helpful if you could tell us where this key might have been made and what sort of lock it might fit."

The old man ignored the question and continued to rotate the key slowly between his thumb and index finger. Eventually he gently rested it on Vargas's desk and began his analysis.

"This is a cruciform key. It has three sets of teeth that are located at a ninety-degree angle to each other. While it is very easy to duplicate this type of key, it is incredibly difficult to pick the lock. It's typically used to protect garages or small warehouse doors."

Torres was impressed by the swift diagnosis. "Do you think there's any way of tracking where it was originally made?"

"I'm afraid not. I would guess it's at least fifteen years old and therefore the lock it fits is of a similar age."

Vargas moved across and shook Rivas's hand. "Thank you for coming in, Señor Rivas. You've been a great help. How quickly could you make ten duplicates?"

The old locksmith picked up the cruciform key. "You'll have them by this time tomorrow."

* * *

Nobody in the boardroom mentioned that Herrera wasn't there. Rumours had been flying around the office all morning. The main one doing the rounds was that he had fallen out with Paz and left town in a hurry. An alternative version suggested the Black Scorpion had taken him out, although nobody could think of a valid reason as to why that might have happened. Whatever the truth, none of the men were about to ask Matias Paz if he knew of Herrera's whereabouts, and no one knew quite what to expect when he entered the boardroom.

Paz could sense the anxiety among the men as he took his usual seat at the head of the table.

"Gentlemen, before we move on to the business in hand, I

want to fill you in on some developments. As you know, the Franklin Corporation is our biggest client, even though their headquarters are based in California. I've sent Luci over there to help with a tricky situation that's just come up, and I expect he'll be there for a few weeks. As ever, it's a delicate matter and he will be working undercover. For now, I'll assume his responsibilities, as well as my own."

While the men digested the news with a fair amount of scepticism, Paz's mind flashed, for a brief moment, to the shallow grave in the forest where he had buried his former friend. After a few moments, he switched his mind back to the matter at hand and began the briefing.

"As well as continuing the search for García's hiding place, we have a new assignment that is connected to the same operation. The man running the police investigation into the robbery has become a direct threat to our employer, and we have been asked to eliminate that threat."

Alonso Núñez was the only man in the room brave enough to confront Paz. "Boss, I assume you are talking about taking out Chief Inspector Vargas? That's a line we've never crossed before and we could end up with the entire police department on our case."

Paz's instinct for survival kicked in. He knew he had to quash any sign of revolt before it had a chance to spread. "Alonso, fuck you. I thought you, of all people, would know better than to question my orders or my methods. Your job right now is not to doubt me but to work your police contact and find out everything you can about Vargas's life. I want to know everything there is to know about that bastard cop – his home address, details of his family, his favourite bar, his daily schedule. I even want to know what time in the morning the fucker goes for a shit."

Paz finished his rant, slowly rose from his chair, leaned his hands on the table and stared menacingly around the room at his operatives. "Has anyone got any problems with that?"

Everyone nodded their support and Núñez stepped back into line. "Boss, I'll get on to it straight away."

The potential rebellion was short-lived and well and truly crushed.

Chapter Thirty-Four

21 January 2012

Buenos Aires

The blown-up image displaying a street map of the Villa Lugano district filled the entire fascia of the giant crime board. García's flat was clearly marked with a red dot and drawn around it were three circles of varying diameters. Torres had called a meeting to update his detective team. He and Vargas were standing on either side of the map. The chief inspector held a long plastic ruler in his left hand, which he used as an improvised pointer.

"We've had a major development in the last twenty-four hours, which I believe may be the break we've been waiting for. We think a cruciform key found among Pedro García's personal effects will help us find his secret hiding place. The lock that works with this type of key is typically used to protect a garage or a lock-up warehouse or even a studio apartment. I think García may well have rented a small building to stash his share of the robbery, and the odds are it's located within a three-mile radius of his flat."

Vargas used the ruler to tap the circle closest to García's flat. "This first circle covers a one-mile radius from the location of the flat and the other two show the street layouts up to three miles away. I want to start the search within the first circle and then we'll work our way out until every potential lock has been tried within three miles of the flat."

Vargas nodded to Torres to fill in some more detail. He picked up a large bunch of keys from the nearby table and held them in the air.

"As the chief just said, we think García's hiding place is somewhere in the Villa Lugano district. To speed up the search, we've had duplicate keys made for all of you."

Vargas pointed the ruler towards the map board again. "Somewhere on this street map is a matching lock waiting to be found and opened. The key is a bit like Cinderella's shoe, except we've got ten of them."

* * *

Alonso Núñez had never been granted the honour of a meet with Paz in the Recoleta Cemetery. But, with no sign of Herrera, he wondered if he was being groomed as a possible replacement. As usual, Paz was seated on the stone bench facing the statue of his boxing idol. He spotted his operative approaching through the grounds and gestured to Núñez to join him.

"Alonso, take a look at that magnificent statue. I find it truly inspiring and, at various difficult moments in my life, I've always turned to it for inspiration."

"It's awesome, boss. I can see why you are so drawn to it."

"So what have we learned so far about Vargas?"

"Well, as you know, in the last few days Vargas has been playing things pretty close to his chest and our contact has to be very careful not to risk exposure. His personal file is password-protected, so it's not easy to access the sort of information we want. I'm thinking of setting up our own surveillance team to try and get a handle on his movements, if you agree?"

"For fuck's sake, the last time I checked we were paying ten thousand dollars a month to this contact, so tell them they need to start fucking earning it."

"Understood, boss. I'll get us what we need."

Paz stood up as a way of signalling to Núñez that the meeting was over.

"Alonso, I hope you are not going to disappoint me."

As Núñez watched his boss walk away, he couldn't help but wonder if Luciano Herrera had recently disappointed the Black Scorpion.

* * *

The search for García's hiding place got underway at just after ten in the morning when the detectives set off to the Villa Lugano neighbourhood. There were just over ninety potential sites to check out within a one-mile radius of the flat, and not all of them had direct street access. Torres divided up the properties between the team and each detective was given a duplicate key. Vargas and Torres kept the original and headed off with their specific list of addresses, which contained a mix of garages and small storehouses. By four in the afternoon, every potential site had been checked out, but no one had made a successful match. Torres radioed the team to confirm that the following day they would begin checking the two-mile zone and he would email everybody their lists overnight so they didn't need to come into the station.

* * *

Vargas had just arrived home and cracked open a beer when he received a call from Hembury. He quickly brought Troy up to speed about García's mystery key and the search for the hidden location.

"Troy, do you think I'm wasting everybody's time? Another needle in a haystack?"

"No, I think it's good lateral thinking and, if it pays off, you'll be a hero."

Vargas laughed for the first time in a while. "You know something? I actually dream about what's inside Box 1321. It's become an obsession."

"Nic, even though it's not my case, I can't help thinking about it either. I wonder if Franklin ever made an internal check to discover who on his management team used that direct line."

"I've had the same thought. That individual, whoever he or she is, has been sanctioning multiple executions from six thousand miles away."

"Yep. And that begs two questions. Who is it and why are they doing it?"

Chapter Thirty-Five

22 January 2012

Buenos Aires

Day two of the search also proved fruitless and morale among the detective team was beginning to run low but mid-morning on the third day, everything changed: Detective Pasqual Sosa hit pay dirt. He was working his way through a run of terraced garages located on one side of a quiet cul-de-sac. Standing in front of the last one, he peered closely at the lock. By now, he'd seen over forty different specimens but something about this one somehow seemed right. A surge of adrenalin pumped through his body and, for a brief moment, he delayed trying the key, just in case he was wrong. It slid effortlessly into place and, after two counterclockwise revolutions, he felt the mechanism click open.

An hour later, the cul-de-sac had been sealed off and a white transit van, which took up most of the floor space inside the garage, had been pushed out onto the road. Police cars buzzed in and out, dropping off detectives and forensic specialists attired in white protective clothing. Neighbours in the buildings opposite wondered if the police had discovered an unexploded bomb.

Vargas and Torres stood inside the garage and gazed at the ten cloth bags neatly stacked against the back wall. It was hard to believe this small, rundown garage contained millions of dollars' worth of merchandise.

Torres was totally euphoric and couldn't wait to start working his way through the haul. Vargas seemed slightly subdued and was unusually quiet.

"Chief, what's wrong? Your gamble just paid off big time. We've found García's hideaway."

"Juan, I have a dreadful feeling about whatever is hidden inside one of these bags. It's already been responsible for nine deaths and, even though we've found it, I strongly suspect we haven't seen the end of the killing."

Three hours later, six detectives had carefully opened all the bags and created a number of separate mounds on the garage floor. Cash, stock and bond certificates, jewellery and loose gemstones and small works of art all had their own pile. Vargas showed no interest in any of them. He was drawn to the smallest stack of miscellaneous items that didn't fit into any of the other categories. Among the random items were four different-sized hard drives, two metal storage boxes and a weathered black leather case. He knelt next to the diverse collection of objects and picked up one of the hard drives.

"Juan, the answer is somewhere in this small pile. Let's get this lot back to the station. Everything else needs to be carefully logged and then put into storage."

By the time Vargas and Torres arrived back at base, the department was absolutely buzzing with a party-like atmosphere. The main detective team were ebullient and in full celebration mode. A junior detective brought two bags, containing the random items, into Vargas's office and carefully laid out the contents on the floor. Behind him, two fellow officers struggled to carry a small cast-iron safe, which Vargas had requested be brought up to his office from the basement storeroom. At that exact moment, a phone call was placed from inside the police department to Theodor Consultants.

* * *

Alonso Núñez wasted no time in briefing Paz on the news he'd just received from his informant.

"Turns out the bastard hid his share in a lock-up garage in Villa Lugano. Vargas has sealed off the entire street and there's a small army of cops on-site. Our contact understands that certain items have already been brought back to Vargas's office for examination."

Paz had been sitting on a bar stool by an island in his kitchen, enjoying a beer and a cheese and salami sandwich, when Núñez gave him the update. His trademark temper kicked in and he flung a half-full Peroni bottle onto the tiled floor. The green glass shattered into hundreds of tiny fragments and cold beer splattered onto the white lacquered cupboard units.

He didn't call Franklin immediately, but, an hour later, after hearing the breaking news of the police discovery on his local radio, he knew he had no choice. Paz reached for his mobile, dreading the verbal assault that was coming his way. He wasn't wrong. Franklin was incandescent with rage and Paz had no option but to suck it up.

"Paz, you are a fucking imbecile. I've paid your useless company literally millions of dollars and every time you've let me down. All the way through this fiasco you've constantly failed to deliver. This latest development is potentially catastrophic for all of us, especially my son. You need to come back to me with a plan that will actually work. Vargas needs to be blown away and the contents of our box need to be destroyed before anyone discovers what they represent."

* * *

The four hard drives weren't password-protected and contained various business files and foreign bank accounts, which Vargas figured indicated complex tax evasion by the respective owners of the drives. Hardly a good enough reason to justify a raft of executions. In addition, there were no references to the Franklin Corporation. The two metal storage boxes were locked and needed some work before they could be opened. One of them contained two black velvet-clad trays of uncut diamonds of assorted sizes, while the other revealed a solitary item: a small artwork set inside an ornate gold frame. In the bottom left-hand corner, Rembrandt's signature was clearly legible. The painting was the long-lost and much sought-after self-portrait he had produced just before his death. Vargas held the masterpiece in his hands and marvelled at its perfection.

Eventually he moved on to the weathered black leather case. He stood it upright and flicked the twin catches on the matching brass locks which, to his surprise, sprung open. But then, he figured there wasn't really much point in locking a case that was already secure inside a safe-deposit box. Centred between the locks were two gold embossed initials. Although they were badly faded, Vargas could clearly make out the letters M.B.

He slowly lifted the case lid back to reveal its contents. The first items that caught his eye were three Manila files, bulging with hand-typed papers, personal certificates and a number of black-and-white photographs. The majority of the paperwork was in Spanish, although some of it appeared to be written in German. Underneath the folders were two unmarked round metal cans. Each contained a fifty-foot reel of 8mm film. The remaining item was a small yellow tin box. The outside design was virtually worn away but Vargas could just make out the word "Tabak". He lifted the tin from the case, placed it on his desk and removed the lid. Lying inside were seven antique military medals, which he tipped onto the desktop. Vargas instantly recognised the unmistakable design of a black Iron Cross. He picked it up to study in more detail and, when he read the engraving on the back, his heart missed a beat. It was dated 4 August 1918 and the name of the recipient was Adolf Hitler.

Chapter Thirty-Six

23 January 2012

Buenos Aires

Vargas placed the medal back on the desktop and stared at the bizarre collection of random items that had been stored so carefully for over thirty years in the black case. He didn't yet understand the implications of what was before him but he knew he was looking at the contents of Box 1321. His instincts told him that, for now, he should keep the discovery to himself. He reached for his internal phone and dialled Torres.

"Juan, there's a hell of a lot of stuff to go through, so I'm going to work late. I might even pull an all-nighter."

"Understood, chief. Do you want me to stay and help?"

"No, I'll be fine. I suspect we've got some very long days ahead, so grab some rest while you can."

"Okay, chief. Have you got everything you need?"

Vargas glanced down at the two film cans lying on the office floor. "Not quite. I urgently need a working 8-millimetre film projector." He paused for a moment. "And some McDonald's would go down well too."

Vargas worked, methodically, through the paperwork in the three files and made copious notes on his laptop. An astonishing picture started to emerge, which was almost too overwhelming to take in. The first file contained papers that were over sixty-five years old, documenting the secret arrival of Adolf Hitler, Martin Bormann and Eva Braun to Argentina in June, 1945. Evidently, they had escaped from Europe on a small cargo boat that had sailed to the industrial port of Río Gallegos on the south-east coast.

The documents also recorded the name of a fourth German civilian who had travelled with the Führer on the boat. His name was Doctor Friedrich Hipke. A quick Google search informed Vargas he had been a distinguished plastic surgeon, based in Berlin, who'd disappeared after the war. A black-and-white photograph, which was clearly taken on board, showed Hitler and Bormann standing either side of a third man brandishing a steel scalpel in the air, who Vargas deduced must be Hipke.

There was also a photograph of Eva Braun. She had a huge grin on her face and held her right hand close to the camera lens to show off the gold band on her finger, which was set with three large diamond stones. Another photo showed Hitler and Bormann standing next to a heavily decorated officer, who appeared to be the boat's captain. Vargas suddenly spotted something else in the photo that sent a cold chill through his body. On the floor next to Bormann was a black leather case. He brought the picture closer to gain a better look. There was no doubt about it; the one in his office was the same as that in the grainy black-and-white photo. He moved over to it and slowly ran his fingers over the gold initials which represented Martin Bormann's name.

Vargas returned to his desk and started work on the second file. Mixed in among the papers, some of which were written in German, were three Argentinian photo ID cards. The first one clearly showed the pretty face of Eva Braun, except her name had now changed to Emilia Franklin. The other two cards portrayed the identities of Gerald and Ronald Franklin. Despite the undoubted skills of Doctor Hipke, Vargas could still detect the unmistakable faces of Adolf Hitler and Martin Bormann staring back at him. They all appeared to share the same address; a farmhouse called El Blondi in the town of El Calafate, located in the Santa Cruz province.

Other fake documents confirmed that Gerald and Ronald were brothers, and that Emilia was married to Gerald. The file also contained dozens of photographs, the majority of which featured Gerald in the company of various groups of well-dressed businessmen. One of them was so horrifying it stopped Vargas dead in his tracks. It featured Hitler and Bormann standing alongside a group of three other elderly men. Vargas didn't recognise any of them, but that didn't matter. What he did recognise was the chilling Nazi salute that all of them directed towards the Führer.

Vargas leaned back, took a long slurp of his chocolate milkshake and reached for the Big Mac lying in an open carton next to it. He took a huge bite and spat it out a second later. It was stone cold, having sat on his desk for a considerable time. It was already two in the morning and he had been ploughing through the files for just under four hours. The only interruption had taken place just before midnight when a junior officer had arrived to set up an 8mm projector. He had no idea how Torres had managed to locate one and, not for the first time, he marvelled at the ingenuity of his loyal assistant.

Vargas moved onto the third file, the thinnest of the three but, in many ways, the most revealing. It contained dozens of bank statements detailing transfers of hundreds of millions of Reichsmarks moving between accounts located in Germany and Argentina. Other paperwork listed hundreds of artworks, together with their estimated values. At the back of the file was a thin brown envelope containing two original documents and one photocopy. The two originals were the death certificates of Gerald and Emilia Franklin. The third was a photocopy of the birth certificate of Richard Franklin. Vargas took a sharp breath and did a double take as he absorbed the full implications of the document in his hands. He shook his head in disbelief and dropped the photocopy as if it had suddenly caught fire. It fell onto the desk but his eyes remained transfixed on the birth name. Incredibly, the document revealed that Richard Franklin was the son of Adolf Hitler and Eva Braun. No doubt the original was somewhere in San Francisco, in the hands of the CEO of the Franklin Pharmaceutical Corporation.

The chief inspector had never worked with 8mm film before but he found it remarkably easy to operate the Bell & Howell projector Torres had sourced. He attached the first reel of film and angled the lens towards the white wall behind his desk. He flicked off the office lights, instantly creating his own personal cinema. The film only ran for three minutes but offered up even more remarkable secrets that had lain hidden for over half a century. The first thirty seconds of footage showed Hitler and Bormann sitting in a garden, sharing drinks with yet another two of the most notorious figures of the twentieth century, Juan and Eva Perón. It was well known that the former president of Argentina had been a Nazi sympathiser and this footage, although silent, clearly showed him and his revered wife laughing and joking with the Führer.

The film cut to an interior scene, which Vargas assumed was the kitchen in the farmhouse. Eva Braun was sitting on a wooden chair, breastfeeding a small baby. A few seconds later, Hitler walked into the shot and stood behind the pair, staring straight at the camera. Another scene portrayed Hitler walking through a large field, accompanied by two Alsatian dogs. In the background, he could make out a large farmhouse which he assumed was Hitler's home, El Blondi. The Führer threw a rubber ball past the camera and the two dogs bounded out of shot in pursuit. The final scene showed Hitler enjoying lunch in the garden along with Bormann and three guests. Vargas instantly recognised the men from the photo he had seen earlier, in which they were pictured giving a Nazi salute.

He quickly changed reels, sat back and wondered what further revelations were about to be offered up from the second film. He was slightly disappointed when the next three minutes of footage concentrated on what was evidently the fifth birthday party of Richard Franklin. The patio at the back of the farmhouse was decked out with balloons and a giant blue wooden number five hung from the porch in the back of the shot. Eva Braun was clearly acting as the party hostess to about a dozen adult guests and eight children who looked to be of a similar age to Richard. There was no sign of either Gerald or Ronald Franklin.

The 8mm Kodak film spun off the end of the reel and the office fell into complete darkness. Vargas looked at his watch and the luminous dial told him it was nearly five thirty in the morning, which meant it was gone midnight in California. He reached for his phone and his finger tapped on a familiar contact. Troy Hembury was enjoying a deep sleep when his mobile ringtone kicked into life. He rolled over to grab it from the bedside table and checked the caller ID before answering.

"Christ, Nic. It's five thirty in the morning at your end. What the hell is up?"

Vargas took a moment before replying. "Troy, I've just spent the last seven hours examining the contents of Box 1321."

Hembury switched on his sidelight and jumped out of bed. "Let me grab a coffee and then I wanna hear chapter and verse."

Vargas spoke without interruption for the next hour while Hembury just listened and took in the enormity of the discovery.

"Troy, for the first time in my career, I'm not sure what to do. The implications of this case are huge. I don't know who I can trust, and what's more, is anyone going to believe me? And what if it's all a fake? Do you remember the Hitler Diaries scandal in the eighties?"

Hembury let out a sarcastic laugh. "Nic, to the best of my knowledge, five people weren't executed to keep that particular secret."

"Okay, but we both know how powerful Franklin is in both our countries. Don't forget the Franklin Corporation was founded here, and it must bring in millions of dollars in revenue to the government. He may live in San Francisco, but he still has incredibly powerful network contacts in Argentina. I'm not sure I won't get the same reaction from my chief as you did from yours."

"Nic, what are you thinking?"

"I'm thinking about keeping all this to myself for now and not even telling my second in command. I want to fly to Santa Cruz and see what's left of the farmhouse that was in the film. Find some locals who are still around from that time. Try and learn a bit more."

Hembury took a swig of coffee and wiped his mouth before replying. "Nic, you need to be careful. That bastard Franklin is the most accomplished liar I've ever come up against. The direct line obviously belongs to him. He's the one who's been ordering the executions. He bullshitted me and then set me up for the arse-kicking I got from the chief. I owe him."

Vargas could feel Hembury's anger from six thousand miles away. "Troy, where are you heading with this?"

"Things are pretty quiet here at the moment and I'm due nearly three weeks' leave. Why don't I jump on a plane and we can take a trip to visit the Führer's farmhouse together?"

"Troy, this is really not your problem."

"Are you kidding? As things stand, the next president of the United States is set to be Adolf Hitler's grandson."

Chapter Thirty-Seven

1 September 1969

San Francisco

Alicia Karisson's best friend, Astrid, had set up the blind date with Richard Franklin. She was feeling excited and a little nervous about meeting one of the city's most eligible bachelors. Alicia was a twenty-five-year-old Swedish national who worked as an assistant attaché at her consulate, located in the financial district in San Francisco.

She had the classic Nordic appearance: blonde hair, blue eyes and a long, slim frame. She was a natural beauty. Four years earlier, she'd represented her country in the annual Miss World contest where she'd finished third. Her friend, Astrid, who also worked at the consulate, was dating one of Richard's friends and he'd suggested they get together for dinner as a foursome.

They met at the fashionable Jolly Harbor restaurant, which was only a five-minute stroll from the consulate. Alicia felt an instant attraction to Richard, which appeared to be reciprocated and, in the following three months, they began a whirlwind romance, culminating in her moving into his spectacular penthouse apartment with its three-hundred-and-sixty-degree views of the city and the Golden Gate Bridge. As well as being the natural heir to one of the foremost companies in America, Richard was attractive, charming and extremely attentive and Alicia couldn't believe she'd actually landed her dream man. She had no idea he was also an accomplished actor and was playing his role to perfection.

Six weeks after moving in, she fell pregnant, and, a month after that, they were married. The wedding celebration took place at the prestigious Hotel Fairmont in the bay area and no expense was spared as Bormann wanted to make it a statement wedding. Richard paid for Alicia's entire family to fly over from Europe and five hundred guests enjoyed a lavish reception in the opulent ballroom. Richard had explained his mother was too sick to travel from Argentina and his only family representative at the wedding was his beloved Uncle Ronald.

Ronald, aka Martin Bormann, supervised the guest list and ensured it included the great and the good, including the mayor and governor. It was hailed in high-society circles as the wedding of the year and featured as a double-page spread in the prestigious *Life* magazine. The couple honeymooned in Europe, visiting Paris, Rome and London, before taking the Orient Express to Venice where they ended their trip at the legendary Cipriani Hotel. On the last night, they were relaxing together on the massive queen-sized bed, and, as Alicia lay against Richard's body, he gently stroked her slightly swollen stomach. She snuggled in close and didn't see his face wince when she asked the inevitable question.

"Richard, when it comes to my background, I'm a totally

open book but you never say anything about your family. The only person I've ever met is your Uncle Ronald. I'm desperate to know more, but we never seem to talk about it."

Franklin felt an instant wave of contempt towards his new wife but suppressed it and recognised the time had come to employ his fabricated backstory.

"Alicia, I only have my mother and uncle left. My family originates from Kraków in Poland. They were working-class factory workers and small-time shopkeepers who struggled to make a living. Then the war came, and the city was occupied. They weren't religious but were good Christians who were appalled by the relentless massacre of Jews that they witnessed day after day. My father and uncle got heavily involved with an underground organisation run by a man named Oskar Schindler. He was a wealthy factory owner who'd created a network of anti-Nazi sympathisers offering refuge in their homes to Jewish families. It was perilous work and they knew the penalty of exposure was certain death, or at best a trip to Auschwitz.

"My father enlisted the help of all his immediate family, but in the summer of 1943, they were betrayed by a Nazi informant. Most of them were lined up and shot in the Jewish Quarter as a public warning to others. My parents and uncle got a few minutes' warning of the imminent raid and managed to escape, and, over the next few months, they made a tortuous eight-thousand-mile journey to South America, where they arrived with nothing more than three suitcases. My father was in bad health, so, sadly, didn't live for very long, and now my poor mother suffers from dementia and hasn't recognised me for some years. But my uncle is a truly remarkable man and, in many ways, I regard him as my father.

He's generous, caring and inspirational. During the early war years, he worked in a small pharmacy in Kraków, helping the pharmacist dispense drugs and today, almost forty years later, despite all that hardship, he now runs one of America's biggest pharma companies. And my mother lives in a small town in Patagonia where, thanks to my uncle's success, she has a comfortable life."

Alicia squeezed her body even closer to her husband's, nestling her head in his chest. "My God, Richard, that story is incredible. One day you've got to tell it to the world."

An evil smirk appeared on Franklin's face. He couldn't believe how easy it had been to spin his wife a total work of fiction.

Six months later, Alicia gave birth to a healthy baby boy and was the happiest she'd ever been. Richard and Ronald seemed ecstatic, and Alicia's parents were invited to fly over from Sweden to meet their first grandchild. Richard had booked Alicia into a small, exclusive maternity hospital on the outskirts of the city. He'd insisted on total privacy and her two-thousand-dollar-a-night suite was situated on its own floor, accessed only via a private lift. Richard had been present at the birth and, two hours later, he, Alicia and their newly born son were visited by Bormann, in his guise as Richard's uncle.

At first, everything seemed normal and all three were in a state of euphoria. However, Alicia was physically exhausted after a fourteen-hour labour and was struggling to keep awake. Richard kept encouraging her to go to sleep. She finally closed her eyes but hadn't quite slipped into unconsciousness when she felt the sudden touch and pressure of a cotton pillow held firmly against her face. She was far too weak to resist and her last momentary thought was wondering which of the two men was holding it down. After five minutes, Bormann removed the duck-feather pillow and stared at her beautiful blue eyes, which were now blank.

Two hours later, Bormann's private physician signed a death certificate, recording the cause of Alicia's demise as severe haemorrhage, caused by excess bleeding taking place immediately after giving birth. He normally charged a hundred dollars an hour for call-outs but, on this occasion, his reward was a cash payment of ten thousand.

A week later, Richard Franklin brought his new son home, where a live-in nurse and nanny were waiting in the newly created nursery to greet them. He may have lost his mother but baby John wasn't short of care and attention. Bormann arrived at the penthouse later that day and the two men shared a celebratory drink in Richard's study. They clinked glasses and Bormann began to speak.

"Richard, you've done well. Let's toast your newborn son – the Führer's grandson."

Both men emptied their champagne flutes. John George Franklin had only just entered the world and had already lost his mother. Everything was going according to plan.

Chapter Thirty-Eight

24 January 2012

Buenos Aires

Olivia Bianchi, the deputy head of HR for the Buenos Aires Police Department, sat at her desk, organising her schedule for the day. She had worked for the police for almost twenty years, having joined straight from university as a trainee graduate in personnel. As one of the most qualified figures in the human resources department, she was often called upon to arbitrate on extremely delicate internal matters and the nature of her work meant she had direct access to high-level confidential files on most of the twenty-five thousand police department workforce.

Every day, she scheduled personnel meetings at the fifty-six stations that were dotted around the city. Today she felt under far more pressure than usual as she sat at her desk arranging her daily planner. She ensured that her final meeting would take place at the Twenty-Fifth Division on Avenida Guzmán, where Chief Inspector Vargas and his serious crime squad were based. Bianchi was held in high regard by all her contemporaries, including the chief of police, but none of them were aware she hid two huge secrets: Bianchi was addicted to online gambling and was on the payroll of Theodor Consultants.

The previous night, she had been summoned to a rare face-to-face meeting with her handler, Alonso Núñez, which proved to be one of the worst experiences of her life. It was only the third time in five years they had met in person. Núñez had summoned her to a meet in a quiet bar near the port. He outlined an outrageous plan that involved her initiating a late-night fire in Vargas's station. Bianchi was horrified by the request and argued she was a paid informer, not a criminal arsonist, but soon realised he was deadly serious. Núñez seemed desperate and was obviously acting under enormous pressure from above. He made it abundantly clear that failure to comply would mean a painful death for both her and her eighteen-year-old daughter, who was currently away at university.

Bianchi realised, at that precise moment, she was completely out of her depth and had little choice but to cooperate with Núñez's demands. She had screwed up badly, and now she had to pay the price. The meeting moved on from the bar to Núñez's apartment, where he demonstrated how easy it is to start a fire using minimal props. By the time she left, at two in the morning, she had been fully briefed and her handbag contained everything she needed to carry out the assignment.

* * *

Torres sat opposite his boss in the office, looking slightly bemused.

"Chief, I don't quite understand what's going on. You spent all night going through the materials, yet you won't tell me what you actually found. What the hell was in that box?"

Vargas was feeling exhausted, having only caught a couple of hours' sleep, catnapping in his office chair.

"Juan, you are just going to have to trust me on this one. I have found something, but it's too sketchy to share with anyone yet. Not you or the team, and not even the chief. A lot of people have died already, and I want to be very careful that I'm not responsible for more deaths. The good news is we have now recovered all the contents that were stolen in the raid. The bank will be happy and so will the box owners. I want you to front a press conference later today explaining we will now begin a process where the owners are reunited with their possessions."

Torres had worked with Vargas for over three years and had total trust in his boss's judgement. "Okay, chief, but the press are still chasing for answers on the killings of the three robbers, especially the sniper shooting."

"That may be, but, for now, we won't contradict the speculation about two rival gangs falling out over the robbery."

Torres nodded and walked across the office towards the door. "And, Juan, I've got an old friend from Los Angeles arriving in town tonight. He's spending a short time over here, so I'm going to take a couple of days' leave. Obviously, if anything new comes up, let me know straight away."

Torres found it highly suspicious that Vargas would even contemplate taking time off at such a moment, but made no comment.

* * *

Bianchi finished her last meeting of the day at just after six. She said her goodbyes to the commander of the department with whom she'd discussed two internal disputes that had been rumbling for a while. She made her way along the main corridor towards the exit but at the last moment veered off to enter the ladies' toilet. Inside was a run of six cubicles and she promptly walked to the one at the far end of the cloakroom. Now, she had a long wait.

* * *

Vargas was leaning against a stone pillar outside the giant Starbucks in the arrivals terminal at Ezeiza International Airport when he spotted the unmistakable face of Troy Hembury exit a set of electric doors, wheeling a small red suitcase. His sculpted features were set off by a thick mop of black hair and penetrating brown eyes, which combined to striking effect. He spotted Vargas at just about the same time and a huge smile broke out on his face.

A few minutes later, the two detectives were sitting side by side in Vargas's Peugeot, heading into the city.

"Nic, I'd love to take a look at some of those old photos. Not to mention Adolf Hitler's Iron Cross. Where are you storing everything?"

"For now, it's all secure in a safe in my office but I took quite a few pictures on my phone, so when we get back to my place we can run through them."

"Who else knows?"

Vargas flicked the left indicator as they entered the street where he lived. "Literally no one. My assistant, Juan Torres, who is a great detective, is highly suspicious but has cut me some slack for now. The problem is the media are all over the story. What started out as a high-profile robbery investigation has now become a murder case, with multiple killings. Until last night, I had no idea who was behind it, but now—"

Hembury cut in. "Now we know it's the Third Reich."

The two men sat across the breakfast bar in Vargas's kitchen and devoured a takeaway from his local Italian deli. Hembury had seen all the photos on Vargas's mobile and was now totally up to speed on the case.

"I did some research on the flight over and it turns out Bormann was a real piece of work. The guy was totally in control of the Nazi Party and its finances. Many conspiracy theories claim he squirrelled hundreds of millions of dollars' worth of Nazi gold over to South America in the last two years of the war and that he made it out of Berlin and lived in hiding somewhere in Argentina. The official tale goes that he was shot trying to escape in 1945. German authorities claim that a skeleton found near Hitler's bunker in 1972 contained matching DNA to one of his living relatives but, the fact is, no one really knows for sure what happened to him. This whole case is beyond mind-blowing. What are you thinking?"

Vargas downed a last spoonful of tiramisu before replying. "I've booked us on a direct flight tomorrow afternoon to El Calafate, which is where their farmhouse was based. That's if it's still standing. After Hitler and Braun died, it might well have been pulled down as part of a cover up. That's over forty years ago now. Anyhow, it's about a three-and-a-half-hour flight and, once we land, we'll pick up a hire car and then, who knows?"

Chapter Thirty-Nine

24 January 2012

Buenos Aires

B ianchi had waited inside the cubicle for a torturous six hours and no one had entered for the last three. She opened the door, walked across to the nearest sink and began her work. Everything she needed was inside her large brown leather shoulder bag. She eased out of her blue cotton dress and slipped on a pair of black joggers along with a black T-shirt. Then she pulled on the black woollen balaclava Núñez had given her. Next, she took a single cigarette from the soft Camel pack and attached it with a rubber band to a book of fifty matches. She removed the top from a 35ml bottle of Chanel N°5 and carefully poured the contents onto a small white cloth. Earlier that day she had switched the perfume for pure gasoline. The entire operation took less than two minutes.

Once her props were ready, Bianchi walked back into the corridor and headed for the main open-plan office area where Vargas's team was based. It was almost midnight and no one was around. She quickly located the door to Vargas's office, which was positioned just off to the side. Bianchi tried the door handle just in case, but, as she'd expected, it was locked. From about ten feet away, she secured the final piece of her jigsaw: a small metal rubbish bin, stuffed with paper, sandwich wrappings and a few empty polystyrene coffee cups. Next, she held the filter end of the cigarette to her lips, which was quite tricky to do because it was now attached to the book of matches. She lit the end and took a long drag. Finally, she carefully placed the gasoline sodden cloth into the bin and positioned the lit cigarette on top. Thirty seconds later, she left through the back entrance of the station, which she knew would be unmanned after midnight.

* * *

Vargas and Hembury were still in the kitchen, discussing the case, when a call came in informing the chief inspector that a fire had broken out at the station. Vargas grabbed his car keys and headed for the door. Hembury shouted after him.

"Jesus, Nic, I hope that safe is fireproof."

By the time Vargas arrived at the station, the blaze was well under control. Two large fire engines were parked at the front and firefighters were working both inside and outside the building. There was a great deal of smoke bellowing out of the windows, but no sign of flames.

Vargas spotted the fire chief, who was standing on the pavement barking instructions to two of his men. He introduced himself and asked for the state of play.

"It's not too bad, chief inspector. The internal alarm system kicked in and sent an automatic alert to our station which, fortunately, is only three minutes away. We've already put the fire out but obviously there's still going to be a lot of damage inside."

"Chief Carizzo, I urgently need to retrieve some items from the safe in my office. It's crucial evidence in a multiple-murder case. I have to get it right now."

The fire chief instinctively shook his head and was about to rule it out, but could hear the desperate sense of urgency in Vargas's appeal. "Grab a safety helmet and an oxygen mask from one of the trucks and come with me."

Vargas led the chief through the main corridor directly towards his office. The smoke levels got worse the further inside they went. It was obvious the fire had started in the open-plan area and the partition wall to his office had completely burnt down. Through the smoke, he could make out the small iron safe in the far corner of the office. At first sight it appeared intact. As he approached, he could feel the extreme heat levels emanating from the cast-iron casing, so he gave the combination to Carizzo, who was wearing fire gloves. Vargas held his breath as the fire chief pulled open the door.

The small black case appeared unscathed and, although it was warm to the touch, Vargas was able to hold it with his bare hands. He thanked the chief and made his way out of the station as fast as he could. As soon as he emerged onto the pavement, he placed the case on the ground and flipped open the top. The files were as he'd last seen them and none of the contents had suffered any damage. He puffed out his cheeks and let out a huge sigh of relief.

By the time Vargas returned to his apartment, it was almost three in the morning. Hembury had been dozing on the living room sofa, but stirred as soon as he heard the front door open. Vargas walked in and placed the case on the small oval dining table. Troy immediately fired off a bunch of questions.

"Nic, what the hell happened? Is that Bormann's case? Did everything survive?"

"Luckily, the firefighters got there before things got too wild."

Vargas started to open the case. "There's a lot of damage at the station and my office is burnt to a crisp, but this baby and its secrets survived intact."

"Nic, yesterday you pulled an all-nighter and whoever did this may have assumed you would be doing the same tonight. Was it aimed at you or the case?"

Vargas thought for a moment. "Probably both."

"You told me you suspected there was an insider working for Franklin's people. Well, they've just raised the stakes to a whole new level."

Hembury got some coffee on the go while Vargas placed the three files on the table, along with the two film cans and the tobacco box containing Hitler's war medals.

"Troy, we've got a lot of work to do. Other than the photos I showed you on my phone, there isn't a comprehensive copy of these documents. If they had gone up in flames, along with the film, the only proof we'd have had left would have been the military medals, which, on their own, may not be enough. We need to scan in all the key paperwork along with the pictures and create a safe file we can place in the cloud, with a couple of backups."

"Got it. Sounds like another all-nighter."

Vargas smiled at his friend. "There'll be plenty of time to sleep on the plane."

Hembury poured them both some steaming hot coffee and passed a mug to Vargas. "What time are we heading for the airport in the morning?"

Vargas carried a handful of papers over to the scanner that was sitting on top of a small cupboard. "We need to leave by eleven thirty but, before then, I have one more job to do."

"Which is?"

Vargas held a wad of papers up in the air. "Find a safe place for this stuff."

Chapter Forty

19 July 1975

Zurich Airport

The Grumman Gulfstream touched down on the tarmac with its trademark silky landing and the two VIP passengers immediately disembarked and walked across to the waiting blacked-out Mercedes 600 limo.

Richard Franklin relished his foreign trips with Bormann, especially when it was just the two of them. He would regale him with stories of the glory days when the Third Reich was in its pomp and his father was riding high and looking invincible. Richard loved hearing first-hand accounts of the Anschluss – the unification of Germany with Austria; the unopposed seizure of Czechoslovakia and the spectacular Nazi parade down the Champs-Élysées after the French capitulated. Then came the betrayal. The arrogant generals who stubbornly refused to follow the Führer's military orders. Finally, the reality, in late 1944, that the war was lost and the recognition that Nazi treasures would inevitably fall into the hands of the communists and Western Allies. Bormann explained to Richard how, at that time, he looked for a safe haven and began shipping Nazi gold and priceless artworks to Switzerland and South America.

Goehner and Roths was one of the oldest private Swiss banks, having been established in 1865. Their motto, engraved on the gold oval nameplate above the main red-brick entrance stated "Personal Service and Discretion". Discretion was a code word for secrecy. The bank, which was situated on Bahnhofstrasse, one of the most exclusive avenues in Zurich's business quarter, also operated a small number of undisclosed vaults that were hidden in underground bunkers built into the foothills of the Alps. These secret facilities were not subject to normal banking regulations and were only available to clients who held over a billion dollars on account. They couldn't be accessed by road or foot and therefore the bank laid on a helicopter for those "special" clients who desired to visit their secret possessions.

After a short fifteen-minute flight, Franklin and Bormann, accompanied by the bank's chief executive, Christian Keller, passed through the various security protocols and finally reached the entrance to their private vault. Richard felt as though he were entering a classic Bond villain's lair that had literally been carved out of the side of a mountain.

Keller was a smooth operator; his wiry six-foot frame was coated by a light blue designer linen suit, complemented by a crisp white cotton shirt and matching blue silk tie. He had a sharp, angular face dominated by heavily defined cheekbones that created a rather gaunt but nevertheless striking appearance. His thick brown hair was perfectly coiffured and held in position, courtesy of a generous amount of product. He moved with remarkable elegance, appearing to glide over the shiny concrete floor of the underground corridor that led to Bormann's vault. The three men came to a stop, facing the massive circular entrance door, which was slightly ajar. Keller, who had led the way, turned and addressed Bormann.

"Mr Franklin, welcome back to your vault. I will leave you now and return to the waiting lounge upstairs. Please take all the time you require and, when you are ready to leave, as usual, simply press the red button located just inside the entrance and I will return to collect you. I trust you will find everything in order."

Keller slightly bowed his head and wafted off down the long narrow corridor. It was the first time Richard had visited the vault and, as he followed Bormann inside, he was immediately surprised by how vast it was. It needed to be. It housed a collection of unique treasures with the combined value of hundreds of millions of dollars. Bormann ignored the high stacks of gold bars that spanned floor to ceiling and covered nearly a quarter of the entire space. Instead, he walked directly to the back wall where dozens of artworks were neatly positioned in upright piles, determined by size. He knelt down and picked up a large oil painting, partially covered by a white dust sheet. It featured a stunning display of red poppies, set in rolling green fields, underneath a crystal-blue sky. The ornate gold-painted wooden frame added an air of authority and beauty to the artwork and Richard immediately recognised the unmistakable brushstroke work of the artist. Bormann gently touched the painting with his fingertips.

"This Van Gogh is one of my personal favourites. It used to hang above the fireplace in a baronial mansion owned by the

Weichmann family in Munich. They ran a massive chain of jewellery shops across the country and for years they ripped off the German people with extortionate prices. Like all Jews, they exploited and manipulated our economy, always looking to feather their own nests. Naturally, as with all the artworks in this vault, it rightfully belongs to the Führer, and, therefore, it now belongs to you and your family."

He carefully handed it across to Richard, who was stunned by its natural beauty and provenance.

Bormann uncovered a number of other paintings, all works of grand masters. He smiled to himself as he appreciated that the hidden vault contained one of the greatest art collections in the world. Another secret only he, and now Richard, knew about.

"Remember, Richard, the gold and gemstones can be leveraged at any time, should you or the corporation need an injection of capital, but these artworks are never to be sold. They are your legacy and one day will hang in your home and the home of your son."

Richard nodded and closed his eyes. He thought about the master plan for John's future and couldn't help but wonder if, one day, the Van Gogh would hang on a wall inside the Oval Office.

Chapter Forty-One

25 January 2012

Buenos Aires

Paz and Núñez met at a small bagel café in the centre of Recoleta for a breakfast update. Both men opted for the toasted smoked salmon and cream cheese poppy-seed special, along with black coffee and fresh orange juice. Paz picked up his white mug and took a large gulp.

"Alonso, tell me about the fire."

"Boss, our contact set it off right outside Vargas's office and, although the firefighters were on-site within a few minutes, they believe that anything that was near the heart of the fire must have been destroyed."

"Alonso, be straight with me. Do we know for sure the stuff was actually there?"

Alonso desperately wanted to be the purveyor of good news but was cautious about lying to his boss. "We believe so, but can't be totally sure. Our contact says Vargas spent the previous night alone in his office working through some of the items from García's haul, but no one knows exactly what."

"Fuck it, Alonso. We have to know for sure. Where are we with Vargas? He has to be taken out."

"Our contact is still trying to get details of his home address. They have access to most police staff files, but not those at chief inspector level and above, so it's proving difficult."

"Failure is not an option, Alonso. Lean on this contact of yours and find a way to get the information."

* * *

Hembury raided the fridge in Vargas's kitchen and cooked himself some scrambled eggs and tomato along with a couple of slices of granary toast. It was almost eleven and his friend had been gone for nearly two hours. He was making good headway on his breakfast when Vargas called him on the mobile.

"Troy, sorting out a safe place for the case is taking a bit longer than I thought. I left my overnight bag on the bed. Would you grab it for me, please, and take a taxi to the airport. Meet me at the LATAM check-in desk in Terminal C."

"Nic, where are you? What are you doing with the case?"

"Don't worry. I'm putting it somewhere really safe."

* * *

The flight on the A320 Airbus from Buenos Aires to El Calafate was uneventful and favourable tailwinds brought the journey time down to just under three hours. Vargas and Hembury slept for most of it and, by the time the wheels touched down, they were feeling rejuvenated. Both men were travelling light and, a few minutes after landing, they collected their Hertz hire car. The red Nissan Micra weaved its way out of the rental car park zone and headed west towards the small city of El Calafate. Although it had developed somewhat since the days of Hitler's residency, it still only had a population of ten thousand, which made it one of the smallest cities in Patagonia.

Vargas was driving, with Hembury in the passenger seat studying a photo on his camera of Gerald Franklin's ID card, giving the address of the farmhouse.

"Nic, you realise there is no street name on here? It just says the name of the farmhouse, El Blondi, and the town, El Calafate."

"Back in the forties, Troy, when our friends set up home, El Calafate wasn't even really a town, let alone a city, so there were no streets. It was just a stopping off place for wool traders travelling across country and the population was less than two hundred, so it was the perfect setting for a hideaway."

The centre of the city was only a thirty-minute drive from the airport, and Vargas parked up on the front drive of the Esplendor Hotel, located just off the main street. They checked in and then set off by foot, hoping to find some inspiration. It was a charming, bustling city that tourists used as a convenient hang-out to visit the nearby Glacier Park, which housed one of the most spectacular glaciers in Patagonia, a 240-foot high monster named Perito Moreno.

The pair worked their way across the north and south districts of the city, stopping off at various bars and restaurants to enquire if anybody knew the whereabouts of El Blondi, but drew a total blank. After four hours of fruitless footwork, they called it a night and consoled themselves in an upmarket steakhouse where they ordered a couple of giant fillets, accompanied by a bottle of Argentinian Malbec.

Back in the hotel room, the two detectives pondered their next move.

"Troy, let's split up in the morning. You work the east side and I'll take the west. Before I start, I'll check in with their city hall and see if they have any old records that might help."

Following a light breakfast of toast and coffee, the two men headed off in opposite directions to continue the search. Vargas only had a five-minute walk to the city hall and, after a protracted conversation with a highly disagreeable front-desk clerk, he eventually found himself in the housing records department. The young woman in charge was clearly impressed by the credentials of the chief inspector from the Buenos Aires Police Department and was eager to help. None of the property records had been digitised and the original paperwork lay in hundreds of boxes piled on top of each other in a large basement stockroom.

They all had handwritten dates on the side and, after a fifteen-minute search, she located the one dated June to December 1945.

She placed it on the large desk in front of Vargas and opened the lid. The box only contained four documents.

"Quiet times back then, chief inspector. Not many houses were bought or sold." She flicked through the small pile of papers, then pulled one out and handed it to Vargas.

"Here you go, El Blondi. A newly built property, first registered on 10 June 1945. The owner was Gerald Franklin."

Vargas felt like he'd found the holy grail as he held the original document in his hand. He took a photo of it with his iPhone camera and passed it back over to the records clerk. "How do we find out when it might have been sold to a new owner, or maybe developed into a block of flats? There doesn't seem to be any sign of a property called El Blondi anywhere in the city."

"I'm afraid there is no way of cross-checking, other than going through every box until you find a relevant transaction and, as you can see, there are a lot of boxes."

Vargas sat back in his chair and cursed under his breath. He thanked her and made his way to the door, bracing himself for a long walk around the west of the city.

Then an idea formed. He took out his mobile and flicked through his photo library until he found the death certificate of Emilia Franklin, aka Eva Braun. It recorded the death as 28 October 1970. He spun round and called over to the records clerk, who was busy lifting up the 1945 box from the table. "Can I see all the records between October and December 1970, please?"

After sifting through over thirty property sales documents, Vargas found what he was looking for. On 1 December 1970, the property known as El Blondi was sold to a woman named Valentina Suarez and the title of the property was changed. The document also provided a street name. Stapled to the property registration form was a set of architect's drawings that indicated that the new owner had applied for plans to rebuild the property.

Vargas was ecstatic at the find and thanked the young assistant for her help before reaching for his mobile. He speed-dialled Hembury, who picked up immediately.

"Troy, meet me outside a property called 'El Negus'. It's in the north of the city on Avenida Libertador."

The large wooden structure, known as El Negus, resembled a Swiss chalet far more than a typical Argentinian farmhouse.

Its striking facade featured twin gable roofs complemented by exposed black-painted eaves. The first-floor level boasted a wood-spindled balcony running the entire width of the house. The property stood on an enormous plot and was set back from the road by a thirty-metre manicured frontage, as well as enjoying a two-and-a-half-acre garden to the rear. The mini estate was protected by a six-foot high white concrete wall that was only interrupted by a pair of ornate wrought-iron gates opening on to a maroon tarmacked drive. Just inside the gates, on the left-hand side of the entrance, stood a small painted wooden hut, housing a uniformed security guard who was brandishing an AK47 rifle.

Vargas and Hembury stood across the road, studying the imposing residence.

"Nic, are you sure this is right? It doesn't look anything like the house we saw in the old black-and-white photos."

"That's because that farmhouse was demolished in 1970 after Braun died. The papers show that the property was sold by the Franklin estate to a Valentina Suarez, who knocked it down and built this monstrosity."

"I quite like it, actually. A chalet fortress with hot-and-cold -running armed guards."

Vargas smiled as he discreetly used his mobile camera to take a few pictures. "Let's have a stroll to the back of the house and see what's what. Hopefully, it'll offer us a way in."

An hour later, they were sitting at a pavement café table situated on the opposite side of the street, about fifty yards away from the front gates. It was the perfect spot to view any comings or goings, although so far nothing had happened at all.

Vargas drained his bottle of Peroni and placed it down on

the table. "So, as far as we can tell, the house is only lightly protected by one armed guard at the front. But it raises an interesting question – what's inside that needs defending by an AK47?"

Hembury was nursing a Diet Coke and dragged on the straw.

"It's like the guard is there to make a statement to warn off potential intruders, but, in reality, the place is not exactly an armed fortress."

They agreed they would wait until nightfall before paying an uninvited visit to El Negus. The plan was to scale the back wall and then find an entry route once they were inside the grounds.

Meanwhile, they continued with the daytime surveillance to see what they could learn. Nothing had happened during the three hours they had been monitoring the house, but then, for the first time, they saw some sign of movement. The front door opened and a middle-aged woman, dressed in full nurse's attire, made her way towards the front gates. As she reached the wooden hut, the security guard stepped out, and they appeared to enjoy a friendly exchange for a few seconds before he returned to the guardhouse and opened the electric gates. The nurse crossed the road and walked directly towards the café where the two detectives were based. As soon as she passed their pavement table, they rose as one and began to follow her on foot. Other than a quick stop-off at a small supermarket to pick up a few groceries, she made her way directly home. She lived in a small apartment located above a parade of shops about a ten-minute walk from El Negus.

As she opened her bag and reached for her door keys, Vargas

and Hembury approached. Vargas held his badge clasped in his right hand so he could immediately show her his ID.

"Excuse me, Señora. My name is Chief Inspector Vargas from the Buenos Aires Police Department and this is my colleague. We'd like to have a brief chat with you about an investigation we are currently working on which has brought us to El Calafate."

Nurse Andrea Gabriel felt her face flush bright red, and she instinctively felt scared, even though she had no idea why the police wanted to interview her. She studied the badge for a few moments and then put her key in the front door lock. "You'd better come in, inspector."

A few minutes later, the three of them were sitting in her cosy living room. Vargas was running the questioning.

"Señora Gabriel, I'd like you to tell us who lives in El Negus and what your work entails, and also why the house needs an armed security guard?"

The nurse had regained her composure and her response was surprisingly feisty. "What is the purpose of your investigation?"

"Señora, it's my job to ask the questions, so please cooperate, and we will be out of here before you know it."

Having been firmly put back in her place, she agreed to help the chief inspector. "I'm a private nurse and I've worked at the house since 1999. I attend to the owner, Señora Suarez. She has been confined to a wheelchair for the last ten years and suffers from a slow degenerative condition that is similar to Parkinson's disease. She takes complex medication, which I administer every day. I work from eight until six and then a night nurse arrives at eight and I relieve her every morning."

"Thank you, Señora. Who else lives inside the house and

why the need for the guard?"

"Other than the night nurse, Señora Suarez lives on her own. She is a widow of many years and has no surviving family. She is a very wealthy woman, and the house contains many valuable artworks that need protecting. She has two security guards, Antonio and Javier, who do alternate twelve-hours shifts."

"What time is the evening handover?"

"They usually swap over at eight."

Vargas thought for a moment before asking the next question. "Does she ever have any visitors?"

"Not that I've ever seen, chief inspector. She doesn't have any friends that I'm aware of."

Vargas glanced at Hembury to see if he wanted to ask anything.

"Nic, I know it's a long shot, but can you ask her if she knows anything about the people who lived in the house prior to Suarez."

Clearly the nurse didn't speak English, so Vargas translated the question. Gabriel nodded towards Hembury before answering.

"She once told me that El Negus was built to her own design with the help of a leading architect from Córdoba. She said the previous owners were close personal friends and, when they died, she bought the land, which included an old farmhouse, from the estate. Obviously, that was pulled down. I think it all happened back in the seventies."

Vargas jumped in. "Do you recall the name of the previous owners?"

The nurse shook her head. "No, I don't recall her ever mentioning their name. Is it important?"

CHAPTER FORTY-ONE

Vargas and Hembury stood up to signal the interview was over.

"Thank you, Señora Gabriel, you've been very helpful. Please keep our meeting confidential. Is there anything else of interest you want to tell us?"

The nurse stood up and began to usher them towards the door. "Only that, in eleven days' time, Señora Suarez celebrates her one hundredth birthday."

They returned to their hotel room and raided the small fridge for some peanuts and Hershey bars. Both men were working on their laptops when Hembury broke the silence. He had been researching everything he could find online about Hitler and his supposed suicide.

"Christ, Nic, Hitler's dog was called Blondi. He named the bloody farmhouse after his pet Alsatian. In fact, the official story goes that Himmler gave him cyanide capsules, which he tried out on the dog before giving one to Eva Braun. The name of the house was a tribute to the dog he poisoned."

Vargas closed his own laptop and glanced at his watch. "Further proof, if we needed it, that the Führer lived right here in El Calafate. Let's allow a good hour for the new guard to settle in and then we will pay Señora Suarez a visit."

"Yes, I can't wait to wish her many happy returns on her upcoming birthday."

It was just after nine in the evening when Vargas and Hembury scaled the back wall of the El Negus estate. Vargas positioned the spare wheel, which he'd taken from the boot of the hire car, against the base of the wall and used it as a prop to stand on and gain leverage. Hembury followed and, within seconds, they were both inside the sprawling grounds. Vargas led the way towards the rear of the property.

"It's weird, Troy, but there's absolutely no sign of an alarm system inside the grounds."

"Let's hope that's the case or our friend with the AK47 might suddenly pop up to welcome us."

A couple of minutes later, they were standing on a large wooden rear porch and working out the best means of entry. There was a pair of double doors that were firmly locked, flanked either side by large casement windows. Vargas held the barrel of his Beretta against one of the square glass panels and glanced at Hembury, who nodded his approval. He smashed the gun against the window and the glass immediately shattered. Both men ran back into the bushes and waited to see if the noise aroused a response. They held their position for two minutes, but there was no sign of activity from inside the house. Vargas stealthily led the way back onto the porch, eased his hand through the new opening and smoothly released the window catch. Moments later, both men were standing inside what appeared to be a large kitchen breakfast area.

Hembury flicked on a small LED torch and panned it around the room in order to get their bearings. It lit up the doorway into the hall and as they made their way towards it, Vargas's arm brushed against a large white circular box positioned on the corner of the oak kitchen table. He cursed as he failed to prevent it toppling onto the tiled floor. Hembury tilted the torchlight downwards and focused on the remnants of a chocolate birthday cake. Although it had broken into pieces, the main section was still intact and the white icing on top clearly spelled out three lines, "Happy Birthday, Valentina, One Hundred".

As they moved into the massive hallway, Hembury was able

to switch off the torch as four sets of wall lights had been left on, providing an eerie illumination. Two other doors led off the hall, but Vargas made straight for the imposing staircase that also benefitted from low-level lighting. The wall to the side of the stairs was covered with Renaissance artwork and Hembury stopped on one of the treads to examine a striking painting of the Madonna cradling the baby Jesus in her arms.

"Nic, I'm no art historian but even I've heard of Botticelli."

Vargas had also stopped on the staircase and was examining a different artwork. "I can trump you with a self-portrait by Titian."

They made their way onto the upper landing, with its two white-painted doors on either side, which they assumed must be bedrooms. Directly facing them, at the end of the landing, was an imposing archway framing two huge walnut doors. Vargas was instinctively drawn towards them and Hembury followed him along the corridor. The intricately carved gold door handles were totally incongruous with the rest of the door fittings in the house. Vargas reached inside his jacket to his shoulder holster for his Beretta. He nodded as Hembury slowly opened one of the doors.

A soon as they were inside, Hembury shut the door behind them and reached for the light switch. The room illuminated, and both men gasped at the disturbing sight that greeted them. It was a large pentagon, and all five walls were decorated with massive black-and-white photographs blown-up to ceiling height. They portrayed giant images of Hitler in a selection of animated poses, standing behind a raised podium with thousands of supporters in the foreground. The photos had been taken at the 1938 Nuremberg rally, which had been attended by over one million Germans.

The white marble floor was broken up by a huge red swastika in the centre. A number of glass-fronted cases and cabinets housed an assortment of Nazi memorabilia. Five marble plinths were symmetrically dotted around the room, supporting smaller items, including a First World War spiked helmet and a mounted copy of *Mein Kampf*. The centrepiece of the entire collection was a life-sized mannequin, fully kitted out in Hitler's distinctive grey uniform, together with black boots and a three-inch wide brown leather belt, set off with a silver buckle. The left hand of the dummy held the Führer's grey cap, edged with a brown leather trim.

Either side of the mannequin stood floor-mounted photo collages, featuring Hitler, Eva Braun, and their dogs, together with personal friends, enjoying private time at Berghof, the Führer's Bavarian hideaway. Vargas was reeling from the sight of the macabre memorabilia when he suddenly spotted something even more spine-chilling: a small matt black urn standing on a white marble plinth in one of the five corners.

Hembury was the first to speak. "Jesus, Nic, this place is a living shrine to Hitler."

"Yeah, possibly topped off by his ashes."

Vargas took out his mobile and spent a few seconds capturing the grotesque images. "The whole vibe coming from this room is sinister. Valentina Suarez is obviously a Nazi and a big fan of the Führer."

Vargas and Hembury exited the pentagon room and continued the search for Valentina Suarez's bedroom. It didn't take long. Vargas could see a glimmer of light coming from underneath the bottom of the first door on the right-hand side of the landing and reached for the handle. It was unlocked, so he gently pushed it ajar and peered inside. The bedroom was larger than he expected, and the furnishings inside were sparse. A king-sized bed with an impressive carved wooden headboard, edged in gold, dominated the room. A large double wardrobe stood to the left of it and, to the right, just in front of the bay window, a dressing table completed the matching set.

Valentina Suarez was ensconced in a motorised wheelchair near the window. Her head was bowed and she was deeply absorbed in a book. She hadn't heard the two men enter her bedroom and, when Vargas spoke, her body stiffened with shock and the book slipped from her feeble grasp.

"Good evening, Señora Suarez."

Vargas and Hembury looked closely at the old woman who was now staring back at them with an expression of sheer contempt. Her grey features were gaunt, her face heavily wrinkled and covered in liver spots. Her cheekbones were pronounced, her thin skin drawn tightly around them. Wisps of grey hair protruded from the white cotton nightcap pulled over her head. Her thin lips were tightly pursed and her blue eyes, framed by a pair of rimless glasses, flicked around the room as though she were desperately looking for a way out. Vargas placed the gun he was holding back into his shoulder holster and walked closer to her.

"Señora Suarez, my name is Chief Inspector Nicolas Vargas from the Buenos Aires Police Department. Please don't be alarmed. We are here to ask you a few questions."

Finally, the old woman spoke and, when she did, her voice was imperious and full of disdain. "Why have you broken into my house and what have you done with Javier?"

"Your guard is safe, and we wish you no harm. But we do need to ask you some questions."

She closed her eyes and thought for a few seconds before answering. "What questions?"

"Señora, what do you know about the family who lived on this site before you bought it. I understand you were close family friends."

Her waspish reply was instant and told Vargas that, however badly age had ravaged her body, her mind was still sharp. "They were wonderful people. True friends to me and my late husband. I owe them a great deal."

Vargas glanced at Hembury before continuing his questioning. Hembury's concerned expression confirmed his own instinct that this frail old woman was somehow dangerous. "What were their names and what did they do?"

Suarez noticeably relaxed and moved into autopilot as she began reciting the story she had told many times before. "Gerald and Ronald Franklin were brothers. They were successful businessmen, as was my late husband. That's how we first met. Gerald was married to a delightful girl called Emilia who I became very close to. We spent a great deal of time socialising at their house. The brothers died in the sixties and when Emilia died in 1970, I bought their house. My husband and I decided to knock it down, and we jointly designed El Negus."

Vargas had heard enough and decided it was time to play his ace in the hole. "Señora Suarez, my colleague and I have just visited the pentagon room."

The old lady appeared to jump out of the chair as she let out a piercing scream. Her entire body began to shake violently, and the scream evolved into a guttural howl.

The connecting door next to the wardrobe burst open and the night nurse ran into the room. As soon as she saw the two men standing close to Suarez, she became rooted to the spot. Vargas could see the sheer look of terror in her eyes.

"Señora, I am a chief inspector with the Buenos Aires Police Department. We are here to interview Señora Suarez. Please return to your room and stay there until we leave."

The nurse nodded and slowly left the room. Suarez had stopped screaming and was now venomously glaring at Vargas, her body still shaking. He walked towards her and then leaned forwards, his face only a few inches from hers. "Tell us what you know about the Führer and his friends, Señora."

Suarez's right hand lashed out and Vargas was taken by surprise at the speed of her movement as she caught him around the temple. He reeled back and instinctively pulled away. His forehead stung with pain as one of her rings had drawn blood.

"Get out of my house. I have nothing more to say."

He touched his head and felt the warm wetness of the blood.

Hembury stepped across to take a closer look. "It's only a graze, Nic. Let's get out of this madhouse. I think we've learned everything we can."

Vargas nodded, and they both turned away from Suarez and walked towards the bedroom door. Hembury opened it to leave but suddenly Vargas stopped. He spun around and ran back towards the old lady in the chair, grabbing her right hand in a tight grip.

"Show me your ring, Señora Suarez."

He stared at the thin gold band, broken up by three large diamonds. The ring hung limply on her shrivelled finger. Vargas slowly looked up at the wizened face of the old lady, now fixed with a mask of terror. At that moment, he knew he was looking into the eyes of Eva Braun.

Chapter Forty-Two

26 January 2012

El Calafate

Liliana Flores had returned to her room and locked the door. The night nurse had no idea if the two men threatening her employer were really who they said they were. What would the police want with Valentina Suarez, and why would they break into the house to interview her? Hard as she tried, she couldn't remove Suarez's piercing scream from her thoughts. Whatever was happening, it didn't feel right. She leaned across her bedside table and picked up the internal phone. She dialled the front guardhouse and Javier answered after just one ring.

Vargas reached for his iPhone and scrolled through the photos until he found the black-and-white image of a young, vibrant Eva Braun who was showing off her new wedding ring to the camera. It was almost unbelievable that the old woman sitting in the wheelchair in front of him was the same person. He held the mobile with the frozen image close to her face. She turned her head away and refused to acknowledge it.

"Nice photo, Eva. You look so happy there. I guess, despite all the subterfuge, it was the one thing you couldn't bear to give up. But why the need to pretend you were—"

The bedroom door flew open and Javier Hernández burst in, his AK47 locked and loaded. He pointed it directly at Hembury, who was only a few feet away from him. "Place your hands in the air and don't move. Señora Suarez, are you okay? Have these men hurt you?"

Vargas was itching to make a move for his Beretta, but knew the guard could kill Hembury before he even had a chance to draw it.

Eva Braun summoned all her inner strength to push down on the armrests of her chair to raise herself into a standing position. As she digested the sudden turn of events, her mouth formed a malevolent grin. "Shoot them, Javier. They came here to rob and kill me."

Hernández was just a security guard, not a trained killer, so for a brief moment he was stunned by Braun's command. His eyeline darted from Vargas to his employer. That was all the time Hembury needed to act. He spun on the spot and took off like a guided missile. His left foot slammed into the right arm of the guard, who instinctively started firing his weapon as he fell backwards. The bullets sprayed into the ceiling and caught an ornate chandelier, which sent splinters of crystal across the room. Hernández rolled sideways and readjusted the AK47, aiming it directly at Hembury, who was also on the floor. A single gunshot rang out and struck the guard just above his right eye. His body slumped to the side, and the rifle slipped from his grasp, silently falling onto the thick-pile carpet.

Hembury glanced over his right shoulder and saw Vargas crouched in a firing pose, the Beretta clenched in his right hand. As he stood, Hembury gave a nod of thanks to his fellow detective, walked over to the body of the slain guard and picked up the AK47. Vargas re-holstered his pistol and turned to Braun, who was now sitting back in her wheelchair. He perched himself on the bed next to her.

"Far too much blood has been spilt protecting your family secrets. It's time to talk."

For the next fifteen minutes, Eva Braun simply sat and listened as Vargas chronicled the information he had discovered in Box 1321. A few times, she closed her eyes and shook her head as if she couldn't believe what she was hearing. He showed her a number of photographs on his mobile, including her own forged death certificate. He really struck gold when he referenced the 8mm film of her son's fifth birthday party. Having remained silent for a long period, she finally sparked back into life.

"I filmed most of that and edited it myself. You know, I was a trained photographer. That's how I met the Führer ..." she paused for a moment and then continued "... my husband. I was just seventeen and working as an assistant to Heinrich Hoffman, the Führer's personal photographer. We started seeing each other secretly soon after that but, of course, our relationship had to be kept secret from the German people."

Hembury kept solid eye contact with Braun as he reached for his iPhone and hit the video recording function. He glanced furtively down at the screen for a brief moment to check the framing. He nodded to Vargas, who could sense she was relishing the chance to finally tell her story. It was as if, for the first time in her life, the floodgates were well and truly open.

"Martin planned everything. He was a true genius. He first identified Argentina as a possible future base in 1943 and he invested heavily in creating foundations for us to live here in safety and comfort. He planned our suicides and the escape from Berlin."

She paused for a few seconds and stared at the two detectives as if she were searching for their approval. Hembury was frustrated as he couldn't understand Spanish, but he knew he was witnessing a sensational confession.

Vargas broke the silence. "Tell me about the Franklin Corporation."

Braun was only too happy to continue with her story. "Martin shipped over five hundred million dollars' worth of gold, as well as a priceless collection of art. He and the Führer talked constantly of building a new empire, a Fourth Reich. He realised the way forward was to create the biggest pharmaceutical company in the world, rather than a physical army. Martin recognised the outcome of the war meant the United States would inevitably become the most powerful country in the world, and that's when he hatched his plan. Franklin Pharmaceuticals would be the perfect vehicle to regain power through legitimate means. A respected, credible corporation that would originate in Argentina and then go on to conquer America. It would also spawn a new Führer for the twenty-first century – a man, with Hitler's blood running through his veins, who would become the most powerful leader of the Western world. Of course, he would have to be born in America, which is why my son, Richard, set up home in California before having a child."

She stopped again, as if the recollection of events was

literally draining her strength away.

Vargas changed the line of questioning. "But why did you fake your own death for a second time?"

She came back to life and laughed at this notion. "Martin convinced me it would be far safer for my grandson's life and future career if he genuinely believed that both I and his grandfather were dead. If I were ever exposed, it would destroy everything. Far better for everyone that I was dead. That way the child would never be tempted to travel here to see me and that part of his life would be closed forever. From the day he was born, John was groomed by Richard and Martin to fulfil his destiny and become the most powerful leader in the world."

"So that's why you razed El Blondi to the ground and created Valentina Suarez?"

"I didn't want to ever leave here because my life with my husband had been truly special. I grew to love this place, but I had to make a clean break and start again with a new home and a new identity. It's been incredibly painful watching John's progress, realising he doesn't even know I exist. I see him on the news channels nearly every day at the moment. He's only a few months away from fulfilling his destiny." Once again, she stopped and thought for a few seconds. "What are you planning to do with this information?"

Vargas didn't reply.

"You realise no one will believe you. My son is one of the most powerful and respected men in the United States. He will destroy you and your bullshit story. You have no idea who you are dealing with."

Vargas had heard enough and rose from the bed. "Actually, I know exactly who I'm dealing with, Frau Braun."

Vargas and Hembury left through the front, now unguarded, entrance and walked around to the rear of the house where they'd left their hire car. On the way back to the hotel, Vargas gave Hembury a literal translation of the Braun interview, including the veiled threat at the end.

"Nic, she is a total piece of work. Every history book in the world says she committed suicide in 1945 and yet here we are, over sixty-five years later, having our lives threatened by her. Do you think we might face problems with the authorities here over the shooting of the guard?"

"I can't imagine she would let the police anywhere near that place. I suspect our friend Javier will never be heard of again."

Javier's dead body was lying in the corner of the room when Nurse Flores returned. She tried somehow to ignore its presence while she slowly moved Eva Braun in her wheelchair into the spare room. She was shaking with fear but was far too scared to ask her employer any questions

"Señora Suarez, you must be extremely tired. You need to sleep and recover your strength."

Braun was clearly exhausted, but she knew she had one more task to carry out before she could rest.

"Liliana, you must promise me you will never speak of this incident to anyone outside this house. Everything will be taken care of in the next few hours. I will ensure you receive a generous bonus this month."

The night nurse nodded. "Of course, Señora. You know you can rely on my discretion and loyalty. Do you require anything else from me?"

"Yes, I need you to fetch my mobile phone from my dressing table."

Chapter Forty-Three

23 June 1981

San Francisco

By 1981, the Franklin Pharmaceutical Corporation was almost thirty-five years old and had broken into the elite group of the top-ten pharma companies in the world. Richard Franklin was now its CEO, having taken over the role from his Uncle Ronald, who'd moved to the post of chairman. Richard was the same age as the company and, in recent years, his insatiable drive and energy had been at the heart of the corporation's rapid expansion across the globe. He'd opened offices in London, Paris, Berlin, Istanbul, Cape Town and Cairo and the Franklin Corporation had become a star player on Wall Street, as investors rode on the back of their continued global expansion and ever-rising profits. He'd carefully followed the key elements of Bormann's plan and recruited senior management figures who were either covert Nazi sympathisers or direct descendants of his father's contemporaries.

After the death of his wife, Richard never remarried as he

knew it would be far too much of a risk to share his life and intimate secrets with a partner. He lived with his ten-year-old son, John, who had inherited the enviable combination of his father's unyielding confidence and ambition, along with his mother's stunning good looks. His sky-blue eyes and slightly unruly mop of strawberry blonde hair created a striking combination. He was also a model pupil: academically gifted with outstanding sporting prowess.

Richard's personal life was complicated. He kept three full-time girlfriends in fully funded luxury apartments in different areas of the city. Although they didn't know each other's identities, he made it very clear that none of them could claim an exclusive relationship with him. In addition to his three mistresses, he enjoyed numerous casual relationships with random women who crossed his path in the upper echelons of society life. Like his uncle, he also had a predilection for young actresses and regularly attended shows at the Golden Gate Theatre on the hunt for young rising talent who might be in need of a rich, influential man to help develop their careers.

Martin Bormann was now eighty-one, and, although his mind was still sharp as a razor, his ailing body was fighting a losing battle against prostate cancer. He lived alone, other than a couple of staff, in a gated mansion that overlooked Nob Hill, one of the city's most exclusive districts. He hadn't been well enough to go to the office for over a year but Richard visited his home twice a week to keep him in the loop. He was a great sounding board and Richard constantly marvelled at the old man's astute brain and business acumen, which invariably helped him with major strategic decisions.

In the first twenty years of building the business, Bormann

had laundered huge sums of money from secret numbered accounts in Switzerland and South America. He didn't need to refer to records, as his computer-like brain knew the location and numbers of all these dirty accounts. Most of them had been opened in the last few months of the war and, thirty-five years on, they still contained the best part of a billion dollars. Then there were the stolen artworks, hidden in various bank vaults around the world, many of which were priceless. Bormann knew the precise location of all of them.

Richard arrived at the house for their scheduled morning catch-up. Bormann was usually waiting for him in his study but today the housekeeper escorted him straight upstairs where the old man was sitting in bed, propped up by a couple of pillows. It was the first time Richard had looked at his beloved mentor and seen a frail, dying old man staring back at him. The usual spark behind his eyes was gone and his skin tone had turned a light shade of grey, almost as if he were wearing a death mask. At that exact moment, Richard realised he was about to lose the anchor in his life, and he experienced a rare stab of fear at the thought of being cut loose. Bormann gestured for him to sit down on the chair that had been placed by the side of the bed.

"Richard, I can tell by the look on your face that you aren't going to be shocked by the news I need to impart. Last night, my physician came over to discuss the results of my latest blood tests. The bottom line is the drugs are no longer working, and the cancer has spread from my prostate to my liver." He paused for a moment and slowly reached for the white porcelain coffee cup on his bedside table. He took a small sip and carefully placed it back on the saucer. It was painful to watch. "Richard, I'm looking at two weeks, maybe less."

"Martin, I'm so sorry. Somehow, I've never really prepared myself for this moment. I'm not ready for you to go. There's still so much I need to learn from you." Bormann tried to manage a smile but couldn't quite achieve it.

"We'll need to spend the next few days together so I can pass on certain crucial information. But I'm happy the plan your father and I hatched in El Calafate all those years ago is firmly on course and it will be down to you and John to ensure its ultimate success."

Richard lifted Bormann's limp hands and held them gently between his own. "Martin, you have my word that we will both fulfil our legacy to my father, your Führer."

Bormann cleared his throat before continuing. "Richard, there is one thing on my mind that I need to discuss with you first and you will need to make a judgement on what you do with this knowledge. I have kept some mementos from the past which, perhaps in hindsight, should have been destroyed. For me, they carry huge sentimental and personal value but I also believe their historical authenticity could, at some point in the future, be crucial, when the time comes for John to declare his true lineage to the world. Right now, their sheer existence is a massive threat to our plan, and by the time you see them for yourself I will be gone. That's why you will need to make the decision as to whether to destroy them or hide them safely for the future."

Richard smiled at Bormann. Even though he was so close to death, the old man never failed to amaze him with his vast store of secret revelations.

"After my funeral, you will need to go to Buenos Aires and visit my apartment in Recoleta. In the master bedroom, there are fitted wardrobes that run the length of one of the walls. Open the one furthest from the window and look carefully at the back panel. You'll see that it has fake screw heads and can be easily removed. Behind it, you'll find a large safe embedded in the wall. The combination is the Führer's date of birth and, inside, you'll find a black leather case, embossed with my initials. Once you have examined its contents, you'll need to make a decision. I trust you to make the right one."

Richard squeezed Bormann's hands as a signal that he understood the importance of the request.

"Richard, right now we have plenty more to discuss."

Bormann only survived for three more days. During that time, Richard hardly left his bedside and slept next door so he was always on hand whenever the old man was awake and lucid. The funeral took place ten days later and Richard ensured it reflected the gravitas and status of the man known to his contemporaries in San Francisco as Ronald Franklin; formerly known to the world as Martin Bormann.

Forest Lawn Memorial Park was set in the Hollywood Hills and offered stunning vistas of the San Fernando Valley and the Los Angeles skyline. It was the final resting place for some of the most iconic names in America, including Walt Disney, Buster Keaton, Clark Gable and Humphrey Bogart. The cost of a custom-built mausoleum was north of one hundred thousand dollars, affordable only for the rich and famous. Franklin thought it a fitting venue for a man of Bormann's stature, who had made such a huge impact on world events. Richard hoped, one day in the future, the engraved headstone would be able to be altered to reveal his true identity.

The guest list reflected the who's who of California commerce and industry, as well as high-ranking politicians from both the major parties. A number of senior corporate executives arrived from Argentina to pay tribute, and the most notable dignitary to attend was the Argentine Ambassador, who flew in from Washington with his wife.

Although Bormann was an atheist, Franklin had decided that, as with his father's funeral, social convention required a Christian service. He was the only person to speak during the ceremony and gave an impassioned eulogy, invoking the fantasy backstory of his uncle arriving in South America, as a penniless refugee, and building one of the world's greatest corporations from scratch.

Only two former Nazis, who were hidden in plain sight among the hundreds of guests, knew the true story of the man they had come to pay their final respects to. Franklin's son, John, sat in the front pew next to his father and cried throughout the ceremony, as he was now old enough to understand he would never see his beloved uncle again.

Bormann used to spoil Richard's son with wonderful gifts and surprise VIP trips to exciting places such as Disneyland and the San Diego Zoo. For his ninth birthday party, Bormann had organised a behind-closed-doors experience at the Pirates of the Caribbean attraction, which he knew was the boy's favourite. Instead of the usual two-hour queue, John and his friends were able to enjoy the ride countless times. Bormann even arranged for one of the seventy-three audio-animatronic pirates to lead the chants of "Happy Birthday". That special event was facilitated by a hundred-thousand-dollar payment from the Franklin Pharmaceutical Corporation.

Unlike his school friends who had large families, John only had two relatives and one of them was now gone. After the ceremony, he stood next to his father outside the majestic mausoleum and took his hand.

"Father, when you spoke inside, you said Uncle Ronald was a truly great man who history would remember. What made him great?"

Franklin leaned down so he was face to face with his son. "John, one day soon I'll tell you just how truly great a man he really was."

Chapter Forty-Four

26 January 2012

Buenos Aires

Olivia Bianchi left her third-floor office and made her way to the rear fire escape. She stood on the platform, aimlessly staring out at the city below and instinctively lit up a Marlboro Light. She inhaled deeply and, as smoke billowed from her nostrils, she reached for the burner phone in her handbag. The contacts list only contained one number and, as she typed the text, she vowed this would be the last time she would ever use it. When Alonso Núñez heard his phone ping, he was sitting in Paz's office discussing Vargas. He read the new message and stood up, shaking his fist in jubilation.

"The bitch finally came through with his home address. The bastard lives in Palermo on the Avenida Santa Fe."

Paz leapt to his feet. "At fucking last. Good work, Alonso. So, what's the plan to take him out?"

* * *

Richard Franklin was enjoying dinner with a couple of his senior management team at his favourite seafood restaurant in the Bay Area. His personal wealth had increased by over fifty million dollars in the last few hours. The share price for the corporation was soaring and earlier that morning had hit an all-time high. Ever since his son had secured the Republican nomination, the share price had risen every day. It was almost as if the two were inextricably linked by an invisible thread. The incoming text on his mobile displayed a number that instantly set off an alarm bell. The message only contained three words and was in Spanish. It simply said *Call me, Richard.*

Franklin instantly made his excuses, left the restaurant, and walked down onto the marina. He stared across the bay at Uncle Sam's Devil's Island, better known to tourists as Alcatraz, and pulled out his mobile. He looked up the text and hit the callback icon to speak to his mother. Braun had regained her usual composure and methodically took her son through the events that had played out earlier that night. Her short-term memory was truly remarkable and she recited the lengthy exchanges with Vargas, word for word. Franklin was clearly stunned by this unexpected turn of events and a surge of disbelief and anger raced through his mind. Somehow, his instincts for control and order kicked in and he managed to keep his rage subdued while he replied to his mother.

"Firstly, I will arrange for the immediate removal of the guard's body. We will dump it somewhere downtown and make it look like a mugging that went wrong. Now, I have some questions for you. What was the name of the man who accompanied Vargas? Did Vargas actually say he still had the original items in his possession? And, most importantly, did he indicate what he planned to do with them?"

Eva Braun's body may have been ninety-nine years old but her brain was as sharp as ever and she relished the intense questioning from her son. It made her feel alive and relevant.

"Richard, he hardly spoke, but I think he was an American. Vargas never addressed him by his name. As for the items, all I know for sure is what I saw on his phone. He didn't actually say what he planned to do but clearly he is coming after you."

"Mother, can you describe the other man to me?"

Braun shut her eyes and allowed her mind to conjure up a clear image of the American. By the time she had completed a detailed description of his features, Franklin had no doubt that she had just had an encounter with Lieutenant Troy Hembury.

* * *

Paz listened intently as Franklin filled him in on the episode in El Calafate. Even he didn't know the true identity of Valentina Suarez, and Franklin kept it that way. He painted her as a close family friend who lived on a property on the former estate. He asked him to sort out the removal of the guard's body as soon as possible and then turned his attention to the ongoing problem with Vargas.

"I told you before, he needs to be taken out and now it's even more important than ever that it happens quickly. It also appears that the lieutenant from California who interviewed me was with him in El Calafate. It would be a bonus if you can manage him as well."

"Señor, we've had a major breakthrough in the last twenty-four hours. Our source has provided us with Vargas's home address, and I've recruited two military vets who have no connection with the agency to carry out the work. They're high-class specialists and are making plans as we speak."

Franklin was clearly impressed by the latest developments. "That sounds encouraging, Paz. Just don't mess up. There's too much at stake."

* * *

After dropping off the hire car and checking in for their return flight to Buenos Aires, Vargas and Hembury grabbed a bite to eat in the small airport coffee shop. Hembury was deeply engrossed in his laptop, while Vargas was catching up on the latest messages on his iPhone.

"Nic, you are going to love this. You know Hitler named the farmhouse after his beloved Alsatian. Well, Eva pulled exactly the same trick when she christened the new house. It turns out, while she was living in the Führer's bunker, she owned a Scottish terrier called Negus."

Vargas looked up from his phone. He'd just been reading a text from Torres, saying he had a strong lead on the police station arsonist.

"Nothing about this case surprises me any more. But I've been thinking and I'm really not sure if the world is ready to hear the news that Eva Braun is alive and well and that—"

Hembury finished the sentence. "Her grandson is about to become the next president of the United States."

"Troy, Braun's right about one thing. Franklin is incredibly well connected and will do absolutely anything to protect the truth about his heritage. Although we can't prove it, we know he ordered the executions of the bank robbers in an attempt to keep the secret. We have to assume that, by now, she's told him about our visit."

Hembury downed the dregs of his cappuccino and closed his laptop. "Yes, and that means that both of us are now targets."

Chapter Forty-Five

27 January 2012

Buenos Aires

The two detectives caught the internal flight to Buenos Aires and took a taxi from the airport back to Vargas's apartment. Throughout the journey, they began to formulate a plan of action and agreed that, inevitably, they would have to face up to Franklin and confront him with their findings. Both of them had doubts about taking the case to their respective police chiefs as they still had no concrete evidence to prove Franklin was behind the murders in Buenos Aires and they wondered if anyone would accept the evidence in Box 1321 as proof of a giant conspiracy.

Vargas had just ordered a takeaway when a call came in from Torres that sounded like it might be a game changer. He brought Hembury up to date before leaving for the station.

"Troy, my assistant has just arrested a woman named Olivia Bianchi, who is the deputy head of HR for the force. He says he has conclusive proof she started the fire in the station. It sounds like she may well have been the informant who's been feeding intel to Franklin's people over the last few weeks. If we can get her to talk, we might finally have a direct line of sight to that son of a bitch Franklin."

"Okay, Nic. Understood. I'm going to keep researching online and see what more I can find out about his early years in Argentina. From what I can tell already, his Uncle Ronald, alias Bormann, forms the Franklin Corporation in 1946 and, within five years, it establishes itself as the leading pharmaceutical company in South America. Richard joins the board when he's just twenty-five and leads the charge to expand in the States. There are dozens of articles on the internet that reference Nazi gold being shipped over to South America, so clearly Bormann had unlimited funds to build the company into a giant corporation."

"Makes total sense. Let's hope Bianchi gives him up as her employer. That'll be one huge nail in his coffin."

Just as Vargas made for the front door, the entry buzzer sounded. "That'll be our Chinese. Keep mine warm. I'll be back later."

Because of the fire, Torres and the detective team had migrated to a smaller office in a nearby station. Olivia Bianchi sat alone in the basement interview room, working out her tactics. She had no idea what evidence the police might have against her but she had every intention of proclaiming her innocence. Her extreme fear of Núñez and his fellow thugs meant she had no plans to betray them.

Directly above her, Vargas was being briefed by Torres, who had lined up some viewing footage on his laptop.

"Chief, many of the hard drives recording the internal cameras in the station were written off in the area by the fire but the one monitoring the main hallway was undamaged.

Take a look at this."

Torres had three files cued up on the screen ready to play and he clicked the top one which displayed a time code of 18.05.24. It showed Bianchi walking along the corridor leading to the front entrance of the building and disappearing from view as she entered the ladies' toilets.

Vargas felt a sudden surge of emotion as he realised he was looking at the woman he had mistaken for Sophia a few days earlier. Even the way she walked was strangely similar but, when he saw her face for the first time, he was massively relieved to discover she shared no real resemblance to his wife after all.

Torres hit the stop button. "So that footage was taken at just after six in the evening. During the following five hours, four other women enter and depart the same washroom but Bianchi is never seen leaving." He then placed the cursor on the second file, which displayed a time of 23.55.05. "Now, chief, watch this."

The locked-off shot of the dimly lit empty corridor filled the computer screen once again and, after five seconds, a woman opened the toilet door and appeared in the hallway. She was dressed from head to toe in black, with a balaclava completing the disguise. She turned away from the camera and walked back towards the main office area. The clip froze and Torres lined up the final file.

"There's absolutely no doubt that the lady in black is Bianchi. This final clip shows her leaving the station just after the fire started."

The new image covered the door at the rear of the station and the steps leading down into the car park. The figure, dressed in black, was clearly seen walking out through the door and disappearing into the night. Torres closed the laptop and opened a blue file that was sitting on the desk.

"There's more, chief. We first saw this footage twenty-four hours ago and since then we've gained access to Bianchi's private bank and savings accounts. They make interesting reading." He took out some loose papers from the file and handed them across to Vargas. "Seems like our HR lady loves a bit of online gambling. The pity is, she's not very good at it. Over the last two years, she's racked up huge debts but they are offset every month by incoming payments from a foreign account that we haven't yet identified. The IT boys are working on it but they think it may be impossible to trace the source."

Vargas closed the file and nodded. "That's good work, Juan. Let's go and have a chat with Señora Bianchi. I have a pretty good idea who her paymaster might be."

Vargas and Torres entered the interview room together and sat down opposite Bianchi, who had now been joined by her lawyer. The chief inspector placed a file on the table and flicked open the cover, revealing the incriminating bank statements. He saw Bianchi glance down at the papers and then instantly look away. He still felt slightly unnerved by her similarity to his wife but could almost smell her fear and decided to go straight in for the kill. He pressed the button on the tape machine and sat back in his chair.

"Señora Bianchi, we have irrefutable video evidence that proves that, on the evening of 26 January 2012, you wilfully committed the crime of arson at the Twenty-Fifth Division Police Station. We know you waited for over five hours in the washroom before starting the fire, once you thought everybody had left for the night."

He paused to gauge her reaction. Her eyes began to well up, and her left arm, which was resting on the table, began to shake. He had no intention of letting up and turned the screw.

"We also know about your gambling debts and the illicit payments you have been receiving every month. We believe you have been abusing your position to provide confidential information on current police investigations to a third party."

Bianchi was now crying uncontrollably, and her head slumped forward onto the table.

Vargas then went for the coup de grâce. "As a direct result of your actions, six murders have taken place. Plus, one of my fellow officers has been killed, as well as two criminals. We plan to charge you as an accessory to murder and you will face a minimum prison sentence of twenty-five years."

Bianchi was now a complete wreck. Vargas switched off the audio recorder and stepped away from the table. "Olivia, it doesn't have to go like this. There is another way. You need to tell us everything you know about the people you've been working for. I suggest you have a good think about it. I'll be back in an hour."

Vargas didn't need to wait an hour. Fifteen minutes later, Bianchi's lawyer sent a message saying his client was ready to trade. Torres and Vargas resumed their positions behind the table and the interview continued. Bianchi had managed to compose herself and began by asking Vargas a question of her own.

"How will you protect me and my daughter from harm?"

Vargas deliberately left the audio recorder off before answering. "Olivia, we will put you both under our protection. Your daughter will be collected from university and taken to a safe house where you will be able to join her. How helpful you prove as a state witness will ultimately determine your future. Now, shall we begin?"

Bianchi nodded her understanding that an informal deal had been reached and Vargas switched on the recorder.

"How and when did they first make contact with you?"

"It was about five years ago. I'd racked up huge gambling debts and couldn't make my house loan payments or cover my daughter's college fees. I received a text from an unknown source who seemed to know every detail of my personal finances. They suggested there might be a way out if I were prepared to take on a second job. I was desperate and curious and, after a few exchanges, I met with a man in Recoleta Cemetery. His name was Alonso Núñez and he explained he worked for a respectable security company called Theodor Consultants. He said they wanted to recruit me as a confidential source. After the first meeting, he took me across the road from the cemetery to his offices, which were incredibly impressive."

Vargas and Torres glanced at each other when Bianchi mentioned the company's name. Finally, they had a proper lead.

"What sort of information did Núñez want."

The floodgates were open and Bianchi was keen to give up everything she knew as fast as possible. "At first, it was pretty innocuous stuff – personal details on certain officers, like salary levels and career history and sometimes home addresses. Of course, I knew it was wrong but I told myself it wasn't actually causing any real harm and the money was allowing me to pay off my debts." She paused for a brief moment to take a sip of water and collect her thoughts.

"After the bank robbery, everything changed. Núñez turned incredibly aggressive and demanded I report in every day with anything I could discover about how the investigation was progressing. On two occasions, I visited your station late at night and took photos of the crime boards in the open-plan area. Where I could, I tried to source internal email chains that discussed the case. Then, last week, he summoned me to a late-night meeting, and that's when he hit me with the arson plan. He made it clear, should I refuse to cooperate, they would kill me and my daughter. I was in far too deep by then and felt I had no choice."

She paused again and Vargas jumped in. "Olivia, did Núñez ever mention the name Franklin?"

"No, never. Why?"

Vargas switched off the recorder and indicated to Torres the interview was over. His parting shot to Bianchi exhibited a complete change of tone. "Your cooperation at this point is noted and you'll need to sign a written statement. Señora Bianchi, your deceitful behaviour may well have contributed to the deaths of nine victims, so I suggest you think about that."

Ten minutes later, Vargas conducted an emergency meeting with the entire detective team. On the crime board behind him, the name Theodor Consultants loomed large.

"Let's spend the rest of today learning everything we can about this outfit, and tomorrow morning we'll pay them a visit. Odds are they'll be at work on a Saturday given what's going on, so I want a search warrant in place for their offices and arrest warrants for Núñez and whoever the CEO happens to be. Somebody give them a call and confirm they'll be there. Plus, I want to know if they have any connection to the Franklin Corporation."

Vargas arrived back at his apartment just after five and found Hembury in the same state he had left him several hours earlier, sitting at the kitchen breakfast bar in his underwear, working away at his laptop.

"Troy, that's not a good look to come home to."

Hembury laughed for the first time in a while. "You should be so lucky. How did it go with your arsonist?"

Vargas brought him up to speed on the interview with Bianchi and handed him a small file containing three pages of typed notes. "This is the outfit behind the killings, but, so far, we can't find a direct connection with Franklin. The CEO is a guy called Matias Paz. The holding company that owns Theodor Consultants is based in the Cayman Islands and the shareholder breakdown is cloaked in secrecy. We're going to raid them in the morning and see what we can find."

Hembury studied the information in the file and then threw it down on the table. "Theodor is such an unusual name, yet that's the second time today I've come across it. But what the hell was the reference?"

He returned to his laptop and, for the next ten minutes, retraced his history. Vargas opened a beer and waited.

Suddenly, Hembury snapped the laptop shut and rose from the chair. "Nic, at last we've got a connection with Franklin. I think this security company was founded by Martin Bormann, in his guise as Ronald Franklin. This morning, I spent a couple of hours researching Bormann. His father's name was Theodor."

Vargas punched the air in triumph. "Thank God for Wikipedia. This may not stand up in court but it's another link to Franklin. It's weird how these characters all felt the need to use names from their past as a way of coping with their new identities."

Hembury grabbed a couple of fresh beers from the fridge. "Nic, I've been doing a lot of thinking today about our next steps. I'm going to book my flight back to LA for the day after tomorrow. I want to set up another meet with Franklin and it would be good if you were with me. We need some leverage over him, and I've got an idea for a play."

Vargas sat back in his chair and nodded to Hembury to continue.

"An old English girlfriend of mine is the political correspondent for BBC World News and works out of Washington. She is incredibly well respected and I think we could trust her to break this story on the international stage. If we can't bring Franklin down by normal means, maybe we can use the media."

"Why don't you call her and see if she's willing to meet us in LA?"

"I already have and she's up for it."

"And, while you're dreaming of your ex, I'm off to see Sophia's parents.

Since her death three years earlier, he had never missed the once-a-month visit to his in-laws. They weren't Orthodox Jews but loved hosting the traditional Sabbath meal for their immediate family. It was an emotional roller coaster, and although he dreaded going he always left feeling invigorated by the warmth and support he received from Sophia's family. He slid open the top drawer of the bedside table and grabbed the blue velvet skullcap that always joined him on his monthly Friday night outing. It was a treasured gift from Sophia, who had bought it for him prior to his first visit to her family home, five years earlier.

Despite his usual misgivings, an hour later he pulled up in his white Peugeot directly in front of the tiny garden of the modest detached house, situated in the middle-class Almagro district in the city centre. He put his "Friday night" face on and headed for the front door. He was greeted warmly by Sophia's parents and sister as usual, and, after exchanging pleasantries, they made their way into the small dining room at the back of the house.

The circular mahogany table was neatly dressed, covered with a pristine white lace tablecloth. The four place settings were evenly spread and the starter plates containing home-made chopped liver were already in place. The centre of the table was dominated by two ornate silver candlesticks, holding unlit candles. A matching silver platter housed a large plaited loaf of challah, which had been pre-sliced. Alongside it, was a cut-glass decanter containing sweet red kosher wine, a concoction that Vargas found undrinkable.

The only other piece of furniture squeezed into the room was a matching mahogany sideboard, displaying a prized collection of framed family photographs, a number of which featured Sophia. There were five in total, and, although Vargas had seen them on countless occasions, he always felt a sucker punch in his stomach every time he encountered them. The pain was always the same; almost unbearable, which was the main reason he dreaded the monthly visits, but his sense of duty and love for Sophia's family left him with no choice.

Vargas took his usual seat at the table, opposite Sophia's younger sister, Nadia. Her parents, Rebeca and Gabriel, took the other two seats and his father-in-law recited a short Hebrew prayer before they set about tackling the chopped liver. Gabriel was a second-generation immigrant whose parents had escaped from Germany in 1937, four years after Hitler's election as chancellor. At that time, Jews were not yet stigmatised as enemies of the state, but the writing was clearly on the wall as the Nazi Party tightened its grip on power and began to seed its poison among the German people through relentless propaganda.

Vargas winced slightly as Gabriel leant across and filled his wine glass, then braced himself and took a sip. Gabriel smiled knowingly, shook his head, and downed his in one.

"Nic, seems like you are working on the hottest crime in history. The papers are full of it. Two gangs killing each other to get their hands on the contents of those stolen boxes. They say the haul could be worth over a hundred million."

Vargas wasn't sure if the last comment was a statement or a question but knew he had to keep to the official story. "Well, one thing's for sure. It's a bloody mess and at the moment we have more questions than answers. It's still early days in the investigation but we'll get there in the end."

Gabriel didn't seem happy with the bland reply but before he could follow up, Vargas switched the subject with a massive gear change. "I've never really asked you about your parents before, of their lives in Germany. I know they left in the nineteen thirties. Did they lose family members?"

Gabriel was clearly stunned by the question, and there was a gaping silence before Rebeca spoke. "What a strange question. You've never brought this up before. Why now?"

Vargas could sense the tension he'd unwittingly created and leaned forward towards his father-in-law. "Gabriel, the last thing I want to do is upset you, but I'm really interested in your family history and it's a strange thing that we've never discussed it. But if it's not the right moment—"

"They escaped just in time. My father's three brothers and two sisters were arrested a few months later and sent to Treblinka, a death camp in Poland. They were all married and between them had nine children, my cousins. None of them survived the camp. The Nazis butchered all of them."

Gabriel's voice began to break, and his eyes welled up as he slumped back in his chair. Vargas was stunned by Gabriel's story and amazed he'd never heard it before. But, then again, it had always seemed a taboo subject and, selfishly, he'd never really thought about it, as the events seemed to have happened so long ago.

"Gabriel, I'm so sorry to have upset you, but thank you for sharing it with me. I should have asked you before."

Vargas took a deep breath before continuing. "Now, why don't I tell you a bit more about the case and see if you can come up with any ideas to help me solve it."

The mood took a while to lift but everyone was fascinated by the titbits Vargas revealed about the infamous safe-deposit robbery. He regaled them with stories of the carpeted tunnel and Café Torino, where the thieves had based themselves for eight months, and described the sheer carnage he had witnessed in the depository. He knew it was all pretty innocuous information, but, nevertheless, they lapped up the fascinating details.

By the time he left, everyone was enjoying playing armchair detective, speculating on the motives of the thieves who were involved in the killing spree that was dominating the news.

An hour later, Vargas entered his apartment feeling mentally and physically exhausted. Hembury was already asleep and Vargas was desperate to wash away the taste of the kosher red wine, so grabbed a beer from the fridge and pulled up a stool by his kitchen worktop. He picked up his laptop and opened up the book section on the Amazon site. He typed "Hitler" into the search bar and dozens of entries came up. He worked his way down the listings and two books, particularly, caught his eye, *Hitler: A Study in Evil* and *Martin Bormann: The Man Who Manipulated Hitler*. Two clicks later, both titles were downloaded to his Kindle. He picked it up and walked into the bedroom where he flung it onto the duvet. He flopped down on the bed, knowing he had a long night of reading ahead of him.

Chapter Forty-Six

28 January 2012

Buenos Aires

Matias Paz and Alonso Núñez conducted their regular morning catch-up in the usual setting inside Recoleta Cemetery. They were totally unaware that, less than a mile away, their office was in lockdown. Vargas and Torres, supported by a team of six detectives, raided the offices of Theodor Consultants at nine thirty. There were twelve employees on-site and, surprisingly, Vargas and his team were met with no resistance.

Eleven of the staff were male operatives who were bright enough not to take on the Buenos Aires Police Department in a shoot-out, even if some of them contemplated it. They all remained silent as Torres herded them into the boardroom and took possession of their IDs, weapons and mobiles. It soon became clear that none of them were Paz or Núñez.

The sole female in the office was a young, attractive Spanish student who ran the switchboard and doubled as the receptionist. She was clearly perplexed by the unexpected police raid and was only too happy to cooperate. Vargas interviewed her separately in Paz's office.

"Ana, there's absolutely nothing for you to worry about. We just need to talk to Paz and Núñez about a routine investigation we're working on. Do you know where they are?"

Ana Varela breathed a huge sigh of relief. "That's easy, chief inspector. They're holding their morning briefing in the cemetery. You'll find them near the boxer's statue. I think his name is Firpo."

The giant map by the gates of Recoleta Cemetery provided Vargas with a precise route to Firpo's mausoleum. He'd left two men behind in the boardroom to ensure no one could provide advance warning to Paz. He quickly formulated a pincer movement with Torres, and they split into two groups of three. The cemetery was vast but it took less than five minutes to reach Paz's informal office. Both groups of detectives liaised by radio and came to a stop about twenty yards away from the imposing statue. Vargas led the team from the north and could see the backs of two figures seated on a stone bench, deep in animated conversation.

Torres and his men approached Paz and Núñez head-on from the south. Vargas held his position and, when they were all ten yards away from the statue, he actioned the attack. Torres and his two detectives, weapons drawn, moved forward to confront the two men who had been oblivious to them. Suddenly, Núñez spotted some movement. Instantly, he drew his Glock and began firing wildly at Torres, the lead man.

Bullets slammed into the side of a marble mausoleum but failed to find any human flesh. Torres and his men fired back as they dived for cover. Núñez spun around and raced off in the opposite direction, slap bang into Vargas and his men. He weaved to his left and raised his gun again to shoot but, before he could let off another round, two bullets slammed into his chest. The impact sent his body lurching backwards. Vargas turned and nodded to Lucas Rivas, who had fired the decisive shots. The youngest detective on the team had probably saved his boss's life. Rivas ran forward with his gun still drawn and checked Núñez's body for signs of life. Up ahead, Paz had remained stationary on the stone bench and was now surrounded by Torres and his men. He stood up arrogantly and offered his wrists, the universal gesture for handcuffing. One of the detectives happily obliged.

* * *

Cabellero and Delgado was considered one of the city's top three criminal legal firms and Mario Delgado, one of the founders, was known to be a Rottweiler. At the beginning of the interview, Paz's eminent lawyer wasted no time in rebuking Vargas.

"Chief inspector, my client is the CEO of one of Buenos Aires' leading security firms and is held in the highest regard by his clients and rival companies within the industry. Any charge you may have considered bringing against him involving his employee, Alonso Núñez, is now null and void, thanks to the reckless actions of one of your men. Núñez is no longer alive to defend himself and there is no direct link between my client and Señora Bianchi. I suggest that, unless you have any further evidence against Señor Paz, you release him with immediate effect."

Vargas blatantly ignored the reprimand and kept his eyes fixed firmly on his prey. "Señor Paz, I believe that, for the last few weeks, you and your agents have been working directly for Richard Franklin, searching for the contents of his safe-deposit box, which was stolen in the Banco Estero raid. That work has included the torture and murder of six civilians, the killing of one of my officers, and, I'm guessing, the deaths of two of your employees. I also believe you were behind the arson attack at the police station, where the investigation was based."

Paz maintained eye contact with Vargas the whole time, his face resembling a frozen mask with a slightly crooked grin.

"I think it's only a matter of time before we unravel the true ownership of Theodor Consultants and establish a link with the Franklin Pharmaceutical Corporation. Let me ask you a question, Señor Paz. Do you know the name of Martin Bormann's father?"

Vargas thought he spotted a tiny flicker of recognition in Paz's eyes but the Black Scorpion refused to speak.

Delgado jumped back in. "Chief inspector, as I suspected, you have absolutely no concrete evidence against my client so, once again, I request you release him."

"Señor Delgado, we still have the testimony of a witness who claims she was recruited by Theodor Consultants to—"

The door burst open and Detective Martin gestured from the corridor for Vargas to join him. The chief inspector switched off the audio recorder and left the room.

Martin was holding a small polythene crime bag containing the mobile phone that had been recovered from the home of Sebastian Ramos. "Chief, as you know, when we ran Paz's fingerprints through the computer, nothing came up. The guy is clean and doesn't have a record. But then I remembered the prints we took off this phone. I ran a check and the lab has just confirmed a perfect match."

"Alex, that's a total game changer. Put it on charge for a few minutes. I want the bastard to see that frozen image on the screen."

When Vargas returned to the interview room, Delgado was about to launch into another rant when he spotted the bag containing the mobile. Vargas placed it directly in front of Paz and clicked the power button through the polythene to bring up the gruesome image of Ricardo Gonzales's mutilated body.

"Señor Paz, we found this phone at Sebastian Ramos's apartment. It was left behind by one of his torturers. Do you recognise it?"

The CEO refused to acknowledge the question and avoided eye contact with Vargas.

The chief inspector picked up the package and waved it in front of Paz's face. "Your fingerprints are all over it. This mobile places you directly at the murder scene. The phone log also reveals a call to the Franklin Corporation in San Francisco. Matias Paz, I am charging you with the murders of Sebastian Ramos, Pedro García, Ricardo and Raúl Gonzales and Maria Vidal. And that's just for starters."

The lawyer visibly deflated and stayed quiet for once, while the frozen mask that was Paz's face remained in place. However, the crooked grin had disappeared.

* * *

Following the fire, Vargas no longer had an office, so he

and Torres held their debrief in a small Costa Coffee located across the street from the temporary station they were now working out of.

Torres handed his boss a fresh latte and took a large gulp from his Americano. "Chief, there's still a lot going on with this case that you're not letting me in on. We now know Theodor Consultants were at the sharp end chasing down the security box but we still don't know who they were working for and why they were so desperate to find it. And what's the story with Franklin Pharmaceuticals? Are they running the show?"

"Juan, as I told you before, there is a much bigger picture going on and I still believe it's safer for you not to be directly involved. I want you to find out everything you can about Theodor and pull in the rest of Paz's employees. See what gives there. I promise it won't be long till I bring you fully into the loop. You just have to trust me for now."

Chapter Forty-Seven

6 July 1981

Buenos Aires

Franklin had decided his trip to Bormann's apartment in Buenos Aires should include a visit to El Calafate to see Eva Braun for the first time in over a decade. He spoke to his mother by phone about four times a year, mainly out of duty rather than love or genuine concern. After the birth of his son, he had cut her loose. She was now sixty-nine and living under the alias Valentina Suarez. He flew directly to Buenos Aires and, while in transit waiting to board an internal flight to El Calafate, he called to inform her he was on his way. She was totally shocked to hear from him and couldn't help but wonder what dreadful news he deemed important enough that he felt the need to impart it in person.

Franklin stood outside the property named El Negus and closed his eyes. His memory conjured up crystal-clear images of the house that used to stand on the same plot: the home where he was born and spent the first eighteen years of his life. He visualised Hitler sitting behind his desk in his

278

study listening for hours to his precious Wagner recordings; birthday parties in the sprawling gardens with his school friends, and complex chess games played with Bormann, who taught him the art of strategy. Weirdly, none of his memories featured his mother and he suddenly regretted the impulse that had brought him back to see her.

He was shaken out of his childhood reminiscences by the sound of a familiar voice calling his name. His eyes snapped open and he saw his mother standing outside the front door. At first glance, she looked no different from the last time he'd seen her but then he looked closer and detected a slight frailty in her posture and a distinct look of fear in her blue eyes that didn't sparkle quite as brightly as they used to. His heart instantly softened and he realised he had made the right decision to come home after all.

They sat opposite each other in two highly patterned silk armchairs with a black marble coffee table lodged between them. Resting on top was a large white plate containing a fruit cake and an elegant porcelain teapot, alongside matching cups, a milk jug and a small sugar bowl. He remembered exactly where the table used to be kept in the living room of the old house. She saw him looking at it and instantly read his mind.

"It's one of the few mementos I kept from El Blondi. The Führer and I used to take our afternoon tea on it."

Franklin eased back in his chair and smiled at his mother. It had been a long time since anyone had spoken to him in Spanish. "Yes, I remember it very clearly." He poured them both a cup of tea and then began to explain the reason for his surprise visit. "Mother, two weeks ago Martin died. He was struck down by cancer and, although he fought it for two years, in the end it took him."

"When you phoned me earlier, I feared that might be the case."

Richard reached for his cup and sipped some hot tea as his mother reacted to the news.

"You know, I never really cared for him. It always felt as if there were three of us in the marriage and I could never compete with him for the Führer's affections. As your father grew weaker, Martin's influence over him grew stronger and he controlled all the comings and goings at El Blondi. I know he idolised you and the Führer but he always treated me with disdain, as he did most of the women in his life. Ever since we left Berlin, he manipulated every aspect of my entire existence. After John was born, you know he forced me to fake my death and change my identity, which meant I could never see my grandson." She paused for a moment before continuing. "Richard, will I ever be able to meet him?" She stopped to look for a reaction from her son but he offered nothing in return and refused to meet her gaze. "I see. So, even from beyond the grave, he continues to control my life."

Franklin flew back to Buenos Aires and took a taxi straight to the serviced apartment that the corporation owned and made available for directors visiting from abroad. It was in the fashionable San Telmo district, only three miles from Bormann's home in Recoleta. Franklin had one last task to attend to before he was ready to discover what secrets Bormann had left behind.

In the last few years, he had become increasingly concerned about the relentless pursuit of high-ranking Nazis who had fled to South America after the war. It was led by Mossad and the self-proclaimed Nazi hunter, Simon Wiesenthal. Adolf

Eichmann, one of the infamous three, had been tracked down and smuggled out of Argentina to stand trial in Israel and was later executed. Franklin was aware that Schwammberger and Mengele and a number of other prominent Nazis were living in constant fear of exposure and capture. They had reached out to Bormann for financial and practical help and, now he was dead, that responsibility sat firmly on Franklin's shoulders.

Before he'd died, Bormann had explained it was essential for the success of their master plan that Franklin base himself full-time in San Francisco, from where he could drive the business forward and guide his son on his political journey. The implication of that strategy meant he needed to find a third party, based in South America, whom he could trust implicitly to carry out his requests in a discreet and efficient manner. Franklin sat at the desk in the apartment, reading through the notes he had put together on Paz Securities. He glanced down at his watch, noting his meeting with Matias Paz was due in the next hour.

Paz was only twenty-seven years old but had led an intense and colourful life. At sixteen, he'd left school and joined the Argentine Navy as a cadet, serving on the destroyer, *Hércules*. He'd quickly progressed to the rank of junior officer and, two years later, was recruited to the Amphibious Commandos, the special operations group of the Marine Corps. Operatives were trained in the arts of demolition, weapons and close-quarter combat and their skills were called upon to perform assault raids at short notice. Paz excelled in this role and was involved in a number of covert operations, some of which included hand-to-hand combat and the taking of life.

After two years, he took his highly specialised skills to

the freelance market and was recruited by a private British-based agency. He joined a group of mercenaries, stationed in Angola, who were participating in the civil war. Paz fought for the US-backed National Liberation Front against the Popular Movement for Liberation, financed by Russia and Cuba. The payments he received for six months' work were enough to allow him to return to Buenos Aires, set up his own security company and recruit three former commandos as his first employees. He worked tirelessly to build the company, and by the summer of 1981 Paz Securities employed eight full-time operatives, working out of the Recoleta office, and reported an annual turnover of more than a million dollars.

Paz was obsessive when it came to client research and, when he received the enquiry from Richard Franklin's office for a potential meeting, he set about discovering as much about the owner of the Franklin Corporation as he possibly could. One thing was clear, the man he was about to meet with was a big fish: a veritable whale shark, and by far the most important potential client ever to set foot in his office. Following the recent death of his uncle, Franklin had become Chairman, in addition to his role as CEO, of one of the biggest pharmaceutical companies in the world and, although he was based at the head office in San Francisco, both he and the corporation had been born in Argentina in 1946.

Paz's curiosity as to why Franklin wanted to meet had kept him awake for the last three nights, and he was convinced a major opportunity was heading his way. He just couldn't figure out what it might be. Franklin arrived promptly and the receptionist led him straight through to Paz's office, where the two CEOs met for the first time. After exchanging pleasantries, Paz cut straight to the chase.

"Señor Franklin, I know you are an incredibly busy man and I am fascinated to learn how I can be of assistance to you."

Franklin appreciated the bluntness of Paz's approach. It was how he liked to conduct business himself. "Señor Paz, if you know anything about me, you won't be surprised to hear that I have done my due diligence on your personal background and that of your company. I have compiled a file reflecting some of your more controversial operations, which I think would make very interesting reading for the Buenos Aires Police Department."

"Señor Franklin, if you've come here to threaten me, you've made a very big mistake."

Franklin burst into laughter and instantly the atmosphere changed. "I haven't come to threaten you. I'm here because I want to buy your company."

Paz was now intrigued as to how this was going to play out. "Go on, I'm listening."

"Señor Paz, I have some very important friends and relatives based in South America who need my ongoing protection. Many of them are in hiding, using aliases. They are being pursued by foreign forces who are desperate to hunt them down. I need you to be my eyes and ears on the ground and be ready to step in to help them whenever necessary."

Paz couldn't resist interrupting to let Franklin know that he fully understood the sensitivity of the operation. "Señor Franklin, your late uncle was a very powerful and influential man in this country, but he wasn't without his enemies. There are many rumours about his background. Rumours that go all the way back to the Führerbunker in Berlin in 1945."

Franklin nodded and couldn't prevent a hint of a smile breaking out, as Paz was exceeding his expectations. "Señor

Paz, I think we understand each other, so let me explain how our arrangement will work. You will close down your company and reopen it under a new name, which I will provide. In return, you'll receive a personal payment of two million dollars and a second payment of five million dollars will be paid into the new company. You will be the CEO, but, in reality, the Franklin Corporation will own it. There will be months, maybe even years, when you won't hear from me and you can run the business however you deem fit. There will be zero interference. But, whenever I need your assistance, you will immediately turn over the entire resources of the company to take whatever action is required."

Paz's mind was spinning at the mind-numbing numbers Franklin had just offered. "So what will the new company be called?"

Franklin was well prepared for the question: he'd already decided to name it after Martin Bormann's father, in tribute to his mentor.

"You'll be the CEO of Theodor Consultants. And, in that capacity, you can help me right now with some local advice. Which bank has the most secure safe depository in the city?"

"That's easy, Señor Franklin. It's the Banco Estero on Avenida Cabildo."

Chapter Forty-Eight

29 January 2012

Buenos Aires

Hembury and Vargas were booked on an 8.30 a.m. flight to Los Angeles and were ploughing through an early morning breakfast.

"Troy, these are the best scrambled eggs I've ever eaten."

Vargas used a piece of brown toast to scoop up the remains of his food. Troy grinned back at him. "You can thank Gordon Ramsay. I found the recipe on his YouTube channel."

Over the meal, Vargas brought Hembury up to speed on the Paz arrest and the clear thread that tied Franklin to Theodor Consultants.

"The problem we have is that everything is circumstantial. We need concrete evidence that proves the Franklin Corporation owns Theodor. Our IT guys are digging deep, trying to establish who the shareholders of the company really are."

Hembury's phone buzzed and he glanced down at the text. "That's our cab, Nic. Let's continue this on the way to the airport."

A major crash, involving a transport lorry, resulted in a three-mile backup on the main road to the airport and it was touch and go whether the detectives were going to make their flight. As the taxi crawled towards Terminal A, Hembury unzipped his carry-on bag to check he had his passport and paperwork ready.

"Damn it, I've left my laptop at your place. I know exactly where it is. It's on the breakfast bar in the kitchen. I obviously spent too much time trying to impress you with my culinary skills."

Vargas glanced at his watch, then grabbed his mobile and scrolled through his contacts. "There's no time to head back, but there may be another way. One of my team commutes every day on a very fast BMW bike. It's only six forty-five, so he'll still be at home, and he only lives a few minutes from the temporary station where I've left a spare set of keys. With luck, he could have time to pick them up, get to my apartment, collect the laptop and then weave his way through the gridlock before we take off. It's the best I can offer."

"Cheers, Nic. If he doesn't make it, you gain a new Mac."

Vargas briefed Detective Alex Martin, who relished the challenge, and within seconds of ending the call was donning his black leathers.

* * *

The black Mercedes Sprinter parked up on the Avenida Santa Fe at precisely 7.15 a.m. Hakim and Ahmed Saadi sat in the back and ran through their final checks of the complex military-grade equipment they were about to operate in one of Buenos Aires' busiest districts. The two Algerian brothers had served in the People's National Army before becoming independent assassins. They owned a huge warehouse in Morocco, crammed full of armaments capable of starting a small war. The two C90 RPGs in the back of the van were designed to take out heavily fortified tanks and a single round could penetrate twenty-four-inch-thick concrete from a range of one thousand yards. The target they were about to attack was no more than fifty feet away. It was the apartment block directly across the road from where they were parked. Hakim and Ahmed secured their respective fibreglass launch tubes into place and adjusted the leather shoulder straps.

Detective Martin pulled up outside the front of Vargas's eight-storey apartment block and switched off the engine of his blue BMW 1200 GS bike. He ran through the glass-fronted entrance and opted for the stairs rather than the lift to reach his chief's third-floor apartment. At the same moment, Hakim opened the sliding door on the side of the van and Ahmed moved into position alongside him. They already knew they had a perfect sight line to the kitchen and bedroom areas of their target's apartment and were aiming at both. The brothers made final tweaks to their optical sights and prepared to fire.

Hakim was the first to catch a glimpse of the slim male figure moving through the apartment and entering the kitchen. It was just after 7.30 a.m. and their target was clearly up and about, so he gave the order to his younger brother to shoot. The rocket launchers fired simultaneously, and the two projectiles slammed into the side of the apartment block. The high-explosive warheads blew an enormous hole in the side of Vargas's building. Everything inside the apartment was instantly incinerated, and the floors immediately above and below were completely wiped out. The Sprinter door closed and, a few seconds later, the Mercedes fired up. As the brothers drove away, they had no idea they had killed the wrong target or that Alonso Núñez, the man who had hired them, was dead and his boss in police custody. Also, they didn't know that, even though Paz had processed the deposit payment into their Swiss numbered account, they would never receive the balance.

Hembury and Vargas were still landside in the departure terminal when the tannoy announced the final call for the American Airlines flight to Los Angeles. The two men were sitting by passport control and Vargas made the decision to head through.

"I've tried Alex's mobile three times and he's not picking up. He must be out there somewhere, stuck in traffic. I've just sent him a text saying we've had to board. When we land, I'll ask someone in the office to book a courier, so you should get it tomorrow."

"No worries. I've just had a text from Amanda in Washington. She lands at seven tonight and will head straight to my place. I'll make us some food. She used to love my pasta Bolognese."

Vargas took his passport from inside his jacket and the two men joined the queue. "How much have you told her?"

"I said we're working on a case that could involve the biggest political scandal in modern times since Woodward and Bernstein broke Watergate."

The Boeing 777 left on time and Vargas spent most of the flight working on his laptop, creating a detailed timeline of events that he thought might be helpful to Amanda. It was hard to believe just how much had happened over the three weeks since the robbery had taken place. The case had unravelled at breakneck speed and wasn't showing any sign of slowing down. By the time they touched down at LAX, Vargas had created a five-page Word document that chronicled the whole incredible story.

The detectives quickly cleared immigration and made for the taxi rank, where they jumped into a yellow taxi and headed for Hembury's apartment in West Hollywood. Vargas switched his mobile back on and all hell broke loose.

"Troy, my phone's gone into total meltdown. I've had over fifty missed calls, most of them from Torres. My mailbox is rammed."

"Did you tell him you were coming to LA?"

"No, but it seems like the shit's hit the fan."

Vargas hit the contact for Torres, who picked up instantly. He didn't get time to speak before the detective screamed down the line at his boss.

"Jesus Christ, chief. Where the hell have you been? I've been trying you for over fifteen hours. Are you okay?"

Vargas glanced at Hembury and switched the phone on to the speaker setting. "Juan, calm down. What the hell's happened?"

"Chief, earlier today your apartment was literally blown to pieces by a rocket attack. Two missiles were fired from a van parked in your street. I emailed you a link to the CCTV footage. Six people were killed by the blast in the flats directly above and below yours. I thought you were dead. They've found some human remains in the wreckage that they think came from inside your apartment."

Vargas doubled up as a sharp pain hit deep in the pit of his stomach and his brain felt as if it were about to explode.

He tried to talk but for a few seconds he couldn't actually articulate any words. His mouth was parched and his throat felt as though it were being attacked by a pack of razor blades. Finally, he managed to speak and ask the question that he dreaded the answer to.

"Juan, is Alex safe?"

Torres was clearly baffled. "Chief, what's Alex got to do with this? I haven't seen him all day but I assume he's been out and about, working the case."

Vargas knew at that moment the young detective was dead. "Juan, I asked him to go to my apartment this morning to collect a laptop. I left a message on his mobile early this morning, but he didn't get back to me."

Torres was clearly disorientated by Vargas's story. "Chief, I don't get any of this. There's been a full-scale military attack on your flat in broad daylight, bang in the middle of the city. What the hell are we dealing with here and where the fuck are you?"

Vargas turned to Hembury as he replied to Torres. "I am in Los Angeles, and we are dealing with pure evil."

Chapter Forty-Nine

29 January 2012

Los Angeles

By the time the taxi arrived at the apartment block on the corner of Sunset and Vine, Vargas had begun to regain his focus. He and Hembury had viewed the CCTV footage of the attack at least a dozen times. The camera was positioned about fifty yards down the street from his building and it clearly showed the parked van with two tiny objects poking out of the side. After a few seconds, two large puffs of smoke emerged from the rocket launchers and a massive fireball appeared where his apartment used to be. It resembled a scene from a war-torn Middle Eastern city rather than an upmarket district in Buenos Aires.

As the two men walked towards the building, Hembury leaned across and grabbed his friend in a bear hug. After a few seconds they broke apart and Hembury was the first to speak.

"Franklin's declared war on you and your team and the way to pay him back is to expose his lies and bring him to justice.

Together we will find a way."

"Troy, you realise those bastards must have thought I was at home. They obviously figured all the evidence was in there as well."

Hembury nodded. "Yes, and maybe we can turn that to our advantage."

* * *

Richard Franklin sat at his desk in the oak-panelled study of his Pacific Heights mansion and flicked through the news channels. They were leading with the breaking story that his son had just announced his running mate for the November election. John Franklin had gone for the charismatic governor of California, who he hoped would help shore up the female vote. Richard had produced a list of three prospective candidates for his son, with Shirley Jones being the number one choice. In her former life, before becoming a politician, she had been a hugely popular movie star and was adored by millions of fans across the country.

At that moment, he relished the feeling of knowing he was one of the masters of the world who continued to pull the strings on his son's unstoppable charge to the White House. As he flicked through the channels to check on the prominence of the coverage, he caught the tail end of a news report from Argentina about the rocket missile attack on the home of a chief inspector of the Buenos Aires Police Department. While they didn't reveal the identity of the murdered detective, he knew the name. He reached into his desk drawer and picked up a photo of Vargas, which showed him receiving a commendation for bravery at a police awards ceremony in Buenos Aires four years earlier. After he had received the initial phone call from Vargas, he had downloaded an image online and kept the A4 copy in his desk drawer. He picked up the heavy crystal-cut glass of Jim Beam and toasted the picture in front of him.

Even Franklin was impressed by the sheer scale and audacity of the attack that Matias Paz had managed to pull off. Vargas and the contents of Box 1321 had all been cremated in a couple of seconds and he made a mental note to call Paz later in the day to congratulate him on his outstanding work. He concluded that he may have underestimated the talents of the CEO of Theodor Consultants after all and decided a significant bonus was in order. Fortunately for Franklin, it was a call he never got around to making. Had he done so, his voice and number would have been recorded, as the police in Buenos Aires had placed twenty-four-hour surveillance on Paz's mobile and office phones.

* * *

Vargas stood in Hembury's kitchen and pressed his face against the large glass aquarium housing dozens of stunningly marked tropical fish. Hembury was carefully feeding them and, as they swam towards the food, he began to call out their names.

"There you go, Chauncey ... attaboy, Eric ... come on, Willie, don't hold back."

"What the hell, Troy – you've given them names?"

Hembury dropped in the last of the feed and looked up from the tank. "Each one of these babies is named after a player on the Clipper's team." He pointed at an electric blue fish, whose skin colour was broken up with striking gold-and-black markings. "See that Blue Ram, he's Bobby Simmons, our star forward. What a guy!"

Vargas laughed but could see his friend was deadly serious and clearly adored his tropical family. "Troy, you are full of surprises."

Hembury walked over to a small shelved unit that contained a number of framed pictures. He reached for a particular one and handed it to Vargas. It showed a large and clearly overfed golden retriever.

"That's Ollie. I lost him in the divorce. To be honest, that was one of the worst parts of the break-up. Living on my own and doing this job means it's impossible to keep a dog." He pointed towards the giant fish tank. "So that's where these boys come in."

Vargas was mesmerised by the fish, who were busy enjoying their supper. "I get it, they don't need walking and are perfectly house-trained."

"Yep, and unlike Ollie they don't eat everything they can lay their paws on in the flat." Hembury moved back towards the kitchen table. "Nic, I haven't even asked. How's Sophia? I couldn't help noticing she wasn't living at your apartment. Did you guys break up?"

Vargas felt a sharp twinge in his stomach. Hembury immediately noticed the look of pain on his friend's face. "Troy, I lost her three years ago to a fucking brain tumour. It came from nowhere. By the time it was diagnosed, she had just weeks left."

Hembury was stunned by the news and for a few seconds neither man spoke. Then he walked across and held Vargas in a tight embrace. "Jesus, Nic, I'm so sorry. I remember you telling me how close you guys were and how much you loved her."

Vargas cleared his throat and looked into his friend's eyes. "It's unbearable at times but then you get deeply involved in a case and you forget, until you return home to an empty apartment. Troy, I never told you, but she was Jewish. She used to tell me stories about how her grandparents fled Nazi Germany before the war and started a new life in Buenos Aires."

"Christ, Nic, I had no idea. We really need to nail these bastards."

Chapter Fifty

29 January 2012

San Francisco

Richard Franklin pushed the DVD into the machine and waited for the familiar image to appear on the TV screen. He was in his bedroom and Mucki was sprawled across the bed, happily snoring, dreaming about his next meal.

Franklin sat down gently next to him, careful not to disturb the giant Alsatian. When the image appeared, he pushed play on the remote control and waited for his favourite film to begin. A black-and-white caption filled the screen. It contained five words and a date, "Richard Franklin—Alaska bear hunt—2008".

Franklin's eyes widened as he watched the giant brown bear make its way towards the shaky handheld camera. The video cut to a wider angle that showed him in the foreground aiming his Winchester hunting rifle at the oncoming predator. The footage cut back to a shot of the bear as two bullets pierced its body. It let out a primeval roar and fell backwards, crashing into a large bush. Franklin then ran across to the stricken bear, who was wriggling on its back in agony. He emptied two more shots into its stomach and after that there was no more movement. The next image showed Franklin posing next to the dead animal, cradling its head against his body.

He hit the stop button and stared across the room at the same bear's head, now mounted above the fireplace in his bedroom. Every time he watched the footage he'd paid two of his guides to film, he revelled in the same sensation of total pleasure and power he had felt when he first pulled the trigger four years earlier. He leaned back onto the bed and curled up next to Mucki, being ever so careful not to wake him.

* * *

Vargas ended his call and looked across at Hembury working in his open-plan kitchen, creating an avocado salad to accompany his pasta Bolognese.

"That was Torres. They want me back as soon as possible to head up the investigation into the attack. They haven't formally identified Alex's remains, but no one's heard from him since he picked up my keys from the station. What's left of his BMW was found outside the building. Troy, it's devastating to think I sent him to his death."

"Nic, you can't blame yourself for what happened. We're dealing with a psychopath who has absolutely no boundaries and will stop at nothing to protect his son's ambitions for the White House."

Vargas nodded and stayed silent for a moment, contemplating his next words. "Troy, this whole case is a nightmare. It's become an obsession and Franklin has to be stopped. I told

Torres I'm pursuing a strong lead in California and bought myself forty-eight hours at best."

Hembury nodded and tried to lighten the atmosphere. He started to make a French dressing. "If things go well with Amanda tonight, that might just be long enough to carry out our plan. Do me a favour, there's a liquor store at the end of the street. Would you pick up a couple of nice bottles of French red wine and a few snacks? Her favourite is Nuits-Saint-Georges."

"Am I going to be the third wheel tonight cause I'm really not in the mood?"

Hembury emptied some croutons into the salad bowl, walked across the kitchen and rested his arm on Vargas's shoulder. "Nic, we just need to get her on our side. If she agrees to go along with this, we'll have some very strong leverage to use against Franklin."

By the time Vargas returned from the shop, Hembury had finished prepping the food and was busy setting the table. "Perfect timing. She just texted to say she's ten minutes away. Let's get that wine open."

Amanda Carter was one of the BBC's highest-profile and pre-eminent news correspondents. For five years, she had anchored the UK's prestigious ten o'clock bulletin and, before that, she'd cut her teeth as a war reporter, working on the front line in Bosnia and Lebanon. For the last three years, she'd been based in Washington, where she worked for BBC World News as their senior US political correspondent. At forty-five, she was at the height of her beauty and her stunning figure was complemented by her crystal-blue eyes and jet-black hair. Her exceptionally pronounced cheekbones and Angelina Jolie lips completed the effect. Senior White

House politicians were intimidated by her looks and scared of her sharp intellect.

When Hembury formally introduced her to Vargas, he couldn't help but think of the old adage that his friend had been punching way above his weight. She oozed warmth, with a lively sense of humour and an infectious laugh. Within a few minutes, the three of them were sitting around the table arguing about why Americans were so obsessed by the classic English accent. An hour and a half later, they had demolished Hembury's pasta dish and were working their way through the second bottle of red.

Carter downed a large scoop of chocolate chip Häagen-Dazs and smoothly changed the subject. "Troy, as much as I love your spaghetti Bolognese, I didn't fly over two thousand miles just to sample it again. Nic, are you ready to share your story with me?"

Vargas stood up and left the table. "I'm going to need my laptop."

Although she was a veteran journalist, known for her tough interviewing style, it was telling that for the next hour Amanda didn't ask a single question. She just sat and listened as Vargas took her through the entire story, step by step, concluding with the military-style attack on his apartment. She then spent another thirty minutes viewing a protected online file, containing copies of the most relevant documents and photographs that had been hidden away in Box 1321.

Vargas had also used his phone camera to make video copies of the 8mm films that showed Hitler and Braun enjoying post-war life in Argentina. Finally, he played her the video Hembury had secretly filmed of Braun during their encounter in El Calafate. She sat at the table, totally enthralled, occasionally scribbling down questions in her notebook.

When Vargas finished, she switched into full journalistic mode and reeled off a series of questions, aimed at both men. "Troy, as you said when you called me, it's probably the most unbelievable story I will ever come across in my career and you're not wrong. However, I'm not sure the world is ready to hear that Hitler's grandson is a few months away from becoming the next US president. But, if it is true, this story needs to be told. You won't be surprised to know I have some questions. Firstly, other than Paz's mobile phone, do we have any other evidence that connects Richard Franklin to the murders?"

Vargas was quick to reply. "Not yet. I'm convinced the Franklin Corporation owns Theodor Consultants, but the names of the shareholders are deeply hidden in a group of offshore holding companies that we're trying to break into."

Amanda put down her pen. "We might be able to help your guys with some added resources for that part of the investigation. Do we have anything that ties Franklin to the hired assassin who killed García outside the courthouse?"

"No. Again, I'm sure he was hired by Theodor, but Paz isn't talking."

Carter wrote something down in the notebook. "Nic, if I'm going to put my neck on the line, I need to know that the source material is still around and totally safe – the birth and death certificates, the original photographs, the 8-millimetre film, along with Hitler's medals."

"Amanda, you have my word that every single one of Franklin's attempts to destroy the evidence has failed. All the original materials are stored in a totally safe place. I'll transfer the file to you now so you can show it to whoever needs to see it at your end. Then Troy and I will fill you in on our plan."

Chapter Fifty-One

7 July 1981

Buenos Aires

There was one final task for Richard Franklin to carry out before he could return to San Francisco. He stood in the master bedroom of Martin Bormann's apartment, staring at the fitted wardrobes. There was a strong musty smell hanging in the air, confirming no one had visited in the last two years. He felt a great sense of unease about confronting the parting gift Bormann had presented him with from his death bed.

His mind flashed back to his childhood, and images of Bormann as a much younger man flooded his memory. As a boy, Richard had idolised his "uncle" far more than his own father, who had always seemed remote and cold. During the previous thirty-five years, Bormann had mapped out an intricate plan that had its origins in the Führerbunker, in war-torn Berlin, when all seemed lost. Bormann's genius was undeniable. He was a master of manipulation and misdirection and had planned every significant moment of

Richard's life, including the major event he was about to confront in the apartment. He had no idea what discovery awaited him, except he knew it would be of huge significance to his life and was the final piece of the complex jigsaw that Bormann had created for him to inherit.

He opened the end wardrobe door and carefully slid the line of immaculate Saville Row suits along the metal hanging rail to one end. Bormann had always been fastidious about his appearance and his shirts and suits were handmade by one of London's oldest tailors. It was a poignant reminder to Franklin of his mentor, who had died just two weeks earlier. It only took him a few seconds to remove the fake back panel of the wardrobe and he found himself face to face with a large, grey wall-mounted safe. He didn't need to check the combination, as he knew his father's date of birth by heart. The lock mechanism made a gentle whirring sound and the safe door clicked open. He gently lifted the worn black leather case out of the safe and carried it over to the bed.

The first thing he noticed were the gold initials M.B. He shut his eyes for a moment and tried to visualise Bormann carrying the case into important meetings with his father. He flicked the twin catches, opened the top and peered inside. For the next couple of hours, he scrutinised the carefully filed documents and viewed the black-and-white photos, many of which featured his parents and Bormann. He was particularly fascinated by the pictures that had been taken on board the boat. He'd never seen them before but his mother had spoken many times of the marathon sea crossing and he had always struggled to visualise the true hardship of the journey. The photos confirmed the oppressive, claustrophobic atmosphere of the interior cabins, and, for the first time in his life, he felt able to understand the sheer drama and deprivation that his parents had suffered in fleeing Germany. He noted the two 8mm film cans and figured they probably contained personal footage of his father and Bormann, no doubt shot by his mother.

Finally, he opened the yellow tobacco tin that contained his father's war medals. He placed them in a neat line on the quilt, turning them over one at a time to read the engravings. He'd always known his father had been awarded the Iron Cross but had assumed it had been lost during the chaos of the last-minute escape from Berlin.

On his deathbed, Bormann had left him with an enormous dilemma. The contents of the case were of huge historical value, as they provided unquestionable proof of the authentic chronology of Hitler's escape from Berlin and his post-war existence in Argentina. He fully understood why Bormann had protected the unique collection but he also knew that, should it fall into the wrong hands, the master plan he was in the process of enacting would implode.

In the end, he was guided by his gut instinct and used the landline in Bormann's apartment to book an appointment with the manager of the Banco Estero. Two hours later, he sat in the back of a taxi on the way to the airport, clutching the key to Box 1321 in his hand, wondering if he'd made the right decision.

Chapter Fifty-Two

30 January 2012

San Francisco

Franklin was alone in the boardroom, having just finished a series of management meetings, when his personal assistant buzzed through.

"Sir, the pilot's confirmed everything is in order for your trip to Phoenix this afternoon. The flight time is just over two hours, so if you want to make the Convention Center in good time for John's speech, you need to be airborne by three."

"That works for me. I'll probably stay over, so book me into the same hotel as John."

"Sir, there's one other thing. Lieutenant Hembury from the LAPD has just been on. He says he needs to speak with you urgently."

Franklin had been personally assured by the mayor that Hembury had been well and truly reprimanded following their last meeting and was therefore concerned by this development. His initial instinct was to ignore the message or to call the chief of police but his curiosity got the better of him. Now that Vargas was dead, he needed to know how much Hembury knew.

"Get him on the line, Mary."

Hembury had dropped Amanda off at the airport and was making his way to the station when the call came. Franklin's voice boomed through on the Bluetooth car speaker, exuding an air of arrogance and contempt.

"Lieutenant, I really didn't expect to hear from you again. I can only give you a minute."

"Mr Franklin, thank you for returning my call. I'd like to meet with you and your son to discuss a very delicate matter and it needs to happen in person."

Franklin laughed down the line. "Do you realise that you are talking about the future president? I think you are wasting my time, lieutenant."

Hembury decided to play his ace. "Mr Franklin, it's come to my attention that a major news agency is trying to gain access to some highly sensitive material that I believe was recently stolen from your family. I think it's very much in your interest, and that of your son's, that we meet as soon as possible, or the consequences could be grave."

Franklin was clearly caught off balance and his contemptuous tone morphed into one of guarded concern. "Today is out of the question. My son is making a campaign speech in Phoenix this evening, so the earliest we could possibly meet with you is tomorrow morning. I suggest you come to my Pacific Heights residence at, say, ten."

Before Hembury could confirm, the line went dead.

Franklin glanced at his watch. It was ten thirty, and, following Hembury's call, he now had a great deal to sort out before he could even contemplate boarding his Cessna to Phoenix. With Vargas dead, he believed Hembury was the only person left alive who posed a real and current threat. He thought the news agency line was bullshit and a bluff – a ruse to secure a speculative meeting with him and his son. As far as he was concerned, it was a meeting Hembury would never live to make.

Franklin left the boardroom and returned to his office, where he retrieved a black MacBook from a locked drawer in his desk. He opened up the settings and clicked on the Tor browser, which allowed him to access the Dark Web while protecting his online identity.

He'd only been on it once before, two years earlier, when he'd used it to hire a local small-time anonymous hitman to take out a troublesome girlfriend who had outstayed her welcome.

There was no time to bring in a top-class assassin like The Ghost. He needed to go down and dirty – sometimes that worked just as well. Providers on the Dark Web offered an array of illegal services, including drugs, guns, counterfeit money and even fraudulent lifetime subscriptions to Netflix. Financial transactions were carried out using Bitcoin, the cryptocurrency that enabled two parties to transact without knowing each other's identities. He was pleased to discover the website he had previously used appeared to still be live. It had a memorable domain: removeanyproblemwithaclick. onion.

He moved off the browser for a brief moment to open a file on his desktop, containing Hembury's home address. He'd used his high-level contacts in the LA Police Department to obtain it after his first meeting with the lieutenant, as he'd thought it might prove useful down the line. He highlighted it, flicked back to the website and began his post.

I used your service two years ago for a job in Russian Hill and it was highly successful.

The flashing cursor burst into life almost instantly. *I remember it.*

Franklin continued typing. *I have an emergency job that requires your special skills. It has to happen tonight in Los Angeles. The subject is a male police lieutenant named Troy Hembury. His address is 1554 North Vine Street in West Hollywood. Apartment 16. It's essential the body is removed so it appears to be a disappearance rather than a killing.*

Franklin wondered if the status of the subject would prevent the transaction from happening. The reply gave him the answer.

500.

Franklin understood that to mean the fee was the equivalent of five hundred thousand dollars in Bitcoin, five times the rate he'd paid two years ago, but it was an eighth of the fee he'd paid to The Ghost just two weeks earlier. Under the circumstances, it was a bargain.

Agreed. Let me know when it's done.

Franklin closed his laptop and reached for the intercom on his desk. "Mary, let the pilot know I'll be on time for the flight."

Aaron Wicks was an unusual hitman – a former pharmacist who'd decided, some years before, he could make a lot more money using drugs to kill people than he ever could selling them over the counter. He lived in a small rented townhouse close to Santa Monica Airport, just twenty-five minutes from Hembury's apartment. This latest job would be his biggest payday yet, but with higher rewards came higher risks.

However, this was a returning client, so he knew he would get paid.

The first thing he did was google his target. It only took a few seconds to find a number of postings that referenced the lieutenant. He clicked on images and printed off a couple of colour headshots. Next, he opened the glass door of his Labcold vaccine fridge, which contained a selection of colour-coded ampoules. He knew exactly which two he needed for the job. He selected midazolam and propofol, which he planned to combine to create his own customised lethal cocktail. Both drugs were powerful sedatives used by anaesthetists prior to surgery. Wicks's unique concoction was capable of knocking out a giant gorilla in less than three seconds. Once his subject was unconscious, he would administer two more doses. The recipient would never wake up.

He returned to his computer and sent a brief email to his cousin, a part-time waiter and shelf stacker, who doubled as a driver for him when circumstances dictated.

Be at mine with the Cherokee by 2.30. It's a last-minute job, so I'm paying double rates.

Finally, he opened his small wall safe and took out a large bundle of fifty-dollar bills. He counted out two thousand dollars and placed the notes in a white envelope. He was ready to go to work.

Franklin's private jet touched down at Sky Harbor International Airport in Phoenix just after five in the evening, where a chauffeur-driven Mercedes S-Class was waiting to meet him on the airstrip. The Convention Center was just a three-mile drive away and, as the blacked-out limo passed the front of the building, Franklin saw a large crowd queuing down the street, waiting to be admitted.

He was dropped at the rear entrance where he was met by one of his son's staffers, who gave him an all-access lanyard and escorted him through to the backstage lounge area. He immediately spotted John, deep in conversation with his campaign chief, Cathy Douglas. He made his way across the busy room and greeted the pair, double kissing Cathy and embracing his son.

"Looks like a huge crowd tonight. How's the speech going, John?"

"All good, Dad. Where do you want to watch it from? There's a VIP box on the first level or the live feed will be shown in here."

As ever with his father, John knew you could never second-guess him. "Neither. I'll pace nervously around in the wings."

Cathy laughed on cue. "Richard, I'll sort you out a table with some snacks and a bottle of Jim Beam."

"Sounds perfect, Cathy, thank you. John, I'll see you afterwards. We need to catch up on some stuff. Now get out there and kill 'em."

The Convention hall was rammed to the rafters. Three thousand fervent Republican supporters screamed and applauded and waved their giant placards as John Franklin ran through his carefully rehearsed set piece. As ever, his charismatic personality and clichéd sound bites wound the audience up into a near frenzy.

"For years, under the current regime, our country has been in steady decline as politicians take you, the people, for granted. I intend to unify this great country of ours and bring prosperity to all. I will put the American people first and once again make us the greatest nation in the world."

This line prompted the normal response. An orchestrated chant rang out around the giant hall. "Unify the USA ... Unify the USA."

Richard Franklin downed his bourbon and stood in the wings, lapping up the feverish atmosphere. The Nuremberg rallies may have had over a million live attendees but the power and reach of television meant his son's speech was playing into the households of tens of millions of people across the country.

Franklin spoke for just under an hour and ended his speech with a call to action. "Go out across our great country and campaign with every bone in your body to help me kick out this lame and corrupt administration. Washington is currently run by a political elite who govern for their own self-interest. I will clean them out from top to bottom and head a government that will truly work for you, the people, and not for itself."

The entire crowd rose to their feet and Franklin milked the rapturous applause for the next ten minutes. His father made his way backstage to the lounge where the mood among the young staffers was exuberant. He saw Cathy standing by one of the large TV monitors, watching her candidate's standing ovation, and headed straight for her.

"Another great event. Good job. Cathy, I need a few minutes with John on our own. Is there a room we can have?"

"Of course, Richard. There's a make-up room just off the corridor behind here. I'll ask one of the team to take you there now and I'll bring John through as soon as he comes offstage."

John didn't join his father for almost half an hour, remaining in the hall for a series of meet-and-greets with key donors and posing for dozens of selfies. When he finally made it to the dressing room, he was greeted with a warm hug from his father.

"Best one yet, John. The atmosphere was electric. It felt like a rock concert out there."

"I know, I'm still pumped full of adrenalin."

"John, I need to bring you up to date on events in Argentina." Richard Franklin took a seat and indicated to his son to grab a nearby chair.

"Dad, I caught the news footage of the missile attack that killed the chief inspector. I assume that was Paz's work?"

"Yes, and I now think the materials were either burnt in a police station fire or incinerated in the explosion, along with the man who found them. The nightmare is almost over."

John picked up on his father's apparent caution. "What else is there?"

Richard Franklin told his son about the phone call with Hembury and the request for a meet with both of them.

John flew into a sudden rage. "Jesus, Dad, why the hell did you agree to meet him?"

"I felt I needed to stall him. I promise you in a few hours' time he will no longer be a problem and the potential threat to our family will be eliminated. Both he and Vargas are lone wolves, and I'm convinced no one else knows about the box. John, I still want you to be at the house with me tomorrow, just in case Hembury made a diary note about the meeting and his department sends someone else in his place once they realise he is missing. If no one shows, we can celebrate the passing of the final hurdle."

John seemed irritated by his father's request. "That sounds

highly unlikely to me. If Hembury is out of the loop, no one is going to show."

"John, I agree, but let's just be prepared for all eventualities. I've got the Cessna here, so I suggest we leave at seven in the morning."

"Dad, I'm not sure you've factored everything in. The shit is going to hit the fan in LA when a police lieutenant gets taken out."

Richard leaned across and put his arm around his son's shoulder. "John, don't worry, no one will ever know he was murdered. Thanks to my friend on the Dark Web, he will just magically disappear."

The black Jeep Cherokee passed Santa Monica Pier, turned north onto Sunset Boulevard and headed towards West Hollywood. Wicks sat in the passenger seat next to his cousin, balancing a small insulated thermal cool box on his lap. Resting on the dashboard in front of him was an unopened pack of 3mm Luer lock syringes, his weapon of choice. It was by far his favourite as it offered a secure connection with the needle which needed to be twisted and locked into position to prevent it accidentally slipping off. Next to the syringes lay the deadliest part of his kit, a small pack of stainless-steel gauge needles.

His cousin, Wes, glanced at the sat nav read-out on his iPhone, which was mounted to a sucker on the windscreen.

"We're about twenty minutes away from the location, so should be there by three forty-five."

"That's good, Wes. When we get there, we'll do a little recce and find a place to park up where we have clear eyes on the apartment block."

"Cool, Aaron. Who is the mark this time?"

"Trust me, cuz, you really don't want to know."

An hour later, the Jeep was parked up about thirty yards from the front entrance of Hembury's apartment block, on the opposite side of the road. Three syringes were now prepped and loaded with the deadly concoction. Inside the apartment, Vargas was working on his laptop when a text came in from Hembury.

Dropped Amanda off at the airport. I'm at the station and will get back about seven. Flights are booked for the morning. See you later.

Vargas read the message and checked the time. Hembury wouldn't be back for another three hours, so he decided to head down to the corner shop to pick up a few beers and snacks. On his way to the shop, he spotted Wicks and his cousin sitting in the front of the Cherokee and a sixth sense kicked in to tell him something was wrong. He picked up a couple of Peroni six-packs and, on his way back, deliberately headed along the opposite side of the street in order to walk right by the Jeep.

As he passed the Cherokee, he maintained his rhythm but glanced across at the two men, spotting the cool box that was resting on one of the rear seats. He crossed the road and made his way promptly back to the apartment. Something wasn't quite right about the guys in the Cherokee but he couldn't be sure. He decided to get back to his laptop and see in an hour if they were still there. He checked at five and again at six and the Jeep hadn't moved. He felt a growing sense of unease and decided to call Hembury, who picked up straight away.

"Nic, I'm just about to leave, so should be back about six forty-five. Shall I pick up a few beers?"

"We're sorted on the beer front but I think we have a

potential situation. There are two guys sitting in a black Cherokee parked across the road who haven't moved in the last two hours. I'm pretty sure they are staking out the apartment. I managed to get a closer look at them when I went to the store and I noticed a small cool box on the back seat, which seems a bit odd bearing in mind it's pretty cold out there."

Hembury thought for a moment. "Maybe Franklin's had a change of heart about meeting me tomorrow. I'll call you when I'm a street away and we'll pay a surprise visit to our friends."

Forty-five minutes later, when Hembury turned the corner of Vine on to Sunset, Wicks spotted him in the rear-view mirror and, ten seconds later, had armed himself with a loaded syringe and was out of the Jeep. He nonchalantly crossed the road and fell into place about ten steps behind his prey. His clenched fist managed to keep the syringe totally hidden from sight. Hembury was about twenty yards from the front entrance of the apartment block and could sense Wicks rapidly closing the distance behind him.

As he prepared to strike, Wicks subtly adjusted his grip on the syringe and the needle was suddenly visible in his left hand.

At the last moment, Hembury and Vargas performed a perfectly timed pincer move on the unsuspecting hitman. Vargas had been holding position behind a clump of bushes by the side of the block for the last ten minutes and had kept his eyes firmly trained on Wicks from the moment he left the Jeep. The hitman was less than five feet away when Hembury spun around with his right arm raised, his Smith & Wesson aimed directly at his attacker's head. Wicks had been just a hair's breadth away from striking and was momentarily stunned by Hembury's last-second manoeuvre. Instinctively, he turned on the spot and started to race towards the Jeep. He only managed four steps before he was taken down by a perfectly timed rugby tackle, courtesy of Vargas, who seemed to appear from nowhere. He slammed into Wicks and the sheer impact of the collision sent the syringe flying from his grasp.

Having wrestled him to the ground, it only took a few seconds to position him face down on his front, with his arms firmly pinned behind his back. Hembury knelt down and held the gun inches from Wicks's head. He used his other hand to retrieve a pair of heavy-duty handcuffs and passed them to Vargas. At that exact moment, the sound of an engine fired up and both detectives glanced across the street to see the Cherokee pull away and disappear around the corner.

Vargas pulled Wicks up off the pavement and frogmarched him towards the entrance of the apartment block with Hembury walking alongside, his gun still drawn. Once they were inside, Hembury sat him down on one of the kitchen chairs and reset the handcuffs so his wrists were tied behind the back of it. Vargas was standing by the sink, emptying the contents of the syringe into a drinking glass. He had no doubt the liquid it contained was lethal. He walked across the kitchen and held the glass in front of Wicks's face.

"Fancy a drink? What is this stuff?"

Wicks was clearly shaken and horrified by the dramatic turn of events. He was a former pharmacist who had become a small-time assassin and realised that, with this particular job, he was way out of his depth. Hembury could almost taste the fear coming from his attacker and knew it wouldn't take long to break him.

"As things stand, you are facing forty years for the attempted murder of a police lieutenant and, I can guarantee, you won't enjoy the company of the inmates at Pelican Bay."

Pelican Bay State Prison was a maximum-security institution that housed over two thousand of California's most violent criminals. Wicks knew of its horrendous reputation and had no plans to experience its delights first-hand. Tears rolled down his cheeks as he spoke for the first time.

"I want to cut a deal. I'll tell you everything I know."

Hembury pulled up a chair and sat just a few feet away. "Go on, we're listening."

Wicks was sweating profusely and shaking like a leaf. He made every effort to compose himself, took a deep breath and began to tell his story. "My name is Aaron Wicks and I used to be a pharmacist. A few years ago, I set up a site on the Dark Web and I take money to kill people."

Wicks divulged the entire background to his attack on Hembury, including the highly unusual request from his anonymous employer to act at incredibly short notice. He explained he only agreed to take the job because of the enormous half-a-million-dollar fee.

Hembury signalled to Vargas to join him at the other side of the room. "Nic, the timing makes total sense. Wicks was booked less than an hour after I spoke with Franklin. But, yet again, we can't prove a direct link."

Hembury walked back across the room and sat down opposite the hitman. "You are going to send a message to your employer confirming the job was successful."

Wicks nodded. "I'll need my laptop and it's in Santa Monica."

Hembury leaned across and stared into the frightened eyes of the broken hitman.

"Let's go."

Richard Franklin relaxed on the king-size bed in his Marriott suite and poured himself a large bourbon from the bottle Cathy had especially requested be left in his room. He reached across for his laptop. As soon as he logged on to the Tor browser, a ping sounded to indicate he had a new message: *Operation was a success. Please conclude the transaction.*

He smiled to himself as, once again, he felt he was back in control of events. A few seconds later, he clicked on to his online Bitcoin wallet and completed the payment. He shut the laptop, left the room and headed for the bank of lifts at the far end of the corridor. His suite was on the fifth floor and he took the lift straight down to the basement. He arrived at the underground car park and, as he walked across it, kept a careful eye on where the CCTV cameras were positioned. It took him a while to locate the giant steel rubbish bins, which he'd anticipated he'd find on that level.

There were four grey units positioned together near the exit barrier in an unlit section of the car park. He checked no one was around before opening the black laptop. He raised it high above his head and began maniacally smashing it down against the top of one of the bins, breaking it into dozens of pieces. Parts of the screen and keyboard scattered onto the concrete floor around his feet. He spent the next ten minutes carefully picking up the wreckage and depositing the pieces into the four bins. He emerged from the shadows and made his way back to his suite. Once inside, he downed another glass of bourbon, picked up his mobile and punched in a text to his son.

CHAPTER FIFTY-TWO

All has gone as planned. Sleep well.

Chapter Fifty-Three

31 January 2012

Los Angeles

I t was gone midnight when Hembury and Vargas arrived back at the apartment. Earlier in the evening, Hembury had arranged for two of his senior detectives to meet them at Wicks's townhouse. As soon as the hitman had sent through the confirmation message to Franklin, he was taken away for further questioning and charged.

Vargas grabbed a couple of beers from the fridge as Hembury spoke on the phone with Amanda Carter, filling her in on the latest events.

"Troy, this episode confirms this man is a monster, running totally out of control. I'm not sure you should be walking into the lion's den tomorrow."

"At least we have the element of surprise on our side. He clearly won't be expecting me to show. I think for now we stick to the plan."

A few hours' later, two planes took off from different locations, both heading for San Francisco. Hembury and

Vargas took a scheduled Delta flight from LA, and John Franklin joined his father on board his private Cessna at Phoenix Airport. As they belted up for the two-hour flight, John again queried the need for him to go to his father's house for a meeting he now knew wasn't going to happen.

"Given the news on Hembury, I'd like to go straight to my office. There's so much going on at the moment. I just can't afford the time."

"John, I told you last night we have to play this very carefully. Hembury may have had someone on his team book him an internal flight for the meet, so it's more than possible he made a note of who he was coming to see. Now he has mysteriously disappeared, they might just send someone else along to try and find out the purpose of the meeting. We will obviously play dumb, and as Hembury's body will never turn up it will lead nowhere and become a dead end. So I want you with me."

John recognised his father's tone of voice, and the prospective president knew better than to argue.

Hembury and Vargas landed just after eight and grabbed their pre-booked hire car. They drove north, heading for the exclusive area of San Francisco where Franklin's mansion was located.

Pacific Heights was regarded as the most expensive neighbourhood in the United States and was renowned for its billionaire residents and record-breaking house prices. With a valuation topping forty million dollars, Franklin's residence on Pacific Avenue was one of the three most valuable properties in the area. Hembury parked up opposite the Dutch colonial mansion an hour before he was due to arrive. It was set well back from the street and boasted a magnificent circular drive that led to the opulent marble-columned entrance. Vargas peeled down the electric window and leaned out to take a closer look at Franklin's grandiose pile.

"Amazing what a few tons of Nazi gold will get you."

Hembury was also looking at the mansion. "Franklin's used that stolen wealth to build a business empire that has made him one of the most powerful and influential figures in the country. He's used the platform it's created to manoeuvre his son to within touching distance of the White House. It's just totally incredible."

"Troy, are you still happy to make this play? Maybe we should front up to Franklin and his son together."

Hembury shook his head. "Let's stick with the plan. I'll drop you at the hotel and then FaceTime when it feels like the right moment. When he sees you're still alive, it'll be a double whammy."

Franklin had given his staff the morning off, so the massive house was empty when he and his son arrived back just after nine in the morning. They grabbed themselves some fresh coffee and pastries in the kitchen and made their way through to the study where they sat and waited, wondering if anybody would show.

At precisely ten o'clock, Hembury stood outside the electric gates and pressed the buzzer on the videophone entrance panel. Franklin glanced across at the screen that was fixed to the office wall and gasped in horror as if he'd been struck by a lightning bolt. Staring back at him in black and white was a ghost. Filling the frame was the unmistakable face of the police lieutenant, who he thought was dead. John knew his father well enough to realise something was drastically wrong. Richard Franklin took a few moments to compose himself and then pushed the gate release button.

"That bastard Hembury is somehow alive. The hitman obviously just took the money but never carried out the job."

John was out of his chair and standing next to the screen, glaring at the image. "How much do we think he knows?"

"John, we are about to find out. Let me do the talking. Don't forget, your running mate is the governor of California, so we have the power to shut him down. Trust me, we will crush him."

Franklin left the office and strode through the grand entrance hall towards the imposing front door. He stared at the handle but paused before reaching for it, sensing the physical presence on the other side. He took a deep breath in an attempt to quell the twinge of fear and misgiving that had suddenly overtaken him. Finally, he turned the handle.

The door opened and the two adversaries faced each other for the first time since Hembury had visited Franklin's office.

"Lieutenant. Incredibly punctual. I like that. Please come in, my son is waiting for you in my office."

Hembury had seen the poker face before but this time he could sense a slight discomfort bubbling beneath the veneer of self-assurance that Franklin was so good at portraying. "Good to see you again, Mr Franklin. Something came up at the last minute that almost prevented me making it but, happily, I was able to take care of it."

The coded reply wasn't lost on Franklin, who realised his hitman had botched the job. He turned and gestured to Hembury to follow and the two men walked down the hallway into the huge study, where John Franklin was waiting. Hembury had seen him on television countless times and the first thing that struck him was how much smaller he was in real life than he appeared on screen. His trademark smile beamed as he walked forward and warmly shook hands with the lieutenant. Hembury wondered how many thousands of fake handshakes he had given during the campaign. Richard Franklin eased into the seat behind his desk while his son moved into position, standing next to him, creating a united front. Hembury knew the moment had come to bite the bullet and he opened with the script he had rehearsed with Vargas.

"Two weeks ago, a safe depository in Buenos Aires was broken into and a number of boxes were raided, one of which was owned by the Franklin Corporation. The criminals who took part in the heist were systematically tortured and murdered by agents working for a security company called Theodor Consultants. It would appear Theodor was desperate to locate and repatriate the contents of Box 1321, the box owned by your company. Media reports suggest a rival gang was trying to steal the haul. But that's not true."

Richard Franklin sat stony-faced in his chair while John perched on the end of the desk, looking distinctly uneasy.

Hembury maintained eye contact with the older man. "Theodor was taking its instructions directly from you, Mr Franklin."

"Lieutenant, this is getting very tiresome. As I told you last time, a bank robbery in Argentina does not fall under the jurisdiction of the LAPD, so I can't see why it should be of any interest to you."

Hembury had been expecting Franklin to use the same ploy as last time. "It became of great interest to me and the LAPD last night when you employed a hitman to try and take me out."

Although the blood was visibly draining from Franklin's

face, he managed to keep his composure. "Lieutenant, I would imagine that hundreds of boxes were hit in the robbery, so it's impossible to know what specific box was being chased down by this Theodor company and, secondly, they have no connection either to me or to the corporation. So, right now, I'd like you to leave, and you can be certain I will be speaking to the governor directly to ensure you are seriously reprimanded for coming to my home with this outrageous accusation."

It was time for Hembury to play his first major card. "Mr Franklin, Interpol is now working with the Buenos Aires Police Department and using all the considerable means at their disposal to break through the cloak of secrecy surrounding the true share ownership of Theodor and I have no doubt they will discover a direct link to the Franklin Corporation. In addition, Theodor's CEO, Matias Paz, is currently in police custody. He has been charged with multiple counts of murder and is facing a life sentence. I wonder how long it will be before he decides to cut a deal with the authorities in order to gain immunity?"

Hembury let the last sentence hang in the air for maximum effect. John Franklin went to speak for the first time but his father gestured to him to remain silent.

"By the way, Mr Franklin, we now know that a mobile we found at one of the crime scenes, containing a contact number for your San Francisco office, belonged to Paz. I assume it was a direct line running straight to your office?"

Hembury was on a roll and ready to play his second card. "Last week, I spent a number of hours examining the contents of Box 1321 and now I totally understand why you tried so hard to keep them secret. The original documents and photographs chronicle the story of Adolf Hitler, Martin Bormann and Eva Braun's safe passage from Germany to Argentina by boat. Also included are forged birth and death certificates that show their change of identity."

Once again, Hembury paused to see if either man wished to speak but it was clear he had a captive audience, so he ploughed on. "They assumed the surname of Franklin. Adolf Hitler was your father, Mr Franklin."

Hembury, for the first time, looked directly at John. "And your grandfather."

Still, neither man spoke. They just stared back grimly at Hembury, who was now relishing the encounter.

"I even got to hold seven of Hitler's war medals, including the coveted Iron Cross. But the most revealing insight into their secret existence after the war came from two reels of 8-millimetre film that show them in situ at their home in El Calafate. Trust me, it was far better than anything you'll find on Netflix. Some parts of the film show Hitler and Bormann entertaining other prominent Nazis who also escaped to South America. But my favourite scene from all the remarkable footage will be of special interest to you, Mr Franklin, as you star in it. It shows you, along with your mother, celebrating your fifth birthday at a large party in the garden at El Blondi. I'm sure you must remember it."

John Franklin was clearly struggling to hide his emotions and he looked distraught as Hembury continued with the onslaught. His father was desperately trying to work out a strategy to counter the relentless attack but it was all unravelling too fast.

"What do you want, lieutenant?"

Hembury was buoyed by this first sign of concession and

decided it was time to play his third card. "I'll let you know that shortly, but I haven't finished yet, because I'm about to come to the biggest secret of all."

Once again, Hembury switched his eyeline directly to the presidential candidate. "One that not even you know."

John Franklin's eyes flicked for a moment to his father, who acknowledged the look and had a mystified expression on his face.

"One of the death certificates we found in the box was a double forgery. Not only was the identity of the person a lie but the documentation of their death was an even bigger one."

Richard Franklin guessed what was coming next and avoided any further eye contact with his son.

"Eva Braun didn't die on 28 October 1970. Instead, she changed her identity, for a second time, to Valentina Suarez. After John's birth in America, she was forced to fake her death by you, Mr Franklin, together with Bormann, as you both thought she might prove a liability down the line."

John Franklin turned to his father and spoke for the first time since Hembury had entered the room. "Is any of this true, Dad? I always believed she died the same year I was born."

Richard Franklin spoke to his son as if Hembury wasn't present in the room. "Everything your uncle and I did was done to protect you, John. From the moment you were born, we planned your path to power and it was far better you believed both your grandparents were dead. That way, you had no real ties to Argentina. No reason to ever go there."

Hembury picked up again as he was pumped and ready to deliver the death blow. "John, even a cunning arch manipulator like Bormann failed to foresee one flaw in the plan – Eva Braun's longevity. In a few days' time, she will celebrate her one hundredth birthday."

Richard Franklin's voice roared into life, in a desperate attempt to shield the truth from his son. "That's a lie, John. It's a total fucking lie."

Hembury ignored the hysterical outburst and reached inside his jacket for his iPhone. He set the video function live and held the mobile in the air. An image of Eva Braun filled the screen, and for a couple of tantalising seconds nothing happened. Then the silence was broken by the sound of an old woman's voice. Both the Franklins spoke fluent Spanish and had no problem tuning into her Argentinian accent.

"Martin planned everything. He was a true genius … He planned our suicides and the escape from Berlin …"

For the next few minutes, no one spoke in the room. The only movement was made by John Franklin, who edged closer to the phone to gain a better look at his grandmother. Richard Franklin kept his eyes on the screen but, at the same time, his right hand edged steadily towards the bottom drawer of his desk. He slowly slid it open, without making a sound. When the video file stopped playing, Hembury detected the slight hint of a tear in John Franklin's eyes. He put the mobile away and regained eye contact with Richard.

"Mr Franklin, you asked me before what I wanted. I'm ready to tell you."

Franklin stared back impassively, his poker face restored.

"I'm not sure the American public is ready to learn that the man who might be their next leader is the grandson of the most reviled dictator who ever lived. A man who ordered the annihilation of an entire race and was personally responsible for over thirty million deaths. It would blow their minds to discover their next president was Adolf Hitler's grandson. Make no mistake, I am prepared to release the original documents if you leave me no choice. But I'm prepared to offer you both a way out."

Richard Franklin gave a slight nod and discreetly kept his right hand hovering by the open drawer.

"Tomorrow morning, you will make a joint press statement. John, you will announce that, for personal reasons, you have decided to stand down from public life with immediate effect and therefore renounce the Republican nomination. Richard, you will announce you are retiring, and as the CEO and majority shareholder you are handing the Franklin Corporation over to the government as a gift to the American people. As long as neither of you ever reneges on this deal, the contents of Box 1321 will remain a secret. Any deviation whatsoever and the world media will receive everything."

Richard Franklin managed a wry laugh. "Lieutenant, no one is going to accept our resignations at face value. It's a ludicrous idea and I also think it's a massive bluff on your part as all the evidence you're talking about has been destroyed."

At that precise moment, Franklin produced a gun from the open drawer and aimed it directly at Hembury. "Let me introduce you to a very special weapon that has a secret all of its own." He stood up from the desk and slowly walked across the office towards an alcove supporting a six-tiered bookshelf. He continued to aim the gun at Hembury and used his left hand to reach for a red leather-bound book on the bottom shelf. He raised his arm and proudly held it high in the air. "This is a first edition of Hugh Trevor-Roper's bestselling biography, *The Last Days of Hitler*. It was first printed in 1947, and, ever since it was published, it has been regarded as the definitive biography of my father. When it comes to Adolf Hitler, this is the bible and, for sixty-five years, historians and students alike have paid homage to its contents."

Hembury knew Franklin was a ruthless killer, but now he could see he was facing a level of malevolence he'd never encountered the like of before. Franklin placed the book down and walked back to his desk, keeping the gun raised the whole time.

"This pistol is actually the star turn in Roper's book. It's my father's personal weapon. A 7.65 millimetre Walther PPK. The very gun that Roper claims Hitler used to blow his own brains out. It became so infamous that Ian Fleming decided James Bond should have one. It first appeared in *Dr. No*. I'm a great Bond fan, of course."

Hembury realised that Franklin was crazy enough to gun him down in his own house. Hitler's son continued his frenzied rant.

"As you now know, lieutenant, better than anyone, what you uncovered about my father's post-war life and my very existence tells you the book is full of bullshit, as indeed is your claim to hold possession of the original contents of the box. Unfortunately for you, I know they went the same way as your Argentine friend, Chief Inspector Vargas. Incinerated in a massive fireball. You're bluffing, lieutenant. And what a wonderful irony that I blow a hole through your temple with my father's gun."

Hembury held his nerve and played his final card. "Actually, I'm afraid you're misinformed. Chief Inspector Vargas is alive and well and the contents of Box 1321 are safely in his hands. Right now, he's sitting in the lobby of The Laurel Inn, a mile away, waiting for me to FaceTime him. If I don't call him in the next fifteen minutes, he will release the documents to the media."

Franklin reeled back in shock and his son rushed forward to prop him up. He sat down again behind his desk, the gun still aimed at Hembury. "A fine attempt, lieutenant, but we both know it's a last desperate bluff."

Hembury reached very slowly for his mobile. "There's only one way to find out. Let me call him."

Franklin nodded and Hembury hit the contact.

Vargas had been willing his mobile to ring for the last thirty minutes. He was sitting by a small coffee table in the hotel lounge, nursing an untouched drink. His laptop was open, displaying his desktop. When he saw the incoming FaceTime call from Hembury appear on his screen, he felt a surge of excitement pulse through his body. He clicked on the green icon and Hembury appeared. The lieutenant turned the phone around to face the startled father and son.

"Nic, I'd like to introduce you to Richard and John Franklin."

Richard Franklin instantly recognised the chief inspector from the image he'd downloaded from the internet. His live presence on the screen seemed to deal a fatal blow and he suddenly found himself struggling to breathe.

Vargas assumed the plan he had developed with Hembury had worked so far and it was now time for him to play his part. "Mr Franklin, we had a brief conversation a couple of weeks ago but a great deal has happened since then. I believe the lieutenant has offered you a deal. Before you decide what to do, let me help you make your mind up."

Vargas pointed his iPhone camera directly at the screen of his laptop, a move he had rehearsed a dozen times in the previous hour. "Can you see the file named 1321?" He pushed the phone closer to the laptop and manually zoomed in to the folder. "This file contains copies of all the relevant documents, certificates, photos and medals, as well as videos of the 8-millimetre films."

He double-clicked and a black-and-white image of Hitler and Bormann standing either side of the cargo ship captain filled the screen.

"If you fail to call the joint press conference tomorrow morning, this file will be emailed to a senior journalist at one of the world's leading broadcast networks. I will also give them full access to the original source materials."

Franklin felt the strength draining out of his body. The Walther PPK suddenly felt as if it weighed a ton. His voice was a monotone. "How do I know you really have the originals?"

"Mr Franklin, neither I nor the contents of Box 1321 were anywhere near the apartment when your assassins struck. I'd already moved everything to a safe place."

Franklin spoke again but, by now, he sounded like a malfunctioning robot. "No one will believe it."

Hembury could literally see Franklin disintegrating in front of him. His powerful, physical charisma had vanished and his body shook uncontrollably. "Mr Franklin, we need your answer right now. If this material goes live, both of you will be at the epicentre of the biggest media shitstorm the world has ever known. The internet will transform the story into a global event in a matter of minutes. It will make headlines on every news agency across the world and the city of El Calafate will become the most searched for name on Google. Whatever denials you issue, your reputations will be trashed. It'll all be over for both of you."

CHAPTER FIFTY-THREE

Hembury turned to John, who was clearly crushed and totally dumbstruck.

"The Republican Party will drop you like a hot potato and your political career will be in shreds. People will revile you as Hitler's grandson, and for the rest of your life you and your family will be hounded by journalists following up on the story."

Hembury then switched his gaze to John's father, who had now rested the gun on top of the desk. "As well as releasing the documents, Nic will press charges against you for conspiracy to commit multiple murders in Argentina and file an extradition claim. I don't see either of you having much of a choice."

Richard Franklin glared at Hembury with utter contempt and reached once again for his father's gun. "All of us have choices, lieutenant."

In an instant, he placed the barrel of the pistol to his head and blew an enormous hole through his right temple.

Chapter Fifty-Four

1 February 2012

Los Angeles

T he Stack-'Em-High on Beverly Grove was unusually busy for a midweek lunchtime. Vargas and Hembury sat at the bar munching their way through a couple of house burgers along with draught pints of Heineken. Although it was one of LA's most popular sports bars, the TV screens were set to CNN, awaiting a much-anticipated press conference from John Franklin, scheduled for one thirty. Rumours were flying around the media that he was about to stand down as the Republican candidate, although nobody was sure. His chief of staff had simply announced that the presidential candidate had some grave news to deliver and the news networks obliged by clearing their schedules. Vargas poured a huge dollop of ketchup on his fries and put his arm around Hembury's shoulder.

"I'm booked on the red-eye tonight to Buenos Aires so, once he makes the resignation announcement, I suggest we spend the afternoon here getting totally wasted."

"You'll get no fight from me on that one. I'm wondering what he's going to say about his old man's death. So far, he's managed to keep it quiet. Nic, I've got to tell you, this has been the most insane and dangerous case I've ever worked on. Both of us nearly died. But, strangely, I'm really going to miss you."

Vargas smiled and the two men clinked their pint glasses in a mutual toast. The female news host on CNN announced it was time for the press conference and the screen cut to John Franklin's campaign office to reveal the presidential candidate sitting behind his desk. He had a sombre expression on his face, as opposed to the beaming smile his millions of supporters had come to expect. He stared straight down the lens and began reading the prompter containing his prepared speech. His subdued voice was laced with sincerity and warmth. The man was a talented liar.

"Today, I want to address the American people about a tragic event. Last night, my father, Richard Franklin, tragically took his own life. As millions of you know, his story was the embodiment of the great American dream. Together with my late uncle, he moved the small family pharmaceutical company from Buenos Aires to San Francisco where he proceeded to build the Franklin Corporation into one of the biggest companies in the world. He was a truly inspirational man – a leader of men and a wonderful, loving father. I and my family are grief-stricken by his sudden passing. For many years, he hid a dark secret from the world."

Franklin suddenly paused and appeared to wipe a tear away from his right eye. He was a superb actor, giving an Oscar-winning performance. After a few seconds of silence, he continued.

"My father suffered from extreme mental health issues but, such was his strength of character and generosity of spirit, he kept these hidden from almost everybody in his life. The truth is, he never recovered from the death of my mother, which took place shortly after I was born. He brought me up as a single father and never considered remarrying, as the love of his life had gone. His sudden passing has made me re-evaluate my goals and values.

"As his sole heir, I automatically inherit the majority shareholding in the Franklin Corporation and will become the new CEO. I have decided I want my father's legacy to be the ultimate gift to the American people, so I am going to pass over total control of the company to the federal government. It will take over one of the world's leading pharmaceutical companies, and the American people will enjoy the financial and humanitarian benefits that come with that ownership."

A spontaneous burst of applause echoed around the sports bar, which took Hembury and Vargas by complete surprise. John Franklin had found a way to put a positive spin on his father's death.

"Now, I want to talk about my own personal future."

Hembury was chewing on a cold fry slathered in ketchup. "Here we go."

Franklin left another dramatic pause, big enough to drive a bus through.

"I have decided I owe it to my father's memory to dedicate the rest of my life to the American people. Having divested myself of the corporation and handed it over to the safe hands of the nation, I now pledge to serve my country in the ultimate way."

Once again, Franklin paused and maintained eye contact

with the camera without blinking.

"I intend to be the next president of the United States."

Pandemonium broke out in the bar as diners spontaneously stood to applaud and cheer the Republican candidate, who had just won the hearts of the whole country.

Vargas turned to Hembury, who was wearing a bemused expression on his face. "Troy, what the fuck just happened?"

Chapter Fifty-Five

1 February 2012

Los Angeles

Moments after Franklin wrapped the live press conference, Amanda Carter was on the phone to Hembury. "Well, that didn't play out the way we expected. That man is full of bullshit. You realise his poll ratings are going to go crazy after this. He's just donated a company, with a turnover of thirty billion dollars a year, to the American people."

Hembury knew she was right. "Amanda, I think this tells us he has the same innate cunning as his father. Maybe he's an even bigger monster, hiding under a cloak of respectability. The truth is, he's taken a calculated risk. He probably thinks it's doubtful we still have the original materials and has decided to call our bluff."

"Troy, I've got a conference call in thirty minutes with the managing editor of BBC World News and our head of legal. They are also bringing a leading historian into the loop. Bottom line is, we will all need to see and examine first-hand those original materials before we can get the green light. I hope Nic has kept them somewhere safe. I'll report back."

Two hours later, following another call with Amanda, an action plan had been forged. Hembury would join Vargas on the night flight to Buenos Aires and, the following morning, they would meet up with her and her team, once they had flown in from Washington. The BBC would sort out a city hotel that would act as the base camp for the trip. In the meantime, the two detectives agreed they might as well stick to their original plan and Vargas ordered a couple of fresh beers.

* * *

The Claridge Hotel, with its neoclassical frontage, was a dominant feature in the centre of Buenos Aires. It was located just a few hundred yards away from Avenida 9 de Julio, the main thoroughfare in the city centre. The BBC had booked six rooms, as well as a large suite that would act as a meeting room.

It was just after midday when Vargas and Hembury entered the luxurious tenth floor suite. Amanda and her team were already there, helping themselves to a selection of sandwiches from a large silver platter resting on a circular glass-topped table. Next to the food was an oblong box containing an 8mm projector, which Amanda had requested the hotel source. As soon as she spotted the two detectives enter the suite, she ran across to greet them. It soon became obvious she was running the show and, once everybody was seated around the table, she made the formal introductions.

Amanda was flanked by two imposing male figures. To

her left sat her boss, Hugo Botting, the managing editor of BBC World News. On her right was Edward Robinson, a top legal brain, whose company was one of the oldest and most respected legal firms in the UK. Next to Botting sat Sir Keith Taylor, a distinguished-looking figure, who Vargas suspected must be well into his eighties. He was a renowned historian who had written three major tomes on the rise of Hitler and the Third Reich. His books were always top of the reading list for students studying that period of history at university. Amanda didn't waste any time getting the ball rolling.

"Troy, everybody in the room is totally up to speed with the backstory. I've also briefed them on your meeting with the Franklins and, of course, we all witnessed the outrageous press conference." She turned her attention to Vargas. "Nic, you know why we are here. The question is, are the materials safe and can you bring them to us?"

Vargas nodded, stood up and walked across the room. He turned when he reached the doorway. "Trust me when I say they are totally safe. Give me an hour to go and collect them."

Amanda seemed genuinely relieved. "Great, now we are here, can I ask where you hid them?"

A small grin broke out on Vargas's face. "I got myself a safe-deposit box."

The HSBC branch where Vargas had rented the box was only ten minutes from the hotel, and he returned to the suite forty minutes later. Nobody spoke when he entered the living room and he could sense five sets of eyes glued to the large object he was carrying in his right hand. There was a collective intake of breath as he gently placed the weathered black case in the middle of the table and carefully removed the contents. For the five other people sitting around the table, the level of anticipation and excitement couldn't have been higher if he'd been unveiling the Crown Jewels. Once all the items were on the table, Vargas opened the tobacco tin and retrieved the seven German medals.

Taylor was the first to react. He reached across and picked up the black Iron Cross, balancing it in the palm of his hand, as if he were weighing it. When he was satisfied, he turned it over and saw that Hitler's name and the year 1918 had been engraved on the back. For a man of his age, his voice was still remarkably strong, and his cut-glass English accent helped give an air of authenticity.

"If this is genuine, and my initial instinct is that it may well be, it is an earth-shattering discovery and turns all our historical understanding on its head."

The next few hours seemed to pass remarkably quickly as Amanda and her colleagues worked their way through the piles of documents and photos. At one point, Vargas laced up the two three-minute film reels and projected them onto one of the walls of the suite. The films had the same effect on everyone in the room as they'd had on him when he first saw them. Although they had all been told in advance what to expect, they watched in complete silence with a sense of incredulity.

Everyone worked on their respective laptops and iPads but all eyes were on Taylor, who used his classic Parker pen to make meticulous handwritten notes in a large leather-bound notebook, which seemed as old as he was.

He carefully catalogued every photograph and document and made detailed notes when he watched the short films, which he insisted on viewing three times each. Finally, he rested the pen on the table and laboriously fitted the top back into place. You could cut the tension with a knife.

Amanda broke the silence. "Sir Keith, to a layperson like me, these materials feel authentic but we all remember the scandal over the Hitler Diaries. What's your first impression?"

The famed historian adjusted his pince-nez and took a sip of water before replying. "My dear, I knew as soon as I saw Martin Bormann's personal case that everything inside would no doubt be genuine. I've seen it before in at least three other photographs featuring Bormann, taken between 1942 and 1945. It seems clear to me that historians have been hoodwinked for almost seventy years."

During the next couple of hours, the meeting of six organically morphed into two smaller groups. Botting and Robinson probed Taylor on the legal validity of his opinion. They required a list of solid facts that would prove, beyond doubt, that the materials were genuine. Carter, Vargas and Hembury discussed the best possible way to break the story to the American people and the wider world. They worked on selecting the key points that proved the direct bloodline between Hitler and John Franklin. As the evening progressed, the two groups merged back into one and they began to discuss timings and strategy. The BBC was one of the oldest and most respected news agencies in the world and, as the managing editor of its World News operation, Botting felt a huge weight of responsibility as he contemplated breaking the biggest story in its long and illustrious history. Although he was racked with doubt, the evidence he had seen was overwhelming, and then there was the personal experience of the two detectives, who had confronted Richard Franklin with their revelations, resulting in his suicide.

Robinson pointed out that, legally, they should stay clear

of the multiple murders in Argentina and just focus on the materials that were discovered in Box 1321. In addition, the phone footage with Eva Braun couldn't be transmitted, as it was obtained without her consent. Also, he wasn't convinced the video was sufficient proof of her true identity. The story he felt that could legally be told, based on the materials in their possession, had four main strands. Firstly, documented proof that Hitler, Braun and Bormann faked their deaths and escaped Germany at the end of the war to begin a new life in South America. Secondly, clear evidence they created fake identities under the alias of Franklin. Thirdly, a clear paper trail that proved, beyond doubt, that the Franklin Pharmaceutical Corporation was founded by Bormann using illicit Nazi funds. Finally, the extraordinary truth that the man who was the favourite to become the next president of the United States was, in actual fact, Adolf Hitler's grandson.

Nobody knew what John Franklin's next move would be, so it was agreed that time was of the absolute essence and Amanda would prepare a news package that would break the story within the next forty-eight hours. Taylor agreed he would put his reputation and career on the line to substantiate the authenticity of the materials that had been hidden away for the last sixty-seven years. Botting chartered a private jet to take everyone back to Washington. It allowed them the freedom to work non-stop on the story during the twelve-hour flight and, more importantly, they could take the materials on board and keep them safe.

As soon as they hit Washington, Amanda decamped into a small edit suite, deep in the bowels of the BBC news studio complex. She hooked up with Roland Thompson, a brilliant news editor she'd known for most of her career. She trusted him implicitly and the two of them set to work on creating a one-hour package. Carter had called him a few hours earlier from the Learjet to explain she needed his help on what would undoubtedly be the biggest story of their respective careers. He asked her if she'd discovered Elvis was still alive and was stunned when she replied that the story he was about to cut was a hundred times bigger.

She insisted Hembury and Vargas stay at her two-bedroom apartment in Georgetown, as she planned to remain in the edit suite until the piece was ready to go live. The detectives spent the following few days debriefing each other and writing up the reports that they knew would be requested by their respective superiors as soon as the story broke. They worked through the night, methodically processing the sequence of events, starting with the bank raid and ending with Franklin's suicide.

"Troy, I never asked you. How did John Franklin react when he saw his old man blow his own brains out?"

"It was strange. He let out a primitive-type scream and then, almost instantly, he seemed to regain his composure. He picked up the pistol, which was coated with blood splatter, and began to clean it with a white pocket handkerchief as if it were a precious jewel. I tried to speak to him but he ignored me as if he were in some kind of weird trance. Finally, he put the gun back down on the desk and turned to eyeball me. Nic, it was the most chilling stare I've ever experienced. I thought he was going to speak but all he did was hold the gaze. I realised, at that moment, I was looking into the eyes of a monster."

Chapter Fifty-Six

6 February 2012

Washington D.C.

At midday Eastern time on Monday, February 6, 2012, BBC World News did something it had never done before. Without any warning whatsoever, it ditched its rolling news coverage. Amanda Carter appeared on-screen and delivered an opening piece to camera that shook the nation to its core.

"In the next hour, we are going to show you incontrovertible proof that John Franklin, Republican candidate for the post of president of the United States, is not the man he claims to be. He is, in fact, the grandson of the most evil man in history – Adolf Hitler. Irrefutable evidence has come to light ..."

Hembury and Vargas sat on the sofa in Carter's flat, glued to the live transmission. They had their laptops open and followed the development of the story online as the internet went into complete meltdown. Within two minutes the Google search engine showed over fifty references to the story that hadn't existed moments earlier and that figure grew exponentially. Fifteen minutes into the broadcast, just as the first clip from the black-and-white 8mm footage was being shown, the figure had grown to over ten thousand. Ten minutes later, the story chain had exceeded a million and "Hitler" became the most searched for word in the world on both Google and Yahoo. Every news broadcaster across America followed the story and began ripping clips from the BBC broadcast, even though it was still transmitting. The story went global and was the lead on news networks in over one hundred and twenty countries.

At the precise moment Amanda went live, John Franklin was in his office at campaign headquarters, working on his latest rally speech. He was still basking in the afterglow of the press conference, which had triggered his personal ratings to soar. They were up by an incredible fifteen points. The Republican candidate now held a massive lead over the incumbent of the White House. His inbox was overflowing with supportive emails and the national press and television stations were lauding the generosity of his actions. In addition, the revelation of his father's tragic suicide had gained him a huge sympathy boost from female voters. A nice bonus.

Even though his office door was closed, he could normally hear the general hubbub generated from over a hundred staffers working outside in the huge open-plan area. He suddenly realised all he could hear was his own thoughts and the distant murmur of a TV. Something was wrong and, as he stood up to investigate, he caught sight of one of the giant wall-mounted televisions in the distance. As he focused on the screen featuring two headshots, his brain felt an instant surge of panic and disbelief. He was looking at a picture of his own face next to one of Adolf Hitler.

Everyone in the office appeared hypnotised by the transmission and, as he opened the door, a four-way split came up showing shots of the Argentinian ID cards for Gerald and Ronald Franklin, alongside grainy photos of Hitler and Bormann. Although his mind was now submerged in a murky fog, he recognised the voice of Amanda Carter, the reporter who had interviewed him many times for the BBC World News. Suddenly, he found himself running through the office at breakneck speed, heading for the bank of lifts. Weirdly, he felt as if he were moving through quicksand and was conscious that all eyes in the office were glued to him. As the lift doors closed, he felt a brief moment of respite and he breathed out for the first time since seeing the TV images.

A few minutes later, he was driving out of the underground car park into the busy morning traffic. His mobile, which was resting on the dash, appeared to be having a seizure, as it manically vibrated with incoming calls and messages. He flicked it on to silent and floored the accelerator. Instinctively, his reflex thought was to call his dad, and then, a millisecond later, he remembered he couldn't. He felt alone and desperate and needed some time to think. The unimaginable had happened and now he had to find a way to process and deal with it. He caught a glimpse of the read-out on his iPhone and saw six missed calls from his wife, along with over twenty others. He couldn't bear going home to face the inevitable questioning, and he pictured a hunting pack of reporters and cameramen waiting outside his house to assault him. Instead, he headed for the sanctuary of his father's mansion in Pacific Heights.

Amanda Carter's wrap-up was perfect in every way. It was delivered in an authoritative tone, combining the sensational and grave aspects of the story.

"The man who many of us believed could be the next president of the United States is an impostor – a counterfeit candidate. From the day he was born, he was groomed by inherently evil people, obsessed with world domination and the creation of a super race. I want to end this report with the grotesque words of Adolf Hitler, a vile monster who we now know escaped justice and planned to build a new dynasty. 'The sacred mission of the German people is to assemble and preserve the most valuable racial elements and raise them to the prominent position.All who are not of a good race are chaff.' These are the words of John Franklin's grandfather, Adolf Hitler."

John Franklin sat in the kitchen in his father's house and flicked through the messages on his phone. He had muted the TV and was using the remote to hop through the news channels. There was only one story in play. He was in free fall and everyone was deserting him. The only person left he felt he could trust was Cathy, who had also been chasing him down. He called her and she picked up instantly.

"John, what the fuck? Everything has gone to shit. The party is about to announce your deselection as their official candidate. Donors and supporters are dropping us like a stone and heading for the hills. I know this story can't be true, but the evidence looks compelling. Tell me what the hell's going on?"

Franklin suddenly saw live shots of the front gates of his father's house appear on Fox News. Someone must have spotted his car on the drive and a huge media crowd was gathering outside. He felt like a rat caught in a trap.

"Cathy, of course it's bullshit. You need to issue an instant denial and set up a live press conference for me to publicly rebut the allegations."

Cathy knew Franklin well enough to know, instantly, that he was lying to her. She paused for a moment before cutting her losses.

"John, it's over."

Caroline Franklin was shell-shocked. She sat on the bar stool in her kitchen watching CNN, transfixed by the breaking news. She had missed the initial BBC broadcast but it was impossible to avoid the blanket coverage revealing her husband's true identity. Her life lay in tatters, shattered by the incredible revelations. Her marriage to the presidential candidate had been exposed as a sham. He was not the man he made himself out to be. Her mind flooded with questions. Could the revelations possibly be true? Was John's grandfather actually the most reviled man in history. The questions kept coming, but she had no answers. She glanced down at the copy of *Vogue* lying open on the breakfast bar and bit down on her lip. The exclusive double-page spread displayed a stunning photograph of her posing in her bedroom, wearing a gorgeous ten-thousand-dollar Armani trouser suit. She stared at the headline: *Is This the Next First Lady?*

Caroline stood up, walked out of the kitchen and made her way into the large breakfast room as though in a trance. Her twelve-year-old son didn't sense her presence, as he was totally absorbed in the *Tomb Raider Legend* game he was playing on his Xbox. She came to a stop a few feet behind Bill and stood there, frozen to the spot, just staring at him. There was only one question now dominating her thoughts: was she really the mother of Adolf Hitler's great-grandson?

Franklin was struggling to catch his breath and felt as though he was experiencing a distorted nightmare. He glared at his mobile for a few seconds as if it had betrayed him, then snapped back to reality and placed it back inside his jacket pocket. He knew he had to buy himself some thinking time and that meant getting out of the media glare. His father owned a secluded sea ranch in Carmel that very few people knew about. It was situated on the beach and enjoyed spectacular one-hundred-and-eighty-degree views of the Pacific Ocean.

He'd stayed there many times with his own family and remembered his father kept a set of keys for it on a wooden rack in the main hallway. He grabbed them and made his way through the house to an internal door that led to a large triple garage, positioned to the side of the property. Inside were a Rolls-Royce, an Aston Martin convertible and a black Range Rover. He knew the keys for all three would be resting on the passenger side sun visors and opted for the relative anonymity of the Range Rover.

The mansion had a rear entrance, which he hoped the media scrum out front weren't yet aware of. He gunned the four-litre engine into life and used the remote on the dash to open the garage door. A minute later, he hit the code for the rear electric gates and headed south on the coastal road to Carmel.

The one-hundred-and-thirty-mile drive took just under three hours and, during the journey, Franklin worked his way through more than twenty local radio news stations, desperately trying to escape the relentless media coverage of the BBC revelations. By the time he parked up on the drive outside the sea ranch, his mood had severely darkened and he was desperate for the sanctuary it offered.

As soon as he was safely ensconced inside, he helped himself to a large tumbler of his father's favourite bourbon, and it took him less than an hour to drain the bottle. The alcohol started to kick in and, as his mind began to become slightly cloudy, his thinking became more confused. He wondered if he had the mental strength to emulate his father and take his own life, but realised he wasn't brave enough. He decided he would try and reach out to Cathy once more. If he could get her back on side, he had a chance of mounting a fightback. He tried her continuously for the next hour but, every time, her voicemail kicked in.

Franklin found a second bottle of bourbon inside the antique walnut drinks globe and poured himself another glass. He stood in front of the curved floor-to-ceiling windows and gazed out at the sheer vastness of the ocean. The tide was in and the sea was rough but he suddenly felt an irresistible urge to be down on the beach, to be closer to the water.

Fifteen minutes later, he found himself, fully clothed, wading waist-high through the crashing waves. In one hand he held a bottle of bourbon and, in the other, a plastic bottle of barbiturates he had found in the medicine cabinet in his father's bathroom. A wild wave stopped his momentum, knocking him over, and he went under for the first time. When he emerged, he struggled to regain his balance, but after a few seconds he managed to stand upright and stare straight-ahead, out to sea. He held his position for a few seconds and then began walking.

By the time Amanda signed off, hundreds of millions of people around the world were coming to terms with a new reality. Hembury and Vargas were stunned by the display of sheer journalistic brilliance they had just witnessed.

"Troy, she nailed that bastard to a giant cross. There's no coming back from this. I can't believe it's finally over."

"What are you going to do now, Nic?"

Vargas sat back on the sofa and closed his eyes. "I don't know about you but I feel like I want to sleep for a week. I really need to get back home and help Juan and the team as they work their way through the car crash I left behind."

"Listen, Nic, before you go back and catch up on your sleep, I have an idea. How about not sleeping and pulling an all-nighter in Vegas?"

Vargas's face broke into a huge smile. "Bring it on. Who needs sleep?"

* * *

Six thousand miles away in a small city in Patagonia, an old lady sat up in bed and watched events unfold live on TV. She glanced away from the screen and stared at the small white plate on her bedside table with its slice of birthday cake. Next to it sat a tiny green onyx jewellery box. Her bony fingers slowly prised open the lid and fumbled around inside until she found what she was searching for. Her grip was pitifully weak but she managed to lift the glass vial out of the box, balancing it between her forefinger and thumb. She used her tongue to help position it between her back teeth and then crunched down, releasing the cyanide.

In the afternoon of her one hundredth birthday, sixty-seven years after she had first faked her own death, Eva Braun finally took her own life.

Epilogue

6 April 2012

Washington D.C.

I t was a crisp spring morning and Hembury and Vargas relaxed in the back of the black unmarked Chevrolet Tahoe as it smoothly navigated its way through the traffic on Pennsylvania Avenue. The SUV was driven by Danny Sullivan, a special agent who formed part of the president's Secret Service unit. He was tasked with delivering the detectives to a confidential meeting in the Oval Office. Vargas had flown in the night before from Buenos Aires, joining Hembury at the eminent Jefferson Hotel, a convenient five-minute drive from the White House. Hembury leaned forward to speak to the driver.

"Agent Sullivan, what can you tell us about the meet? Is it just us and the main man?"

"Lieutenant Hembury, I'm just your driver, but I am at liberty to tell you that you'll be meeting with the president and the director of the FBI. My job is simply to get you there safely and on time."

Fifteen minutes later, at precisely 11 a.m., Sullivan escorted the two men into the Oval Office, swiftly made the formal introductions and then departed. President Edward Powell greeted the two detectives with warm handshakes, as did FBI Director Gideon Mueller. Powell gestured for them to sit on a large black leather sofa while he and Mueller took their places in single armchairs, facing them. The president eased forward in his chair and picked up a blue folder from the glass coffee table positioned between them. He waved it in the air before speaking.

"Gentlemen, this folder contains the confidential reports you presented to your respective police chiefs and tells a remarkable story. To be honest, I found much of it a very difficult read. I think it's fair to say the American people are still in shock from the fallout of the Franklin revelations but they would be absolutely horrified if they knew what else was in this file. Richard Franklin was evidently a calculating sociopath who sanctioned countless murders. It's a miracle you survived his machinations. He and his so-called Uncle Ronald were clearly evil pieces of work but, equally, very smart. In fact, and I'm sure you know this, Bormann was one of the highest-ranking Nazis to escape justice after the war, despite all Mossad's best efforts to track him down. Last month, we exhumed Ronald Franklin's body from Forest Lawn and DNA taken from one of Bormann's surviving relatives in Germany confirmed his true identity."

The president switched his eyeline towards Vargas. "Chief Inspector Vargas, I owe you a huge debt of gratitude. Your bravery and perseverance were truly remarkable, and of course I share your sadness regarding the deaths of your two officers."

Vargas nodded, and the president turned his attention to Hembury. "Lieutenant, the fact that you ignored huge pressure from above to drop the entire investigation is of great credit and demonstrates huge integrity on your part. No words from me can really sum up my gratitude to you both for the actions you took on behalf of the American people but I can at least try and express it. Later today, in a private ceremony, I will be presenting you both with the Presidential Medal of Freedom, the highest honour this office allows me to bestow."

Before the detectives could react, the FBI director spoke for the first time. He held a black file in his hand. "Gentlemen, that's not quite it, I'm afraid. Firstly, I have to report that, although we strongly believe John Franklin took his own life at sea, his body has not been found and therefore we have to seriously contemplate the possibility that he left a false trail of clues at the Carmel house and, in reality, may have fled and is now in hiding. He certainly has the financial resources and contacts to disappear, so he remains part of an ongoing investigation. But now we need to talk about Richard Franklin."

There was a distinct change of tone in the director's demeanour, signalling a sense of foreboding. "We know Franklin was a complex man whose life was cloaked in a web of secrecy and lies. Initially, we believed the information you uncovered told the whole lurid story. But, I'm afraid to say, it didn't."

Mueller paused for a moment and glanced over at the president, double-checking he had clearance to continue. Vargas and Hembury shot a look at each other, both wondering what on earth the new revelations could possibly be.

For a few seconds there was an uncomfortable silence, eventually broken by the president. "Director, please continue. These men have more than earned the right to hear your findings."

Mueller nodded and retrieved a small sheaf of stapled papers from the file. "Gentlemen, our initial search of Franklin's Pacific Heights mansion uncovered a wall safe in his study that contained various business papers and over two million dollars in cash but nothing untoward or unexpected. However, one of our men was searching the garage when he discovered a second safe, ingeniously hidden under the terracotta tiled floor. It had been embedded into the concrete and covered with a one-metre square panel of tiles which, at first glance, meant it was perfectly concealed, unless you knew exactly what you were looking for. It was sheer chance we found it."

The FBI director glanced at the papers, which he handled like a stick of dynamite. "It took us a while to break it open but the pay off was worth it. The documents it contained were highly disturbing and, evidently, Franklin intended they would only ever be for his eyes. It turns out, among other things, Hitler's son was a serial womaniser. For many years he maintained relationships with a string of women who lived in a number of luxury apartments, situated across different districts in San Francisco. He kept in-depth files on all of these women – their entire life stories are chronicled in these documents. They were all carefully vetted by private detectives before ever meeting Franklin, and, what's more, they all shared something in common. In every case they had no surviving close family to speak of and few close associates in their lives."

Hembury couldn't resist butting in. "How many women are we talking about here?"

"A great many, lieutenant. The paperwork covers the last forty years, and they reveal the identities of twenty-five women. However, the fact that Franklin was something of a Lothario is not really of interest to us but the files also revealed other information that is deeply concerning. In four instances, it appears a child was conceived, three boys and a girl. In every case, shortly after the birth, the woman concerned simply disappeared without trace, leaving the baby parentless. We know from our interrogation with Aaron Wicks, the hitman who tried to take you out, that he was employed by Franklin to murder one of his girlfriends two years ago. On that basis we have to assume a similar fate befell the mothers of his children."

Vargas just beat Hembury to the obvious question. "So what happened to the children?"

"Chief inspector, it appears that in all four cases a highly respected private agency specialising in inter-country adoption placed the babies with who, at first glance, appear to be suitable and respectable families. The boys were sent to New York, London and Sydney and the girl to Buenos Aires. However, after further investigation, we discovered the male partner in each household was a senior employee of the Franklin Corporation. Also, it transpires that Richard Franklin was on the board of the adoption agency and held a controlling financial interest in the holding company running it. Once again, he was pulling the strings behind the scenes."

Hembury nodded grimly at the FBI director. "So what you're saying is, even though we believe John Franklin may be dead, Hitler has four surviving grandchildren, living on different continents. Probably being brought up by Nazi sympathisers."

"That's exactly what I'm saying, lieutenant. It appears Richard Franklin took out a bizarre insurance policy to protect the future of his bloodline, and I'm afraid there's more. Other paperwork we found in the safe stipulates that in all four cases, when the child reaches the age of twenty-one, they will receive a payment of fifty million dollars, courtesy of one of Franklin's highly secretive Swiss bank accounts. At this time, it appears none of them is aware of their impending wealth."

"How old are the kids now?"

The director studied his papers. "The boys are 15, 17 and 18 and the girl is 19."

The president rose from the armchair, walked across to his desk and sat on the front of it in order to face the three men. He had remained silent throughout Mueller's briefing but was ready to take back control of the meeting.

"So now you both know the full story. Clearly this information is highly sensitive and must be kept from the American people."

The president paused for a few seconds and stared at the two detectives who were processing the implications of these latest revelations. "Gentlemen, the question is, what do we do about it?"

Author's Note

I have always been fascinated by conspiracy theories: the Roswell UFO incident, JFK's assassination, the moon landings, Princess Diana's car crash, all come to mind. But they don't come much bigger than the one surrounding the apparent deaths of Adolf Hitler and Eva Braun. It's a highly controversial topic that has generated many books, articles and documentaries and the truth is that, even today, views differ on what really happened.

As a student, I studied Hitler and the rise and fall of the Third Reich at London University, where I completed a degree in history and modern politics. Part of my academic research included reading Alan Bullock's *Hitler: A Study in Tyranny* and Hugh Trevor-Roper's *The Last Days of Hitler*. I always had a gut feeling that Hitler wasn't the kind of man to take his own life, but, then again, there is a great deal of compelling evidence, and eye-witness testimony, to suggest he did. For the purposes of writing *The Counterfeit Candidate*, I went with my gut. I couldn't help wondering, what if ...

What if Hitler escaped from Berlin at the end of the war and sixty-five years later his grandson was in the running to become president of the United States?

Now you've read the story, I thought it might be helpful to try and separate what we know to be fact from fiction. Firstly, let's look at the facts that are in the common domain.

It's well recorded that in July 1945, just three months after Hitler's supposed death, Stalin threw doubt on the official story, speculating he had escaped from Berlin and was possibly hiding in Spain or Argentina. The genie was out of the bottle and the conspiracy theory was born.

In 1945, and in subsequent years, we know many high-ranking Germans fled to South America, including infamous Nazis such as Mengele and Eichmann, who make cameo appearances in my story. It's also an open secret that the Argentine regime at the time welcomed dozens and possibly hundreds of Nazis, looking for sanctuary, into their country in return for significant payments.

Between 1943 and 1945 Bormann, in his elevated role as party secretary found himself in total control of the Nazi government's purse strings and it's believed he transferred huge amounts of money to banks and businesses all around the world, including millions to banks based in Switzerland and South America.

For *The Counterfeit Candidate*, I created a fictional account of Hitler's escape from Berlin. The early morning drive, heading north from Berlin, through Russian lines to the Baltic port of Kiel and the confrontation with the Red Army soldiers, is an invention. As is the dilapidated cargo boat, *Santa Cruz III*. It never existed. Neither did its German captain, Hans Küpper, or the plastic surgeon Dr Friedrich Hipke.

However, El Calafate in the province of Santa Cruz, in Patagonia, is a real city, but El Blondi, the Argentinian farmhouse is another invention. I liked the conceit that the name of Hitler's new home would be a permanent memorial to his beloved dog, who he left behind in the bunker. I tried my best to get inside Bormann's head and those creations were the end result. I spent a great deal of time researching Bormann and concluded he would never have left his Führer's side, so I made him part of the three escapees, along with Hitler and Braun.

In reality, most historians believe Bormann died in Berlin, on 2 May 1945, trying to escape the Red Army. As I mention in the story, in 1972 a skeleton was discovered in Berlin and DNA tests appeared to prove a match with Hitler's notorious deputy.

The idea of Hitler and Bormann creating and building one of the biggest pharmaceutical companies in the world seemed plausible to me. It would provide them with a huge multinational vehicle, perfect for laundering the vast sums of money they had taken out of Germany. It would also give them a platform of power and respectability for Hitler's son, enabling him to set up a new home in the United States, where he could father an heir, who could go on to become a world leader, achieving the ultimate prize of the presidency.

The Franklins and the Franklin Pharmaceutical Corporation are of course another fictional creation, but I suspect if Bormann and Hitler really did escape together, they may well have looked at the United States as being the obvious location for a future Fourth Reich.

The basic idea for *The Counterfeit Candidate* has been buried inside my head for over forty years, but it took the totally unexpected arrival of a three-month lockdown to turn it into a reality. Like millions of other people, when the virus struck and the world shut down, I lost all my work and found myself at home wondering what to do. I was a television director with nothing to direct, so I decided to finally have a go at writing the story. I had no idea if I was capable of doing it and, trust me when I say, no one was more surprised than me that the book finally got written.

Acknowledgements

Many people helped bring this book together and I'm eternally grateful to them. Paul Feldstein, of The Feldstein Agency in Belfast, was the first literary agent to show any real interest in the project, after he read the synopsis. He loved the idea straight from the off and always believed in the story.

As a first-time writer, who naturally expected rejection, the two-line email I received from Verena Rose, the Acquisitions Editor at Level Best Books was truly awesome.

"I have read THE COUNTERFEIT CANDIDATE and loved it. If you are still interested in publishing with Level Best Books, I would like to discuss a contract with you."

Verena and Shawn Simmons at Level Best have been incredibly supportive and wonderful to work with as a Publisher and as individual Editors and I couldn't have wished to work with two nicer or more experienced people. We may have been based three and a half thousand miles away from each other but the world of lockdown and zoom combined to allow the creative process to work incredibly smoothly. I'd also like to thank Victoria Woodside for her fantastic proofreading and fact-checking.

My wife Charmaine has been unbelievable from day one. Firstly, she put up with me basically not doing a thing in the home but write, twelve hours a day, seven days a week, for three months during the lock-down and then she was the first person to read the manuscript. After that, she became the best Editor I could ever have wished for, working with me every day, improving and honing the book with her inspiring, creative ideas and incredible eye for detail, all of which helped take the book to another level.

My daughter Jessica was also an inspiration as her love of historical thrillers meant she also had plenty of exciting ideas to throw into the melting pot. Finally, I want to thank the gorgeous Georgie, Jessica's Frenchador, who moved in with us at the beginning of lockdown and whose daily walks on Hampstead Heath proved to be a welcome respite from relentless periods of writing.

About the Author

Brian Klein is an award-winning Television Director, with over twenty-five years' experience in the industry. His work regularly appears on Netflix, Amazon Prime, BBC and Sky. Amongst his directing credits are twenty-five seasons of the iconic car show, "TOP GEAR" and five seasons of "A LEAGUE OF THEIR OWN ROADTRIP", Sky One's highest rating entertainment show. He has also directed two feature-length films for BBC Worldwide and five entertainment specials for Netflix.

THE COUNTERFEIT CANDIDATE is his debut novel.